Andrew was born and grew up in Cambridge, until he left school to join Hertfordshire Constabulary in 1972. Some years later he transferred to Suffolk and after twenty years' service, was retired early upon medical grounds. He then retrained and qualified as a Costs Lawyer now running his own business. He is married with one daughter.

Born in Norwich, George grew up in the Suffolk seaside town of Southwold. He moved to Hertfordshire in search of fame and fortune and was privileged to have served the people of the county for over thirty years as a Police Officer. He is married with children and currently works in local government.

HARDER YET!

HARDER YET!

Andrew Brasher and
George Smith

Vanguard Press

A CIP catalogue record for this title is
available from the British Library.

ISBN 978 1 784651 90 9

This book is a combined work of fiction and fact. Names, characters,
places and incidents are either the product of both authors' imaginations or
are used fictitiously, and any resemblance to any persons, living or dead,
business establishments, events or locales is entirely coincidental.

Vanguard Press is an imprint of
Pegasus Elliot MacKenzie Publishers Ltd.
www.pegasuspublishers.com

First Published in 2017

Vanguard Press
Sheraton House Castle Park
Cambridge England

Printed & Bound in Great Britain

"To our wives who have shown great understanding and patience over the years"

Acknowledgements

The co-authors are very grateful for all the help and assistance given during the research of this book.

Particular thanks go to:

Tim Bonfield, Geoff & Gloria Brendling, Christine & David Brooks, Jon Caldwell, Colin Clare, Jean and Paul Cox, David Horan, Ian Fraser, Lesley Griffiths, Ian Jenkins, Peter Mileson, Alistair Muir-Howie, Sonia Parsons, Terry Pearce, David Penasa, Murray Rogers, John Thorogood, John Thorn, Paul Watts, Jackie Wells, John White, Jerry and Jacquie Wyatt, Phil Wynes and Paul Burns Photography.

Foreword

This story charts the lives of two seventeen-year-olds who first met in the early 1970s when they joined Tinkers Hill County Police Cadet Corps. It maps their journey over the course of a three-year period, taking in their different family and schooling backgrounds, changing attitudes, their ups and downs, the immense challenges they faced and their overall teenage experiences with females before exploring their developing friendship. It covers Harry and Ed's mid-teenage years, Harry's endurance in becoming a cadet, before concentrating on their year in training together.

The story engages with some of the main characters who were instrumental in their development and the influential and important part they played in the lives of two young, fairly naïve and impressionable teenagers. It also examines the area that surrounds honesty and integrity after one of them owned up to a misdemeanour, resulting in their resignation, whilst the other remained tight-lipped.

Chapter One
Harry

"Why the colour yellow?" she asked?

"I don't really know," replied Harry looking straight into his mother's eyes. "I suppose it's because it is so vibrant and cheerful," he said. Yellow was Harry's favourite colour; as a youngster he loved playing with anything yellow. It may well have had something to do with his first teddy bear which was more yellow than brown and which he loved well into his early teens. Alternatively, Harry seemed more appreciative of life when it was warm and sunny rather than cold and miserable; it therefore made much more sense to him that as the sun was yellow everyone and everything seemed much brighter, happier and people generally seemed less grumpy.

Harry's mother was a very friendly, hard-working and proud woman. She met and married Harry's father in Holland at the end of the Second World War before moving to the UK to set up home in one of the new government-subsidised prefabricated properties in Norfolk. What she lacked in height, she made up for in grit, determination and enthusiasm and was the typical stay-at-home mother tending to all her family's needs. During her pregnancy with Harry she suffered terribly with her back and following his birth was left with a long-term problem which, in later life, resulted in a double hip replacement. Harry's father was head chef at a local hotel and most days he was only home for a couple of hours during the afternoon before disappearing at around five p.m. to ensure dinner was being prepped for hotel guests. He was a private and sometimes withdrawn individual and Harry attributed this to his slightly miserable persona, but it was more likely to do with his experience from the Second World War. Harry did not know until his mid-forties that his father had been with the Royal Army Medical Corps who had 'cleaned up' the Bergen-Belsen camp in North West Germany after the genocide atrocities. This subject was never discussed by Harry's father and only became apparent after his death; this may have been partly responsible for his father's standoffishness. He too was a proud man but was not the kind of person to shout it from the rooftops; he was also very dedicated to his work although the hours away from home meant little time for a complete family life, resulting in Harry either having to do things on his own or with just his mother. Harry's brother was five years older, having left home at sixteen to join the Merchant Navy and the two saw very little of each other for several years.

Having failed his eleven-plus Harry finished his secondary schooling in July 1971 where he concluded this invaluable part of his life with seven Certificate of Secondary Education qualifications, otherwise known as CSEs. St Bede's wasn't a huge school in terms of students but it taught Harry the basic principles of life: respect, dignity, hope and charity. It was a very close-knit school with only 110 students; on the whole staff were terrific, although at times he felt victimised by Mr Jack, the science master who threw a wobbly each time Harry turned up late for the first lesson on a Thursday morning. Harry tried to explain that he had little control over bus timetables or over the speed that buses ran, but any excuse seemed to fall on deaf ears and just enraged Mr Jack even more, to the extent that he occasionally lost the plot by throwing a board rubber or whatever came to hand at anyone who found the situation amusing. During his last year in particular, Harry found these outbursts more and more unpleasant. Harry used to indulge in silly games at breaks and during the lunch hour, which involved kneeing someone on the outer thigh to give them a dead-leg. Pain was instantaneous and whilst Harry gave as good as he got he also suffered the same fate from others. Part of this 'activity' involved avoidance of the main protagonists as well as being able to spring a surprise on those who appeared to be daydreaming. Little did Harry know that this 'game' would have a profound effect on his health later in life.

Whilst Harry endured five years preparing for his CSE examinations they did not go exactly according to plan, although it wasn't entirely clear in Harry's mind what the plan was. He had been at the same Catholic school for what seemed an eternity and the mention of exams only seemed to register in his head at the beginning of his final year. The science teacher did little to help and there were few prospects so, after the exams, he was expected to leave as there was no sixth form opportunity. The choice was stark: either find a job or apprenticeship or go into further education at college. There was little in the way of careers advice and, even with the full backing and enthusiasm shown by his mother, he had to think of something quickly.

Other than football, one of Harry's most regular and favourite pastimes was swimming in the North Sea which could be reached by bike in less than ten minutes from his home. With the wind at his back he could knock this down to about seven minutes but this was completely inconsequential during a six-week summer holiday where timing was unimportant and frankly meaningless. Harry was also a member of the local scout troop which he joined at fifteen; he had previously dabbled at being a cub scout when he was younger but he felt bullied and intimidated so he gave it up. By joining the scouts he genuinely believed that he was giving something back to the community in the form of 'bob a job' weeks or by acting as a flag bearer at the annual Remembrance parade. Through scouting, Harry was also able to give up some time to help the elderly and for several weeks held down a couple of grass-cutting jobs although with one it meant performing a 'poop and scoop' role before kick-starting the mower. Having never had a dog of his own he was quite astounded at the amount a little sausage dog could deposit in a week.

Scouting provided a wider dimension to his life as he met lots of different people. He was taught the basics of camping, orienteering and learnt to tie all sorts of knots from the simple reef knot, clove hitch or bowline to the much more complicated, if not impossible sheepshank. He also became used to wearing a uniform and standing to attention when they sang the national anthem at the commencement of a troop meeting. Harry went on several camping trips, one of which was to the Peak District. He tried to impress the younger scouts by showing off his newly acquired skills in the art of wood retrieval, an essential requirement when camping outdoors. He discovered a half-dead tree which was ideal wood for the campfire, but it was a little on the large side and required several people and a hefty rope to detach the dead part from the remainder. Harry attached the rope to the branch using one or other of the aforementioned knots and, with the assistance of five or six younger scouts, started to pull with all their might. For whatever reason, Harry decided he would be best placed at the very end of the rope and was straining with every sinew in his body. Suddenly, the dead branch gave way in a flash causing everyone on the rope to topple backwards like ninepins. Harry, being last in the line fell backwards straight into the middle of the biggest cowpat causing an immediate stink as well as resulting in a big brown stain all over the back of his coat and jeans. The younger scouts, having a right old laugh, soon scattered from the disgusting smell which emitted wherever Harry went. He had to literally scrub his clothes several times in the nearby river with soap in an effort to get rid of the stain as well as trying to contain the smell. Fortunately, Reg the scoutmaster had anticipated such an event and had brought an old pair of tracksuit bottoms which Harry was extremely pleased with in the interim until his jeans and coat were dry.

Harry had a good friend named Ernie who lived opposite with his parents and younger brother. He was nicknamed Ernie because his father was a milkman. This coincided with the Benny Hill sketches and the song from that time so it made complete sense but that was as far as the similarity went. Ernie sported a thick mop of ginger hair, had freckles and bore no resemblance to Benny Hill whatsoever. Ernie and Harry were born one day apart in the same year and when they were younger played football on the local recreation ground close to where they lived. As they grew older they became swimming buddies, spending many of the hot and sometimes cool summer days soaking up both sun and rain. There was of course the added bonus of girls who were visiting the seaside resort for their summer holidays.

Ernie attended the local secondary modern school whilst Harry spent at least ninety minutes on buses each day just getting to a Catholic school which his parents thought was a notch up from the local school. Initially, he too thought it was novel attending a Catholic school and up to the age of thirteen he was a believer in the church and what it stood for. But for the rude intervention of the parish priest, Harry probably would have continued being an altar boy. He had reached that age where he was developing his own mind and the last thing he wanted was an officious priest pushing him into something that he no longer wished to participate in on a Sunday morning. Father Rudd had him in tears, berating him for deserting the faith when all he wanted to do was be a normal teenager; it was as if Harry had committed some heinous crime and the priest was having none of it. It was only when Harry's mother intervened that common sense prevailed. She saw how uncomfortable Harry was and, being the consummate diplomat, she agreed that Harry perhaps should have some time to think about it. With gritted teeth and mumbling to himself the priest left their house: Harry never performed as an altar boy again.

Harry was slightly envious of Ernie who was exceedingly brighter and quicker at maths problems than Harry. This was evident when the two visited drinking establishments where they would partake in a game or two of darts. Surreptitiously, Harry always left the scoring to Ernie for two reasons: Ernie was much quicker in deducting the scores after three darts, meaning they could play many more games in an evening and, secondly, if it was left to Harry he would have easily 'cocked up' which would have been seen as an embarrassment which he was keen to avoid. During that school summer holiday of 1971 both lads spent most Fridays and Saturday nights visiting local hostelries mainly playing darts or bar billiards which at the time was a relatively new form of entertainment, but took up less space than a pool table. Given that both were under age to be in public houses it should be seen as some sort of worthy testament as their behaviour was not once questioned by any of the numerous landlords at any of the pubs they frequented. Whether or not there would be any connection, it followed that their age was never brought into question. In hindsight this was probably something related to where they were brought up rather than their actual age. As long as they paid for their beer and didn't cause any problem the good old landlord was quite happy to take the money from them.

It was during one of those games of darts or during a sun-soaking fest on the beach that the conversation turned to that of a job. Harry shuddered at the thought and glanced quizzically at Ernie. "What on earth are we going to do?" he asked, sounding quite exasperated. Neither lad had any idea at that time but it emerged a couple of days later that Ernie knew of someone who had joined their local police force as a cadet. He had it on good authority that police cadets were part of a truly exciting and enjoyable regime: they played sports most of the time, did a bit of studying and wore a uniform which was guaranteed to impress the girls. In an instant Harry's thoughts were, *what could possibly go wrong?*

They talked it over at length, finally deciding that they would stick together and apply to join what seemed like the easiest job on the planet. Apparently, and neither knew if it was actually true, cadets were financially rewarded – but this was something that had to be formally confirmed. They were about to climb aboard a roller coaster in the hope that neither of them would come crashing down to earth with a bump.

Chapter Two
What Next?

The Police Cadet Corps in the early seventies was seen as a relatively cost effective method of recruiting into mainstream police forces. Various forces recruited from the age of sixteen and cadets were regimented though not necessarily to the same degree as the military – but uniforms were compulsory and they were expected to perform drill exercises as part of their training. Discipline was very high on the agenda. There were also a whole range of sports to choose from as well as continuing with academic studies. Harry was fine with the sporting theme but was less enamoured with being back in the classroom. More importantly, they definitely paid you at the end of each month, which had to be a bonus considering all Harry had earned up until now was from picking blackcurrants at a local farm during the summer months and the very small gratuities he received for grass cutting.

There was mild satisfaction in the minds of both Harry and Ernie as they sat nervously in the waiting room at a local police station. They had both been invited for an interview to judge their suitability and credibility to join the cadet corps of their local force. An hour later they were both on their way home having been given some very stern but sensible advice from a police sergeant who had told them there were no vacancies and that they should both "get a proper job" and the worldly experiences that went with it, and if they remained intent on becoming police officers they should re-apply when they were nineteen. Here were two sixteen-year-old lads experiencing their first job rejection and neither found it a particularly pleasant experience. It was a case of going back to the drawing board or, in the case of Harry and Ernie, back to the beach.

Within a few days Harry and Ernie were back in the saddle with applications to two more forces, one north and one south of their home county. A reply was instantaneously received from the one to the north; it was disappointing in that their policy was not to accept anyone who lived outside the county boundary. Harry was slightly annoyed given they only resided approximately 7.5 miles from the nearest point on the county border. They didn't view this as an outright rejection rather than as an anomaly in a comparatively ridiculous bureaucratic system. It was the first time Harry had heard the word "red-tape" uttered by his father.

The day arrived when both Harry and Ernie's applications were accepted for the Kanga county force to the south of where they lived. They were invited for an examination, medical and interview on the same day. For some obscure and slightly meaningless reason both friends travelled the forty-five miles south separately with their respective parents. Harry was particularly nervous as he knew that maths was his Achilles heel and if anything was going to let him down, it would probably relate to this subject. There was a fair bit of time waiting around but, finally, Harry and Ernie were informed they had passed their medical assessments. They then completed a general knowledge and maths test which was followed by more waiting before they had a short interview to let them know how they had fared. Elation for the Ernie camp followed as he was successful in his bid to join the Kanga Force Cadet Corps. Deflation followed for Harry as he was told that he had failed the examination; it felt like a kick in the teeth. Deep down inside he knew that it was most likely the maths questions which had caused this grave situation. Feedback, as we know it now, was clearly not available in 1971 as Harry was just shown the door without any explanation as to where he had gone wrong or what he could do to improve for next time.

Outside the building, Harry, feeling somewhat subdued, congratulated an overjoyed Ernie in achieving his goal. Harry felt really pleased for his friend but at that precise moment made the conscious decision not to give up and, with the determination instilled in him by his mother, he continued his quest for a position as a police cadet. He had a little difficulty accepting Ernie's appointment and could not resign himself to the fact that Ernie was anything other than an equal and, if he was good enough to be accepted for a post, then so must Harry be.

One more application for Harry followed that summer to a force known as Mid-Shires where all the cadets seemed to be modelled on Geoff Capes, an Olympic shot put champion of the time. On arrival at their headquarters, Harry was met by a dozen or so cadets marching along a shrub-lined driveway. It appeared to Harry that they were clones of one another although to be frank he had never heard the expression until later in life.

They all seemed at least six feet, five inches tall; they each had a huge barrel chest and wore an almost identical rose colour glow to their cheeks. "Bloody huge" was an expression that immediately came to mind as they intensified their marching pace. At almost six feet tall and weighing nearly eleven stone, Harry felt completely inferior and slightly intimidated.

Again, Harry replicated the same type of process during his previous application with the Kanga force where Ernie now had the offer of a job. There were the customary medical checks followed by a formal exam comprising various types of questions including English, maths and general knowledge. Unfortunately for Harry the range of questions was completely different so all that he had to rely on was pure knowledge with a degree of guesswork. After what seemed like a fairly short interview he received the same news as before: there was no job. Harry was even more gutted than before; in a relatively short space of time over a few weeks he had applied to four separate forces who had all, for their own reasons given a resounding "No". Surely, someone with his attributes and skills must have something to offer?

Feeling quite glum, Harry left the interview room. Yet as he headed for the exit he was approached by one of the staff training officers who gave him some words of advice: bulk himself up, go back to school for a year and then re-apply the following year as Mid-Shires would definitely be recruiting again. He also handed Harry a piece of paper with the name and address of yet another force; he happened to mention they were still at the recruiting stage for that year. The address was one that was not immediately familiar to Harry but he soon realised that Tinkers Hill was only a short distance north of the capital; the downside was that it was further away from the comforts of home.

Harry sat in the back of his father's Rover 2000 TC contemplating his next steps. He wiped a small tear away from his eye before it had time to drop onto the worn leather seat when, all of a sudden, his father rescued the somewhat calamitous situation. "You're going back to school!" he said in a loud and commanding voice. Harry was quite shocked at this sudden outburst but, realistically, there seemed no real choice in the matter even though Harry still held onto the piece of paper that he had been given, thinking that something positive might still come from it. Harry had difficulty working his father's comment out, as the school he had just left had no sixth form so whatever school his father had in mind had to clearly be somewhere else. Yet he drove straight to this mystery school and it became apparent from the conversation en route between his mother and father that this was their back-up plan.

They arrived mid-afternoon and at a time when Harry believed anyone of seniority would have either gone home or at least be on their way. The former grammar school named after a former Lord Mayor of London had recently changed to a high school status. Harry's father parked near the entrance and entered the building leaving Harry and his mother in the car. About fifteen minutes later he returned and ushered Harry and his mother into the building, along a dark corridor and up some stairs where they were shown into a large, study-type room.

Harry met Mr Schrader for the first time. He was a tall, lean and clean-shaven middle-aged man who spoke quietly but very clearly and concisely. Harry noticed a large pile of school books on the side of his desk, thinking that this person must be very busy. The headmaster explained that even though Harry's exam results were disappointing he would join the school for one year starting in September and he would study and re-sit most of the CSE subjects taken previously and in addition would take O-level English and French. As Harry had no plan B he hurriedly agreed and it was a done deal. Mr Schrader explained very carefully that Harry would need to work exceedingly hard to get reasonable grades which undoubtedly would help him in finding the right career. It was something that Harry was prepared to try; when he returned home later that evening he placed the small piece of paper that he had been given at the Mid-Shires force into a diary hoping that something good might still come from it.

Over the next few weeks Harry was busy getting new uniform, books and sports kit. It was the latter that primarily excited Harry as he was keen to develop his sporting talents – he still had an eye on joining a career where fitness played a prominent part. This also meant that Harry and Ernie could still share some quality time together on the beach as well as the odd game of darts and bar billiards. It was this summer that Harry met a family from West Yorkshire. They were staying at their grandparents who ran a fishing tackle shop in the resort. The house was very close to where Harry and Ernie left their bikes at the top of the steps that led down to the beach, so each day when they passed the house they had some idea as to whether the family would be on the beach or not. Harry took a shine to the eldest daughter, Diane, who was their age, but the whole of the holiday became a bit of 'cat and mouse' involving the Yorkshire lass and, much to Harry's frustration, it was the mouse who came out on top. The only time he was able to speak to her was when the rest of her family was gathered round, despite his attempts to get her alone. Harry partly attributed this failure to Diane's battleaxe of a grandmother who constantly glared at him in an uncompromising manner on a daily basis as he passed their house. As Ernie used to remind him, there were plenty of other fish in the sea.

Another girl soon caught the eye of Harry who at least once a day would wander the complete length of the one-mile promenade wearing little else than his Speedos. He would keep one eye on where he was walking to avoid embarrassing doggie doodles or more importantly the dreaded broken glass, whilst simultaneously scanning the area for the ultimate beach babe. Harry fixed his eyes on a gorgeous sixteen-year-old. She was visiting the resort from Warwick where she lived with her parents. She had the most amazing long blonde straight hair which reached the middle of her back. She also had the most seductive eyes even if he didn't know exactly what the word meant; he was blown away every time she looked at him. This was precisely why he spent nearly eight hours every day during the summer holidays on the beach. Harry struck up a relationship with the wonder from Warwick, the only problem being that her fortnight's holiday was rapidly coming to an end and he would never see her again. *How disastrous* would that be, he wondered?

It was almost time for Ernie and Harry to part, Ernie was off to join the Kanga force cadets and Harry was starting a new school. They wished each other luck and parted company until the following summer holiday although they briefly saw each other during the Christmas break when Ernie reported that everything was progressing well. Harry was by now a Venture Scout and joined forces with a new recruit called Alfie who had recently moved to the area; they formed quite a bond and were seen as a duo that could be relied on with younger scouts looking up to them. They collaborated in various tasks from laying on a small gang show to preparing three-course meals for a party of four; all done in the best tradition of the scouting movement. If Harry was in any way cynical he would question the amount of work that went into the achievement simply to be awarded a badge which his mother sewed onto his uniform sleeve.

Alfie accompanied Harry on one or two overnight camps where the two relied on each other utilising basic survival techniques and fending for themselves. Harry could see the good in everyone, something which he clearly inherited from his mother and he considered Alfie as a good, all-round type of guy who was utterly trustworthy even though some of the other scouts thought he spoke with a bit of a plum in his mouth. Therefore, it came very much as a shock when Harry discovered, in later life, that Alfie had been convicted of downloading pornographic images of children which resulted in a prison sentence. Harry couldn't comprehend this type of behaviour and just couldn't fathom out what went on in some people's minds.

Chapter Three
Ed and His Interests

Ed was born and raised in an East Anglian city well renowned for its university status dating back to 1209 and is heralded as the world's fourth oldest surviving university. In the late 1960s the city was being developed and slowly the outer districts became entwined. Ed lived on the outskirts of the city with his parents and elder sister. She had attended a school over three miles from their home where she obtained good grades so it made complete sense that Ed went to the same school in the hope that he would follow his sister's achievements. He also felt a certain kind of pride knowing that all his immediate neighbouring peers went to a local school close to the estate, which clearly was not of the same ilk.

There was an added bonus to this; as the school was in excess of a three-mile boundary from his home, the local council paid for Ed to cycle to and from school which in 1966 netted the princely sum of one whole pound per school term. This remained fixed until he completed his education in 1972. Now, whilst this figure may not appear to have been of any significance to the chancellor of the exchequer at the time, the very fact that Ed rode to school, meant, for doing absolutely nothing He was receiving money to maintain his Raleigh small-wheeled bicycle which was his pride and joy, as it had been given to him by his parents as a present.

Ed's father worked as an engineer for the General Post Office, managing the whole of East Anglia whilst his mother worked as a telephonist/receptionist initially with the Pye Group, and then to Rattee and Kett, which was later taken over by Mowlems.

Ed's secondary schooling began at the boys' school close to the city centre. There was a girls' school next door by the same name but neither had contact with each other during school time. After a promising start, in his second year Ed came second out of thirty-three in his end of year exams, meaning he would move up to the A stream the following year. It was here that he met Dudley who became a lifelong friend and whose father coincidentally had been trained by Ed's father many years earlier within the engineering profession. Dudley was one of a twin and all three became known as 'Gruesome, Twosome and Tagalong' although it was never evidently clear who was who. The following year, overall Ed was placed twenty-third out of thirty-three, achieving positions ranging from seven to twenty-five in the class.

In the years leading up to Ed's final year, he and Dudley represented the school in athletics and hockey and also played hockey for a local club at weekends. It was through this club they managed to secure a selection to represent the southeast schoolboys at hockey. They were utterly surprised when an announcement was made thereafter at a school assembly to acknowledge their achievements. Ed and Dudley continued their friendship, culminating in them being made senior prefects as well as librarians. This gave them both unrestricted access to areas of the school normally forbidden and a far greater rapport with the teaching staff, but of course they never abused this privilege. This continued during their final year when Dudley was made head boy and Ed, his deputy.

Ed was the consummate competitor and hated losing at anything. When Ed was in the fourth year he took a particular dislike to a member of the sixth form mainly because the jerk thought he was something better than anyone else, but it also transpired that this individual had been seeing Ed's sister on the quiet. Ed decided it would be a good idea to enter the 'mile' race at the end of year sports day. He needed his head testing as he was only ever considered a sprinter and had never ever run anything greater than 100 yards.

Needless to say, Ed, using all of his guts and determination won against the outright favourite. This vein of fortune continued for another two years where he managed to secure further victories in the mile, and other various notable wins. To encapsulate all this, Ed was eventually awarded in his final year a silver cup for winning the mile. Three in a row and, finally, he reaped the rewards and some highly praised acknowledgement.

Ed's final year beckoned in September 1971 and he had given much thought during the summer holidays as to what he wanted to do when he left school. Some of his friends had already left, starting apprenticeships within industries in and around the city; whilst others went on to do A levels. Dudley's brother had left to do A levels leaving just 'Gruesome and Twosome'. This cleared things up a little as to who was who. After each Sunday lunch Ed's father would recite stories from his days in Egypt as a Royal Military Police officer and it was these stories, along with the desire to continue in a sporting context, that Ed decided he wanted to join the police force as a cadet. He was initially undecided, but after speaking to a careers advisor at school Ed decided not to opt for his local force but went further south to the Tinkers Hill force, just north of London.

Ed received a nominal sum of pocket money from his parents but was actively encouraged to seek work opportunities. He had previously secured a Saturday job as a delivery boy on a butcher's round, which meant early morning starts from the butcher's shop. This included loading the basket on the bike with everyone's meat. If stacked correctly and in a specific order it meant that it would take the least amount of time to deliver. Obtaining payment at the time of delivery was quite important as this formed an opportunity for tips, which seemed to increase towards the Christmas period. Ed was lucky that his delivery round included large private houses in an affluent area of the city. He endured the harsh winter months as it kept him fit and relatively healthy and the joy of riding a delivery bike was great once he had mastered the fact that, as the handlebars turned, the basket cage on the front didn't, causing maximum confusion. Just kicking the front rest down to park the bike was so pleasing, knowing that the sheer weight of meat contained within the basket could easily have caused a calamity had the bike toppled over. Ed was paid the princely sum of one pound to complete the deliveries and if he was lucky this increased with tips. He also had to contend with one of those wonderful 'note' wallets whereby some magic occurred. By opening the wallet and inserting the note and closing again something happened. When it was opened again from the other side – hey presto the notes were held in place; this was almost wizardry for a sixteen-year-old.

Ed also managed to secure a job at the butcher's for Dudley so, once deliveries were complete, it was back to Ed's house for coffee and a snack – then they would peruse the Friday edition of the local *Evening News* looking at various types of cars. The two friends would sit and ponder upon many a car wondering whether their dreams would ever be realised. There were TR5s and TR6s, Triumph Spitfires, Lotuses, Rovers of the P4, P5 and P5b variety; these were particularly of interest to Ed as they were used by members of government at the time. The Rover P4 series cars were produced by the Rover Company Limited in Warwickshire from 1950 to 1964, during which period over 130,000 cars were built. The Rover's design, level of engineering, build quality and general air of refinement earned it the sobriquet 'The Poor Man's Rolls-Royce'. This was a relative term as a Rover 90 cost over £1500 in 1959. The P4 cars were built on a massive ladder-type box section chassis which was immensely stable and contributed to the Rover's feeling of imperturbable solidity and is testament to their durability and longevity that the Rover P4s can still be found all round the world today. It was questionable whether this was attributed to the fact that lots of their body panels were made of aluminium.

There were also Austins and Morrises and some rather posh expensive sports cars. Ed and Dudley deliberated and dreamt of one day owning such a distinguishable vehicle but, in reality, such second-hand cars were often rather cheap and petrol certainly wasn't a worry, let alone insurance. How things have changed. In today's age people are more likely to seek the most economical vehicle, when such a consideration never entered Ed and or Dudley's heads at the time. In particular, the French-polished dashboard, wooden sliding tool tray, leather straps, as well as the front leather bench seat meant that any female acquaintance could almost sit on his lap whist he had one hand on the wheel and the other on the gear stick. Most definitely it was Ed's dream to own such a prestigious type of vehicle and he would do anything to turn that into reality.

In addition to such dreams the two lads would look in the sports section of the paper to confirm who else had been selected to play hockey – the teams were published and occasionally they realised they had been elevated to the 2nd team within their local hockey club.

Chapter Four

Harry's New School

Harry walked into the classroom of his new school full of trepidation. He had been placed into a relatively small group who were all in the same position; they had finished fifth year in their respective schools but, for various reasons, wanted to gain further education and Mr Schrader had given them all what appeared to be a second chance. Harry knew he had to do well otherwise he would inevitably experience the same disappointment which had befallen him the previous year. There was no way he wanted another three interviews and be rejected at each again.

Things weren't too bad as there were a couple of girls from his old school in his class and, to top it off, his form teacher was a county cricketer who had an appetite for all types of sports. He actively encouraged Harry to join all the sports clubs during lunch sessions and supported him by nominating him for the 1st eleven football team. Anything sporting, Harry was there, even playing table tennis against the best Chinese scholar but rarely coming out on top. The school was broken up into five houses each being equally competitive. Harry was overjoyed when he realised that the colour of the house he now represented was no other than his favourite – yellow. He immediately knew he was onto a winner and did everything in his power during inter-house challenges to ensure that yellow prevailed as the top house in the school.

During the year Harry developed a friendship with a sixth former called Sasha who was very pretty and seemed overtly friendly and genuine. She was a 'touchy-feely' gregarious type and on one occasion invited Harry for a private one to one walk. She was quite insistent that Harry accompany her down to a wooded dell near to, but off, school premises one lunch-time. This liaison had come out of the blue and Harry was a little perturbed as Sasha was clearly more intelligent and he viewed her as being well out of his league. Never wishing to miss an opportunity he agreed to chaperone Sasha for a twosome walk in the woods. Harry had a very important inter-house football fixture that afternoon against one of their main rivals, so it was crucial he was back in time for kick-off.

Regrettably, Harry did not wear a watch and was oblivious of the time even though Sasha repeatedly reassured him that he would not be late. Sasha was very flirtatious and soon Harry was in her clutches. He was very much enjoying the occasion but realised time was ticking by. He made the decision to return to school so he and Sasha ambled back up the hill. As they neared the school Harry saw one of his fellow teammates already changed into his yellow football strip, beckoning from outside the gate which led onto the sports field. He then noticed more team members dressed in the distinct yellow colours walking across from the changing room. It suddenly dawned on him that time was of the essence and he started to run, leaving Sasha still dawdling behind.

In his mind he concluded that this was a ploy to prevent him playing against their nearest rivals. Harry scored twice in the game but long afterwards had doubts about Sasha's motives. Was this the clearest case of school inter-house espionage ever or was it simply someone who fancied him so much, she couldn't resist his company?

Harry saw Sasha once more on a weekend before she blended into insignificance as far as he was concerned. Although at the same school their connection lasted little more than a month before she moved on to someone new. He never did learn why she had lured him to the dell on that lunchtime and to date it remains one of those unsolved mysteries.

Harry was intent on accomplishing in his last academic year. He wanted desperately to join the cadet corps and he was already making plans. Whereas his secondary school had no dedicated careers adviser the school where he was now had an excellent service, and Harry visited the careers office regularly to obtain the latest updated information. Try as he might he still found maths a problem but he felt there had been an improvement and he particularly knuckled down during these lessons. The one year at his new school seemed to fly by.

Before he knew it Christmas had been and gone. The words of the last staff officer resonated in Harry's head so wherever possible he was running to keep in shape and, as soon as the warmer weather arrived, he was back swimming in the sea to maintain his aerobic capacity. During that year Harry had also kept in contact with the wonder from Warwick and was pleased to learn that she and her parents would be returning to the seaside resort for a fortnight during the summer. *Now, that's something to look forward to,* he thought to himself wondering if she had changed in any way.

There was a lad in Harry's form group who suffered with mild learning difficulties and it transpired, during a register check one morning that Phil was being bullied by a boy from another sixth form group. This had been going on for some time but as Harry was in a different teaching group to Phil it only became apparent after the Christmas break. By all accounts this other lad had a reputation for this sort of trouble and seemed to relish in ridiculing those with a less academic mind. Harry let it be known to his form that this sort of behaviour was deplorable and someone should perhaps give him a dose of his own medicine. Within a week the procrastinator was looking for Harry as what had been said within the privacy of the classroom was taken literally and it was like a red rag to a bull. To make matters worse Phil had actually aggravated the situation by telling the lad that Harry was going to sort him out. This was never Harry's intention, he had only expressed what all of his class were thinking, but it now seemed as if he was plummeting towards a pasting from the school 'hood'. This was a dilemma, which became an even larger one when Harry was suddenly confronted at lunchtime in the corridor near to the dining room. This rough-faced, generously proportioned and well-built kid stood in front of Harry. He absolutely oozed trouble. "You gonna fight me 'cos of that spaz?" he said threateningly.

Harry's mind was going ten to the dozen, he didn't want to say no as his peers would perceive him as being weak. To gladly confront this brute may have developed into a fight there and then, which may have resulted in Harry's immediate dismissal from school which he could ill-afford. Harry played for time as he could see the deputy head approaching from behind his adversary. Before anything further occurred Harry blurted, "After school – four thirty," and turned and walked away.

Fighting was alien to Harry and was not in his nature. He had one minor scuffle with an older pupil at his previous school but it was nothing to write home about. However, he felt quite strongly about Phil being bullied and thought it unacceptable and there was a principle at stake. Whether having a fight in the street after school was the right way of this resolving this was debatable particularly in light of Harry's wish to join the police cadets. How would they view this situation and would his chances of following Ernie disappear up in smoke? Harry decided to duck the impending challenge but knew that it wouldn't go away.

The next morning during register Harry was asked how he got on. Some of his classmates felt let down when he told them he had not defended Phil's predicament. Unfortunately, the aggressor was even more wound up because Harry had defaulted and yet again came looking for him. Harry talked himself into believing it would be wrong for many reasons but, once again, when confronted chose to invite the bully onto home turf. Harry said, "If you want to fight come to my youth club on Friday night," thinking this might put him off.

"I will be there at eight," was the reply, before walking away with a sickly grin on his face. The situation became increasingly worrying and Harry realised he would have to confront this head-on. Fortunately, word had got round so when Friday night arrived Harry was joined by a few mates. When this particularly unfriendly bully, with a face that resembled a twentieth century Mr Potato Head, arrived to invite Harry outside he found himself outnumbered and decided the whole thing was not worth the effort. Harry never had any contact with this brute again and he never bothered Phil again; this was partly due to the fact that Phil's form teacher took matters into his own hands once he became aware of what was going on. It was a lesson learnt by Harry: in cases where you speak out, make sure that you can deliver even though what you say may be taken out of context.

When it came to the final six weeks at school the intensity rose in relation to the careers office; every time Harry visited it seemed that more and more students were waiting for advice from the advisor, who was clearly over-worked as she seemed to have less and less time available. On one of these visits the advisor suggested to Harry that he might wish to increase and widen his opportunities by applying for a navy cadet job rather than just limiting it to the police cadet role. She seemed very positive about this, which made good sense as Harry's older brother had left home at sixteen and had made a relatively lucrative and exciting life at sea with the Merchant Navy. His brother had visited many fascinating and interesting places around the globe in the six years since joining up, but came home for two to three weeks at a time most of which he spent partying.

Harry completed his final year at school and was quite chuffed with the results he achieved. His maths in particular earned him high praise considering the disaster from the previous year. Whilst not a formal O-level grade, Harry could live with the fact that he was not blessed with an arithmetical mind and would just have to muddle through life doing his best. More importantly, he felt very proud that the overall winning house in the sports arena was awarded to his beloved 'yellows'.

Chapter Five
Second Time Lucky

Two months before the end of term Harry decided to apply for three jobs. The first was back to the Mid-Shires Cadet Corps who had rejected him the year before. Although he had not grown massively he was a lot physically fitter and therefore he considered himself a strong outside bet for a position there. His mother also reassured him that it was not wise to try and gain too much weight as to do so might have a detrimental effect on his health. The second was to the Royal Navy which Harry was cajoled into by the careers advisor from his new school and the third was to the Tinkers Hill Cadet Corps, the address for which Harry still had on the piece of paper given to him from the previous year. He really did not contemplate being rejected by all three so really tried to be positive about an outcome of some sort from at least one of them.

Harry sat an examination for each of the cadet corps applications at his local police station. He did this in a small confined room where there was a small window with bars on the outside. Harry wondered if this room was used to interrogate prisoners as there seemed to be an unpleasant smell lingering. He was left alone by the duty officer whilst he completed them, following which he was told the papers would be forwarded to the respective forces and Harry would hear of the outcome in due course. Whilst at the police station he underwent some basic medical checks such as measuring his height, weight, chest size and checking his eyesight. Harry went home and deliberated over the different questions on each paper, one of which related to the Boston Tea Party which he had never heard of and failed to see how there was any relevance between drinking tea in Lincolnshire and becoming a police cadet.

A few days later he travelled to a Navy establishment to take part in the recruiting process. *HMS Ganges* was very imposing and impressive with lots of naval cadets milling around in uniform. The most noticeable feature at this establishment was the vast 143-foot mast which Harry discovered was used for training as well as ceremonial occasions. The mast was central to columns of ropes that were climbed to music by junior seamen culminating in one of the cadets standing up on the button on the very top to make his salute.

There, too, he completed an examination paper as well as a full medical check carried out by a naval medic. Harry sat a formal interview process, during which one of the panel asked, "Why do you want to be a seaman?"

Harry seemed taken aback by this question and truthfully he would have answered that this was not his first choice in the career stakes. Instead he blurted out, "My careers advisor thought it would suit me."

In hindsight, it was not the most consummate reply but they followed this with, "Your entrance exam results suggest you could train higher than an able seaman, would you fancy being a navigator instead?" This came as a total surprise; he had no idea where this had sprung from and Harry squirmed in his chair before quickly agreeing to their suggestion. Completely having misread the situation it suddenly dawned on him that his original application asked for his preferred position within the Navy and he had chosen the starting rank, without thinking any further forward. It wouldn't be the first time that something like that happened in his life. The interview panel reassured Harry that if he found the training for navigator too intense he could always then fall back to the able seaman role. Without wishing to count any chickens before they hatched Harry left the interview in a very buoyant mood. From the conversation he had just had with the naval hierarchy he felt almost certain that his application was one that would be offered, but was still totally dependent on a final confirmation.

By now it was well into the summer holidays and as usual the beach and town was full of tourists. Ernie had returned home from his first year of training with the cadets; he and Harry met up for some drinks and more importantly some reminiscing where Harry tried to get as much information as possible from him about cadet life.

Harry also met up again with the wonder from Warwick who returned to the seaside town for another fortnight of sea, sun and silly hats and their relationship continued to blossom. Not long after attending the naval process Harry received a letter on what appeared to be formal Navy letter-headed paper. It was formal job offer to join Her Majesty's Royal Navy as a cadet and he was to report to a Navy training facility in the southwest of the country. He was sent a long list of equipment and clothing that he would have to supply himself and he was provided with a starting date in September 1972. Overjoyed was not the word.

A few days later Harry was invited for a formal interview to the Tinkers Hill force headquarters. He made the long trip down and was met by a very cheery uniformed sergeant. Harry sat a series of classroom-based tests which were different to those previously experienced. He also went through a more rigorous medical to the extent that he provided a sample of urine but he had no idea why. *Perhaps they are checking to see if I have a drink problem*, he wondered. He also had his testicles felt before being asked to cough. Again he wondered what this was for but never had the nerve to ask.

Harry waited anxiously in the library of this single storey building. He noticed that all the window frames were metal which was somewhat of a surprise to him. Outside, he noticed some cadets marching up and down on a parade square. The sergeant in charge of the recruiting process was about forty years of age, had a distinctive black moustache, was very friendly, jovial and he made Harry feel instantly welcome along with all the other applicants in the library.

In the afternoon Harry was invited to take part in an interview with three fairly elderly men. The one in the middle did most of the talking and it transpired he was an assistant chief constable. He seemed very austere and relished the opportunity to demean Harry's father's job. "What does your father do for a living?" he asked. Harry recalled that on the application form he had written *Director* as his father's job title but he had only been given this role as a technical director literally one or two weeks before the submission of Harry's application. The interview panel had clearly done their homework and knew that he was a chef by trade but, for some reason unbeknown to Harry, they formed the view that he was trying to enhance his chances of a job by embellishing his father's job role.

Harry stood his ground knowing that he had done nothing of the sort and it just coincided with his father's recent change of title. "Yes," he agreed, "he is a chef but he is also a technical director with responsibility for two other hotels." It was perfectly clear that the assistant chief constable did not want to let the matter rest and continued in the same vein, suggesting that Harry was trying to mislead the panel. Harry was genuinely not trying to misrepresent anything or anyone and, feeling quite browbeaten, he explained very slowly and carefully exactly what role his father played at the hotel where he was employed. By doing so, he showed the board his determination not to wilt under pressure. The superintendent who sat alongside the ACC seemed to accept this as a reasonable explanation. Finally, it was the turn of the third board member who turned out to be the head of academic studies within the cadet corps. He was a studious man and reminded Harry a little of Mr Schrader. Potty Hubbard, as he was known, had Harry's results from the tests which he sat earlier in the day. Lo and behold they were relatively happy with Harry's overall results but, unsurprisingly, maths was highlighted as being an issue. *No change there then,* thought Harry to himself. Potty advised that if Harry were to be accepted into the cadets he would have to improve greatly in this area and a lot of work was needed. It seemed a case of déjà vu as he had heard this not so long ago when starting his last year at school. Harry promised unreservedly to do so and left the headquarters not quite knowing which way the day went.

About three weeks later, having still not responded to the offer from the Royal Navy, Harry received a letter from the Tinkers Hill force. It was a letter confirming his acceptance into the force commencing on 4th September 1972. He was absolutely over the moon; all his hard work and perseverance had paid off and now he had a big decision to make.

The following evening and completely out of the blue Harry answered a knock on the door. It was a police officer from the local station and he was the bearer of good news. It came in the form of a phone call from the Mid-Shires force who confirmed Harry had passed all the tests and were offering him a place with the cadets, starting in September. All of a sudden there were three job offers on the table and he couldn't quite believe it.

He made an instant decision there and then which he had no regrets about. He politely told the officer on the doorstep where to go, turning the Mid-Shires offer down. He then set about formally replying to the job offer from the Royal Navy explaining that he was declining it due to 'other commitments'. It seemed as if Harry's fortunes had changed for the better; one year there was nothing, the following year the offer of not just one or two jobs but of three – life was really looking good.

Chapter Six

Ed's application

In the early 1970s each police force was only as strong as its local authority with regard to finances. Establishing the time frame to make such an application to the cadets, Ed obtained the requisite application forms and attempted to write in his best handwriting; although those who knew Ed well were only too aware that it looked as if a spider has crawled across the pages.

The application was duly posted late April 1972 and Ed later received notification to attend his local Parkway police station to sit his 'entrance exam'. Walking into the front office at the station was extremely daunting but became even more frightening when he was greeted by the gruffest looking front desk sergeant he had ever encountered, not that he had met many up to that point. After some formalities Ed was invited in, by the portly officer, to sit his exam. The postal system during this era was quite efficient so every day, after returning home from school, Ed would hastily check to see whether there was anything from the Tinkers Hill Force Cadet Corps. As time dragged on, Ed became slightly apprehensive but then in early May 1972 he received the letter he was waiting for. With some trepidation he opened it slowly not knowing which way it may go. He was ecstatic when he realised that he had been invited to attend Tinkers Hill

Force training headquarters albeit initially for a medical examination. Could this really be the beginning of the rest of his life? Time would only tell. At the end of May Ed's father drove him the forty miles for what was to be an all-day event.

Ed arrived reasonably early to be met by many other prospective applicants, both male and female, of all shapes and sizes. Ed was exceedingly nervous at the prospect. First of all, there was the customary medical and the supply of the requisite urine sample and 'internal' examination. Ed had never experienced this before. This was followed by an eye test and then an aptitude test. Ed was over the moon when he was told he would be progressed to interview stage before a panel of 'big wigs'. Ed, being in a bit of daze at this stage of proceedings, never could recall who interviewed him or what questions he was asked. It was all too traumatic but, fortunately for him, he was accepted and was sent to be fitted for a uniform. Ed felt extraordinarily jubilant in the knowledge that he was later to commence a career as a police cadet on 4th September 1972. He returned to school the day after the interview feeling a huge sense of achievement and the knowledge that he now had a job.

Whilst this was very good, psychologically it was bad in knowing that Ed had a position of employment to go to: he no longer had to work hard. Ed had been brought up to 'know his place in society'. His parents were working class, although Ed had many heated wrangles with his father over this as he could not understand how his father could consider himself working class as he held a management position at work. Perhaps he was lower middle class, but it was a very socialist house that they

49

lived in and clearly in hindsight what Ed required was to keep his thoughts to himself.

One would have to say at this stage of Ed's life he was courteous, well dressed and well mannered. This stemmed from his parents and he often recalled his mother's phrase *manners maketh the man*. Ed had an unusual surname and repeatedly people would get it wrong, but his father instilled in him that he should always be proud of the name he was born with and to ensure that, when announced, it was always correctly stated. This had always been a 'sore bear' within the family as it occurred so often. This became to a certain extent Ed's nemesis that caused him some grief from his early days in the police cadets and for many years thereafter. People soon learnt that if they did not pronounce his name correctly then he tended not to respond or if he did so it would be to correct whoever was attempting to pronounce it. Sadly, this often involved senior officers who were not best pleased.

Looking back, all Ed ever wanted was to be encouraged to achieve the best possible and such encouragement should always have started at home. Clearly this was not the case as Ed could not fault his parents, for they instilled into him that manners were not necessarily inbred but acquired through one's upbringing. His father was always immaculately dressed and always knew how to wear clothes. Ed followed this lead from his father, ultimately giving him the pride and grace to wear clothes and, more importantly, how to look after them. Ed learnt from a very early age how to iron his own shirts and trousers, a trait that most young people have no idea of.

One Sunday evening just before church, Ed's mother said, "You could cut your fingers on those creases," after he ironed his trousers, making him feel particularly proud. Unfortunately, trouble was about to erupt; as they were leaving Ed's sister decided for whatever reason to pull Ed's tie, putting it slightly out of place. He went absolutely apoplectic and his father suggested that if looks could kill she would be dead. Needless to say, she never pulled that stunt again.

Ed continued in his last year of school but his mind was already elsewhere. He elected to study six O levels and in addition to the academic work there existed the amalgamation of the boys' and girls' schools. As deputy head boy he was often asked to assist teachers in numerous tasks and as the school had their own printing press, such tasks were done in-house and often by the head or deputy head boy. It seemed that Ed had his fingers in many pies, so to speak, although the sporting activities continued both in and outside school. Ed and his best friend Dudley were referred to in the club newsletter once as 'the schoolboy twins'. Quite ironic seeing that one was actually a twin. There were home and away matches in all sorts of weather conditions: bright sunshine, rain and even on occasions snow and it was during a hockey match in the snow that a new coloured ball was introduced to assist with playing the game. It was just as well that the orange-coloured ball was introduced as Ed would never have scored otherwise.

It was after a hockey match that Ed's distaste for beer was identified. He had been sheltered from the abuse of alcohol, albeit his father regularly attended his local on a Friday night; this was then followed by a Sunday lunchtime visit to his local club. This was not to say that on special occasions alcohol was not available at home and Ed sampled a 'ginger wine' one Christmas which almost burnt his throat. Sherry was also on offer or sometimes the odd glass of wine with meals, but his parents were always firm and it was never to excess. Unless Ed went out for dinner, he never drank alcohol.

After one particular hockey match it was traditional for a jug to appear full of beer. Whilst Ed was no expert he tried a sample and discovered it was the most watered-down example he could ever imagine tasting and from that moment onwards he rarely drank beer, later becoming more of a rum and black or a vodka and lime man, which almost became the ruin of him in 1974 when he was in police training in Oxfordshire. Poor Harry was to suffer after that incident.

Chapter Seven

Day of Reckoning

Ed and Harry rolled up in Tinkers Hill on a fine September morning in 1972, having left their respective families and home towns to begin what was essentially, a whole new chapter in their lives. They negotiated the gentle slope leading up from the main road via a barrier to what was, at the time, a relatively new one-storey building which housed the force-training department. What they didn't immediately realise was that the slope they had gleefully ambled up wasn't a feature to be underestimated; it would play a significant part not only in their forthcoming cadet training but also in future courses when they reached the pinnacle of being a police officer. The unmanned barrier was the only official entry and exit onto the site which was busy at certain times of the day; little did Ed know that this point would feature in one of his character-building moments.

Tinkers Hill was a New Town, having been built in the 1920s. It was a far cry from the row upon row of terraced houses seen in many inner city or urban areas as it had been specifically designed and created with many open spaces, an inordinate number of roundabouts and an abundance of delightful blossomed tree-lined streets which dominated many areas of the town. The sun was shining so, as far as Harry was concerned, it was a day to be happy – but there was also a tinge of nervousness as well as excitement etched onto the faces of the youngsters as they carried their suitcases nearer to the entrance. A sense of anticipation prevailed as neither Harry nor Ed had any idea of what to expect and there was a blissful feeling of wandering into the unknown. The nearest comparison that Harry could make was that it felt like starting school for the very first time all over again, but there was no backing out now.

Harry and Ed were entering an important and totally new era that would change their lives. Harry in particular had endured so much to get to this stage, and in Ed's case it was almost as if nothing else mattered. Joining the police cadets virtually overshadowed everything else going on in the world; on their first day there was a little matter of the 1972 Olympic Games taking place in Munich which made the front page of the newspapers for all the wrong reasons. Achievements, such as US swimmer Mark Spitz becoming the first athlete to win seven Olympic gold medals, paled into insignificance when the horrors in Munich unfolded during Ed and Harry's first night as cadets. During the early morning of September 5th, a group of Palestinian terrorists stormed the Olympic Village apartment of the Israeli athletes, killing two and taking nine others hostage. The Black September group demanded the release of Arab prisoners as well as two German terrorists in return for the hostages. In the ensuing shoot-out at Munich airport, the Israeli hostages were killed along with five terrorists and a German policeman. Olympic competition was suspended for twenty-four hours to hold memorial services for the athletes. *What sort of start was this to their cadet career,* wondered Ed?

In the immediate days after, Harry and Ed began to find their feet, integrating with the other new recruits as well as learning their way around what seemed like an absolute vast headquarters complex. At this juncture second year cadets also returned to training, boosting the numbers considerably and in the first couple of days it seemed as if there were literally hundreds of confused-looking adolescents milling around with suitcases. Ed and Harry felt a little disadvantaged as it was apparent that some of the new recruits knew one another from school, whilst others knew some of the returning second years from other ventures.

In a very short space of time Ed and Harry met their respective section leaders who they became reliant on and who were there to help and guide as well as assisting them to overcome any initial jitters or the dreaded homesickness. It was their section leaders who made Ed and Harry feel welcome and showed them to their rooms. Yet it was also the same, so-called leaders who instigated practical jokes on the newcomers. Inevitably, the friendship between Ed and Harry was not instantaneous but was one that would develop over time.

The early seventies was an iconic period and by the time Ed and Harry commenced their cadetship, Stanley Kubrick's film, *A Clockwork Orange* had been showing in cinemas for eight months making critical acclaim most notably for its disturbing, upsetting and violent scenes as well as covering taboo subjects like psychiatry, juvenile delinquency, gang culture, rape and other social, political and economic subjects in a dystopian near-future Britain.

Given Harry's somewhat sheltered upbringing, watching a film of this nature within his first few weeks made him reflect hard about life, the impact and differences people could make on society in general as well as how certain behaviour affected an individual. He also sincerely hoped and prayed that none of the cadets he was still bonding with would turn out like Alex, the film's main sociopath character.

Seventies hippie fashion was all the rage and loose-fitting, flowing maxi skirts and dresses became dominant for young ladies. Disco music and dance also influenced dresses with slender lines, flowing skirts and the shimmering fabrics that would look best in a nightclub. For men, flared trousers, tank tops, Harrington jackets and stacked heels became common, the latter being clearly influenced by the pop group Slade who reached the top five of the charts in September 1972 with 'Mama, we're all Crazy Now'. Staying with the music theme, during its heyday *Top of the Pops*, with its eclectic group of zany presenters, some of whom went on to greater notoriety, attracted fifteen million viewers each Thursday evening. At least half of the viewers tuned in, not only to see and hear the latest from the pop scene, but also to drool over a relatively new dance troupe – Pan's People. If there was one night to guarantee a full house in the cadet lounge it would be when Pan's People were performing on *Top of the Pops*. The World Wide Web was just a twinkle in Tim Berners-Lee's eyes, Diana Princess of Wales was only eleven years old and yet to emerge as an international icon onto the Royal scene and Norway rejected membership of the then European

Economic Union, something they have managed to steer clear of ever since.

In overall charge of the training department was Superintendent Eric Crake; it transpired that he was one of the three panel members who had interviewed Harry and Ed to consider their suitability a few months previously. The superintendent was a slim, thin-faced man with a small moustache who had a wispy manner about him. He looked older than he was and you could tell by his gait that he was probably ex-military. He had a pleasant persona and when he spoke his voice was quite soft, with a posh but regimented accent. Eric, it turned out, had been held prisoner in a Japanese camp during the Second World War and it may have been this experience that accounted for him walking with a slight stoop. As the person in overall command of the cadets Harry, quite wrongly as it turned out, felt that he lacked a strong personality and on the face of things he appeared to be easily influenced by those around him. At least one of the new recruits believed that the superintendent was actually the gardener simply due to how he wandered about the place. It turned out that towards the twilight of his career he liked a tipple at lunchtimes from the bar at headquarters causing him on occasions to take a short nap in the afternoon. Whilst this behaviour was not routine, and certainly not acceptable in today's modern police service, it was probably easier to avoid detection in the early seventies for someone in Eric's position. The suggestion that he kept a case of Double Diamond beer beneath his desk was never fully proven. Whilst the superintendent was the head figure, on a day-to-day basis he barely had any influence on how Ed and Harry fared in their first year, although he did make occasional supporting appearances at athletic or other sporting events or chancing his arm at refereeing an in-house rugby match. Ed, to his detriment, would later discover the true nature of this man's steely persona.

Chief Inspector Broome was Superintendent Crake's second in command. Harry knew very little about him and put him in the same category as Superintendent Crake with regards to being more of a bureaucratic figure. He was very rarely seen on a day-to-day basis, as it turned out he was out busy recruiting personnel for the regular police service. Harry learnt quite quickly not to underestimate the chief inspector after his 'trouser' incident and it was quite clear he was certainly no shrinking violet. The chief inspector's daughter became somewhat of a hit with Ed who ensured that he always used the swimming pool on a Sunday morning after he discovered her liking for a mid-morning dip when she used to knock out a few lengths.

The man with day-to-day responsibility for the cadets was Inspector Paul Broadhurst who was a stern disciplinarian having served with the Cameron Highlanders. He was the epitome of the archetypal police officer, having great presence and bearing and when required he could make his voice travel a tremendous distance. He had been promoted from sergeant that year and was highly respected, later being awarded the MBE for services to policing. At the time, the inspector held an almost spellbinding hold over the cadets and there was a tinge of nervousness from cadets whenever he was around. He was extremely fit, forthright and had a dry sense of humour. He had a particular liking for anyone that excelled at football as previously he had captained the police team. He was also a member of the National Wrestling Association and often engaged on a Thursday evening huffing and puffing on the floor mats in the gymnasium with Roy Rivers the swimming instructor. Inspector Broadhurst was always on the lookout for any behaviour which was likely to lead to a cadet bringing the name of the force into disrepute. This included regular checks around the dormitory blocks for any rowdy behaviour as well as scouring local haunts for any underage drinking.

The sergeant in charge of cadets was none other than Bill Watkin, who had a penchant for rugby. He was a no-nonsense type of man and applied all the rules quite strictly but there was a softer side to him. Sergeant Watkin joined the force in 1963 having served as a navigation officer with the Royal Fleet Auxiliary. As far as small worlds go, during his application to join the police he found himself sitting a compulsory spelling test amongst other types of assessments. The test was overseen by Paul Broadhurst who at that point of his service was a constable at the old headquarters located in nearby Twatton. Bill assumed responsibility for the cadets in 1969 when he transferred into the Training Department. Having already passed his inspector's exam as well as an Intermediate Bachelor of Law Degree he needed to add a further string to his bow. He was keen to pass on some of the expertise gained from his fleet auxiliary days to help train budding officers for their life ahead. Everything about Bill oozed 'spit and polish'; he was always immaculately turned out with his tunic and trousers pressed to perfection and his shoes gleaming to the point where you could literally see your reflection in them.

Constable Mick Green had been with the force for only eight years before becoming a regular cadet trainer. He loved the outdoor life and was one of the first recipients of the gold Duke of Edinburgh award having been invited to Buckingham Palace to receive it. Mick was also a county swimmer and a member of the Round Table. He was seen as a fair-minded individual who wanted the best for the cadets. Whenever he did the early morning shift to supervise the cadet physical training he used to ensure that the kitchen staff were always picked up beforehand to ensure that breakfasts were ready for hungry cadets after their session. This meant arriving earlier than normal and then taking a van to collect both staff. Mick Green was the perfect image of a police officer and his uniform was constantly pristine and worn with pride. Most noticeably he turned up on parade with perfectly shiny shoes; this was something he had picked up from an exchange visit to the United States a couple of years before. He had purchased some 'special' paint to help him maintain the shine to avoid having to clean them the traditional way every day with spit and polish. Mick owned a relatively new cult car which had the appearance of something from the space age known as the Bond Bug. It was a compact three-wheeler produced by Reliant and aimed at the hip motorist of the day. Its wedge-shaped design with a lift-up canopy instead of conventional doors and two seats made it appealing to those with an appetite for fun. It wasn't long before cadets jokingly referred to it as Mick's 'Love Bug'. The relatively small 750cc engine was capable of seventy-six mph, in excess of the UK national speed limit, and was comparable to small saloon cars such as the basic Mini and the Hillman Imp. To some, it was simply seen as a three-wheeler likely to come a cropper at the first sharp bend; to Mick it was his pride and joy and a lot of fun to drive. Harry and Ed always thought Mick had a sense of humour; he would need to as the car was a bright orange tangerine colour and stood out like a sore thumb. The two new recruits wondered if this was his way of being noticed.

Constable Knapweed was employed in an administration role within the training department, with his main role being the completion of probationer reports to divisional stations and helping on recruitment days with eyesight tests and checking urine samples. Part of his duties from time to time included assisting with cadet training which involved him having to take the early morning physical training sessions. It was Harry's and Ed's belief that he was not overly keen at this task; not necessarily due to having to rise to be there at seven a.m., it was more to do with his physical presence and ability. He rarely joined the cadets in an early morning run and was more than satisfied just to give orders to the cadet course leader so he could organise and run any sessions that were required. Knapweed joined the force in 1966 at the age of thirty-one having served as a ground wireless fitter in the Royal Air Force, completing his twelve years in the RAF as a sergeant. He was a test engineer for eighteen months before making the transition into the police force and was a keen camping and caravanning enthusiast. In some ways he was a man of mystery who smoked Condor tobacco in his ever-present pipe. In the eyes of others he lacked presence and authority, wore a shoddy uniform in comparison to Mick Green and Bill Watkin and would often be the subject of ridicule from some of the braver and bolder cadets.

As part of the admin training team Knapweed was required on occasions to drive the mighty force coach, a big old Bedford five-litre monster. The driving school arranged for him to be taken out to assess his standard and he duly drove around the local side streets for about twenty minutes before returning. He thought nothing of it, believing he would be notified as to when he might have a formal course. The following day, the superintendent asked him to take the coach out to collect some police probationers; he quite rightly pointed out that he did not hold the correct driving qualification as he had not had any formal training. His excuses were swept aside and told not to worry as he had passed his test with flying colours the day before. He felt quite aggrieved that no one had delivered this good news sooner.

One of Constable Knapweed's responsibilities before leaving the headquarters site for the night was to complete an inspection of all the blocks to ensure all cadets were accounted for in bed and the lights were out. He started this process in the same way, every time taking the same route. He would light his pipe up at the point of leaving the training department building and the trail of tobacco smoke would follow him from block to block. One evening, Knapweed was informed that male cadets had been seen entering the female block after he had left the site for the night. The informant, a dog handler, had previously observed cadets keeping tabs on Knapweed who would ensure he had left in his car before making their move.

Deciding that he was not going to let these novice cadets run rings round him, he arranged to leave the site one evening as usual, only to meet the dog handler at a prearranged destination down the road and be brought back onto the complex in the dog van. Within seconds of arriving, both he and dog handler witnessed three or four male cadets enter the female block. Knapweed, feeling slightly awkward at catching anyone in a compromising position, duly informed Matron who lived on site and she quickly ousted the culprits, who were supposedly there purely for platonic reasons. Those involved were reprimanded the following day. Knapweed had perhaps unfairly acquired such an unforgiving nickname which originated from *The Herbs:* a 1970s' BBC television series for young children consisting of a fantasy mix of human and animal characters inhabiting the magical walled garden of a country estate. One of the characters in the programme was Constable Knapweed, a policeman who was constantly writing the names in his notebook for no real reason.

Francis Hardyman was the cadets' physical training instructor, commonly known as Staff because he was an ex-Parachute Regiment staff sergeant who during the 1956 Suez crisis acted as the colonel's bodyguard. As a result of the conflict and because of the role he played he was fondly remembered as being the only British citizen to have a full British passport which was not valid for either Cyprus or Egypt as he was described, as was the rest of the regiment, as being persona non grata. He oozed military; he was a short man but what he lacked in height he made up for in real strength. He had been a physical training instructor with the Royal Marines but had an unhealthy desire to have the occasional rolled-up Woodbine cigarette, which was probably not the best advert to a bunch of seventeen-year-olds. One fellow member of the training team recalled Staff as being the only man capable of performing a handstand with one hand whilst drinking a pint of beer with the other. However, this little man with the gravelly face knew his role inside out and there was none better than him with regards to gym work. He liked nothing better than to walk across the stomachs of cadets to test the strength and durability of their muscles. He had a unique catchphrase which used to grate with many a cadet at times when sinews were strained to their end degree. "Harder yet!" he would shout in a concerted effort to encourage cadets to push their bodies that bit harder or run that little bit faster. It was Harry's firm belief that this catchphrase became somewhat of a major contributory factor to not only his success within the cadet scheme but all those who had either gone before or after, and who had encountered this little man who had a touch of the joker in him. Despite his age, there were very few cadets who could match his strength and balance when it came to handstands as he was able quite easily to travel the length of the gym upside down without his feet touching the floor. On occasions he attempted to relieve certain tense or stressful situations with a wisecrack which very few found particularly funny, but laughed in any event to keep the little man happy.

Responsibility for swimming and lifesaving fell to civilian instructor Roy Rivers who Harry and Ed thought was an all-round good guy but could easily show signs of grumpiness which they attributed to his age. Roy had a very deep gritty voice and kept words to a minimum. There was a suggestion amongst the cadets that Roy could not actually swim as he had never been seen in the pool. Yet he was more than eager when cadets had swimming lessons and spent many hours and probably even in his sleep saying the phrase, "Down the outside, back up the centre – eight lengths front crawl – go!" Normally, the number of lengths did not change; it was just the stroke type that varied. He would politely insist that if someone was swimming slower than you then there was no alternative but to swim over the top of them. Following a strenuous session of about thirty or thirty-five minutes, Roy moved onto his speciality which were the one-length sprints, meaning that the first one in was expected to be the first out at the other end. That meant clambering out as fast as possible to avoid the following hordes. Of course, Roy had done this many times before and seemed to enjoy putting the slowest swimmers at the front each time. Roy was also a qualified public service vehicle driver and whenever an away day or week was planned, Roy was always in the driver's seat of the force coach.

Sergeant De-Bris had only recently been promoted to the rank, having been in an administration role as a constable the year before Harry and Ed joined. He was extremely fit and would often be seen out and about cross-country running. He was also an ex-amateur boxer so came in for the weekly evening class boxing sessions as well as acting as referee at the twice yearly boxing tournaments. His vast experience greatly assisted him to enforce the rules during a fight. He gave explicit instruction before each fight and started and stopped the count when a cadet hit the canvas and stayed down. He would also make the decision to stop a fight when a competitor could not continue without endangering their health, although this very rarely happened. Having boxed in some high profile fights, it seemed as if Sergeant De-Bris had difficulty in maintaining his normal everyday deportment without resorting to his former glory days of boxing in some way, shape or form.

This was evident one afternoon when some first-year cadets were sitting in the library supposedly having some quiet reflection reading up on some important material. The sergeant had been across to one of the blocks and was seen returning to the training department, which put those watching from the library on alert. He was walking very purposefully as if he was in a hurry when, for some inexplicable reason, he walked straight into one of the lampposts that was positioned on the path adjacent to the parade square. In a flash, he took half a step backwards and connected a quick one-two shot with his left and then right fists as if he was facing up to someone in the ring. He then took a slow step back, looked round to see if anyone was watching before carrying on walking. Those who witnessed the event were curled up in stitches in their chairs, trying desperately to hide sufficiently low enough not to be seen.

Director of Academic Studies was Potty Hubbard who Harry and Ed quickly realised had also been on their respective interview panels with the reliable Superintendent Crake. He had overall responsibility for the non-police teaching staff who visited the training department on a daily basis to instruct the cadets in the subjects which had been specially selected with the standard being adjudged by some to be between an O level and an A level and included subjects such as: economics, statistics, applied psychology, English, principles of law, sociology, current affairs and geography, which were all taught on site at headquarters. One of the most interesting tutors who visited Tinkers Hill site was Chuck Hebdo, an American who taught English and was a larger than life character with a glimmer of individuality, who did not necessarily follow the establishment pattern as he was clearly a very lateral thinker with his talks about mental masturbation and the like. He was a firm advocate that the idea of articulacy was a form of human freedom and expression. Chuck was not bound by the same rules as the police training staff and, partly for that reason, was held in high regard by the cadets who saw him as somewhat of a cat amongst pigeons.

The female psychology lecturer in Harry's view was completely gaga. Talks about Freudian factors and the reasoning for dreams really got into his head; so much so that initially he rebelled against the message the poor lady was trying to get across, particularly when she asked Harry to describe his re-occurring dream of being trapped in a burning building which she then went on to psycho-analyse for about an hour. By the end of the year he was fascinated by the fundamental concept of operant conditioning in behavioural psychology and the use of reinforcement and punishment to either increase or decrease behaviours.

The modern science classes were conducted at the nearby college in Tinkers Hill, which meant a nice one-mile stroll once a week in all kinds of weather. The instructor was either Austrian or German; his one discerning feature was to talk constantly about diastole and systole concerning the heart cycle. Diastole is the cardiac cycle, period of relaxation of the heart muscle, accompanied by the filling of the chambers with blood. Diastole is followed in the cardiac cycle by a period of contraction, or systole of the heart muscle. Initially both atria and ventricles are in diastole, and there is a period of rapid filling of the ventricles followed by a brief atria systole. Simultaneously, there is a corresponding decrease in arterial blood pressure to its minimum. Ventricular diastole re-occurs after the blood has been ejected into the aorta and pulmonary artery. This was one subject that particularly fascinated Boris, one of Ed and Harry's classmates at the time, but all this information seemed of little use in his later police career when dealing with an irate motorist for a bald tyre.

As with any organisation where young vulnerable females were in residence, Tinkers Hill employed the obligatory matron who backed up the 'all male' cast from the training department. Matron would assist with all health matters relating to both male and female cadets and would be on hand to offer remedies for minor ailments such as athlete's foot or chaffing in the nether regions, both of which were quite common due to the amount of exercising, washing and drying that went on. Her role included being a motherly figure at times when morale was low due to sickness or during prolonged lay-off through injury. Some people saw much more of Matron than Ed or Harry, who were quite happy to avoid lengthy absences due to illness or injury.

Chapter Eight
Home from Home

Life away from home was quite trying with homesickness being an issue for a very small minority of cadets and it was quite difficult to gauge who was suffering, as most if not all the males maintained a façade by portraying a macho image within the regimented framework; to admit this openly would have met with ridicule and rebuke from their peers. Harry and Ed seemed to be fine with it, settling in reasonably quickly although there were a couple of times during the early days that Harry wished his mum was there to talk to. He always made sure there was something to do, which left little time to dwell on things that may have been happening at home.

The cadets were housed in four different blocks. The largest, a three-storey block was divided into two houses: Lower Street, which took up all the ground floor and part of the middle floor, and Upper Street which took the remainder of the middle as well as the top floor. The two other blocks were Dotty Street and Buddy Street, both consisting of a ground and upper level. Buddy Street was set slightly apart from the other blocks with Dotty Street being adjacent to the parade square with access via the main door into both the Lower and Upper Street blocks.

Additionally, contained within Dotty Street block, were the female cadet quarters which were completely out of bounds to male cadets with warning signs being strategically placed at the entrance on both the ground and first floors. It was made perfectly clear from a very early stage that any hanky panky between male and female cadets would not be tolerated and was seen as a disciplinary matter if a male was encountered within the boundaries of the female block, regardless of circumstances. Harry often wondered why it seemed all right for the females to wander randomly into the male blocks yet it was treated extremely seriously if males were caught in the female block, as Ed and others discovered later in their cadetship.

Between the main entrance to Dotty Street and the three-storey block was a fairly large lounge area at ground floor level. There was a TV in one corner and a bar billiards table in the other which reminded Harry of his summer holidays back home with Ernie. There was a plethora of wooden-framed low-back chairs with black plastic cushions to sit on. The cushion was held in place by wide rubbery straps that ran from one side of the chair to the other. At the rear of the lounge was a night kitchen where cadets could make hot drinks. Through a double door there were two steps that led up to the ground floor of Lower Street which had a stairwell at either end of the building. At the very rear of this building there was a laundry room housing a couple of washing machines, a dryer, and ironing equipment. The room opposite was where the weekly haircuts took place.

Just behind the kitchenette lay the little shop which became a hive of activity and was extremely popular with cadets and was normally open in the first hour after classroom sessions finished each day. Occasionally it would be opened at weekends by the duty officer. Not only did it sell chocolate, a big favourite with Harry, it also sold snacks and necessities such as Kiwi black shoe polish, white cleaner for plimsolls and other essentials such as sewing kits and brushes to maintain their uniforms in pristine condition.

Harry was attached to Lower Street block and was allocated a room on the middle floor overlooking a huge expansive field at the rear of the complex. From his room he could just see the tops of trains running along the main north-south line to and from London. Approximately twenty-five metres from the rear of the building was an oak tree which stuck out like a sore thumb as it was the only tree in the vicinity; Harry failed to see the relevance of it being where it was and assumed, maybe wrongly, that one day an acorn had randomly fallen from the sky as there seemed little logic in having planted a seed at this particular spot. The tree, however, would play a pivotal role later in their training. One of Harry's immediate neighbours was a first-year cadet called BJ. He was an exceptional rugby player having represented his school at county level at number fifteen, although when it came to rugby Harry knew not one iota about who did what or even how many there were in each team. He had never had the opportunity to play rugby at school and on the face of things it seemed a far too dangerous game to become involved with. BJ was a quiet, unassuming lad who became course leader the following year. His demure, innocent nature made him a popular character but it was a quite a shock when, late one night, he was summoned by the training staff to contact home urgently as his girlfriend had just given birth. *He's not so unassuming now,* thought Harry. The lengths some people would go, to get themselves noticed.

In the room opposite Harry there was another first year who he nicknamed Mad Kev because of his very strong Cockney accent, his short-cropped hair and his big bulbous eyes that stood out when he stared at anyone. He was a bubbly, effervescent type of guy who was always on the go and nothing appeared to faze him. He was a real happy chappy and always visited Harry's room where he would play his records for hours in the evening on Harry's Fidelity record player, which he had recently acquired from home. It seemed strange that Mad Kev had all these records but nothing to play them on and, whilst Harry was more than accommodating to let Kev make use of his record player, after a month or so the monotony became wearing. It seemed that Kev was spending more time in Harry's room than Harry himself. Harry had no alternative; the only way to get him out of his room without being blatantly obvious was to sell the record player to him. The deal was done and the next monthly pay cheque saw Kev hand over ten pounds to Harry for the record deck which was already a few years old and was in need of a new stylus. Result: Harry had ten quid in his pocket and had reclaimed full use of his room. Mad Kev did not see his year out and left for no apparent reason. Harry was sad to see him go but it was even more of a shock when years later Harry learnt of Kev's untimely death on television, murdered with his body dumped in his own estate car. Such a sad end for such a lovely bloke; what made it even more difficult to comprehend was the fact that no one was ever convicted of this heinous crime.

Ed was housed in Dotty Street under the guidance of Section Leader Heinz who was a general all-rounder and a good guy. It was clear that Heinz was destined for greater things due to his no-nonsense approach but he was not averse to receiving extra duty for minor misdemeanours such as raising the Union Flag the wrong way round. Ed had a first floor room overlooking the west side of Lower/Upper Street block but was also strategically placed to partially see into the cadet lounge and, more importantly, what people who were in his line of sight were up to. Ed would sometimes sit for hours by his window cleaning his boots in a dreamy state not really concentrating on what he was doing. Because of his position, the person in the cadet lounge looking up could see the top part of Ed's head and face but not necessarily what he was doing.

It was after Christmas when Ed gave a little surprise to one of the new female recruits who had recently joined as a senior cadet and was getting some familiarisation training at headquarters. Hazel quickly gained a bit of a reputation as a bit of a girl, making it no secret of her liking for the male sex; she always seemed in a flirtatious mood and on more than one occasion made eyes at Ed, presumably as she had heard about his athletic prowess. Hazel sat on one of the seats in the lounge looking up at Ed's room whilst he was cleaning his boots. The hand motion of Ed's cleaning could not be seen from her position but she could see his upper arm movement coupled with his head moving up and down as he admired his handiwork. Hazel got completely the wrong idea with his arm movement going round and round, believing that he was teasing or taunting her with what appeared to be a very sensitive and sensual sexual motion. Her face was a picture when Ed finally held up his boot for Hazel to suddenly realise that he was not a grubby little pervert drooling over her voluptuous body.

The bedrooms in all the blocks were more or less the same; each had a wooden-framed bed with a thin mattress. The bedroom windows were very large, single-glazed and took up almost all of one wall; in that respect there was no issue with natural light streaming into the room. In Buddy and Dotty Street blocks the windows opened in a traditional way, but in the main Lower and Upper Street block the opening part of the window was a third of the size of the whole frame and consisted of a pivot handle to keep the window secured. Turning the handle and pushing outwards caused it to fully open leaving a huge expanse above and below the actual window. The metal frame meant that in winter the wind howled freely into the bedrooms and the one radiator in the room which was below the frame provided plenty of heat, most of which quickly disappeared into the ether due to the lack of suitable insulation and non-existent sealants. There was a small sink just inside the door and on the wall opposite the bed there was a wooden wardrobe. Between the wardrobe and the window there was a small desk fitted to the wall, mainly to assist cadets with somewhere to do their extra-curricular activities. However, Harry identified quite quickly that it was almost the same size as a pair of trousers and it would make a perfect ironing board. Unfortunately, the melamine tops were not heat resistant and some cadets inevitably caused accidental damage, although the preferred view from senior officers was that any damage was more likely to have been caused by negligence and would have to be paid for. Once Harry had mastered the use of an iron he decided to bring one from home which was more heavy duty and older than the ones available in the laundry room. He considered this a great plan until the day when he became over enthusiastic and burnt his uniform trousers.

All the newcomers were welcomed to the fold. They had two choices: either they fitted in and knuckled down or they fell by the wayside. Second-year cadets were on hand to help and motivate the 'newbies'. One person who fitted into this category perfectly was Peanuts who was of Italian descent and had the traditional swarthy looks associated with someone from a warm Mediterranean climate. Although not overly tall he made up for that with his infectious friendly character and generally strutted about as if he didn't have a care in the world. Being a second year, Peanuts felt totally at ease with the headquarters environment and regime. He was elevated to captain of the lifesaving team, was an extremely accomplished athlete as well as a graceful yet very competitive footballer. Peanuts was no angel and more than once his mischievous nature brought him to the close attention of training staff for breaching rules and regulations. It was fairly noticeable to both Harry and Ed during the first couple of months of training that Peanuts was very good friends with Marilyn, another second year cadet, and could, in this day and age, be classed as an item, as they always seemed to be together and clearly enjoyed each other's company. It was, in Harry's view, a perfect match: he was the Italian stallion, she the blonde, drop-dead gorgeous centrefold pin-up. On occasions Peanuts paid clandestine visits to Marilyn in the female block late at night, returning to his own room in the early hours. One morning he was wandering back through the cadet lounge only to be met by Constable Knapweed meandering in the opposite direction. Both seemed as surprised as the other to encounter someone at that time of night. Immediately smelling trouble, Peanuts instinctively closed his eyes and pretended to be sleepwalking, much to Knapweed's annoyance as, when he started talking to him, the appassionato just carried on walking without muttering a sound. The following morning he was hauled in front of Inspector Broadhurst but managed to convince him that he'd actually been sleepwalking, having absolutely no recollection of the incident.

On their first full day, Harry and Ed were issued with the standard equipment presented to each cadet. They were expected to treat all items with affectionate care and respect, which consisted of a very heavy duty tunic, two pairs of trousers made of equally heavy material, four blue shirts, two pairs of black boots, a couple of snap-on ties, a flat cap with a blue band round it which had a small badge depicting the force crest, black leather gloves and white cotton gloves, the latter being used solely for ceremonial occasions or passing-out parades. The peak of the uniformed cap was expected to shine and glisten in sunlight; it was the one item of clothing that was easily mislaid or mistakenly taken by one of the eighty or so other cadets. There was also a very long overcoat known as a Gannex which extended to just below the knee and for shorter cadets it almost reached to shin level. The sheer size and weight of the coat made it very difficult to manoeuvre properly. The Gannex was predominantly used for extreme weather conditions and Harry was convinced it was manufactured almost entirely from a rubber-type material. Most unfortunate cadets experienced the same thing; a build-up of natural body heat seemed to trigger the Gannex into producing even more heat inside, causing a build-up of steam on the inner lining of the coat. There seemed no natural outlet for the body heat; consequently, anything worn immediately beneath the coat became initially sweaty before soon becoming saturated.

Cadets were also issued with standard white plimsolls which had an unusual red sole with a zig-zag pattern. It was expected these plimsolls were cleaned and maintained in pristine condition and at most physical training sessions they were inspected for cleanliness. Given there were two or three times throughout the day when cadets wore these, the upkeep of the plimsolls was an onerous and often repetitive task.

Plimsolls led to yet another run-in between Peanuts and authority after playing another trick on the calamitous Constable Knapweed during one very wintry evening. A very heavy snowfall had left the flat roof of the training department covered with several inches of snow. It was an open invitation to someone like Peanuts, who decided to make a snowball of magnificent proportions and scaled the roof wearing his size eight plimsolls before Knapweed had completed his final rounds of the accommodation blocks. Peanuts rolled the snowball slowly across the roof of the building towards the entrance from where Knapweed would emerge to start his rounds. He knew full well that the officer would be oblivious to what was going on around as he normally stood momentarily outside the department door to light his pipe. By the time Peanuts had finished rolling the snowball, it was approximately three to four feet across and massive to the extent that he could hardly move it. After great perseverance and strength Peanuts managed to perch it right on the edge of the roof just above the training block door. Within two or three minutes the door opened and right on cue Constable Knapweed emerged and stood momentarily before lighting his pipe. Peanuts knew he only had one chance: he ran and hit the snowball as hard as he could, causing it to tip over the edge, dropping onto poor Knapweed. There were muffled cries from below but Peanuts didn't hang around to witness the aftermath, scampering back as fast as he could to his room.

An investigation was launched with casts taken of the footprints left on the roof, which showed conclusively that the culprit was wearing size eight plimsolls as the zig-zag pattern of the sole was evident. No stone was left unturned in the search for Constable Knapweed's assailant and a comprehensive process began. By the time the training staff had eliminated everyone with size eight plimsolls it left only one suspect: Peanuts, who was again unceremoniously hauled before Inspector Broadhurst and asked for an explanation. Realising his predicament, Peanuts had no alternative but to deny any involvement in the snowy affair. Regardless of evidence Peanuts was given a whole week of extra duty where he was expected to appear at any set time of the day in full uniform at a moment's notice. One of those occasions involved Sergeant Watkin who requested the presence of Peanuts outside the training block at nine p.m. dressed in full uniform including his Gannex coat before marching him round and round the parade square. Just when Peanuts thought it was over Sergeant Watkin marched him into the gymnasium and then into the swimming pool complex where Peanuts stood for a short deliberation at the shallow end. *Surely not,* he thought to himself before being ordered into the pool and being told to march to the deep end, which in full uniform was relatively easy due to the weight of his boots, heavy tunic and the Gannex coat. Being the good swimmer that he was Peanuts could hold his breath for a couple of minutes, so walked as far as he could before returning to the shallow end. He then spent the majority of the night trying to dry his uniform ready for the morning parade. Did he learn? Did he hell as like.

Within the training block there were several classrooms which were cold in winter and stifling hot in the summer months where cadets completed their academia. Although the building was relatively new, no one had the presence of mind to install double-glazing as an investment. There was also a library which overlooked the parade square; this housed many gory forensic science books showing repulsive pictures of bodies at post-mortem stage which many a cadet pored through in some valiant attempt to look macho in front of their peers. The lecture theatre was also in the training block; this was staggered in height from front to back with row upon row of flip-up seats. Harry was impressed with the layout of this room as it enabled everyone to be seen by the person at the front presenting the lecture or seminar. This was completely different to anything he had encountered at school whereby those pupils wanting to have a quick shut-eye would promptly seize the opportunity by sitting at the back behind many rows of other students, thus reducing the chance of being spotted snoozing by the teacher at the front. Although the set-up of the lecture theatre was much more modern, it still didn't stop some cadets snaffling the seats at the back first in order to try and have the occasional forty winks.

The amenity block, otherwise known as the canteen, was where cadets ate their breakfast, lunch and evening meal. This also doubled as the canteen for regular officers who generally refrained from fraternising with the youngsters and there was a rest area to one side where there was a billiard/snooker table for those wishing to become a budding Ray Reardon. The amenity block also housed the bar which cadets were forbidden to enter at all cost. The bar area overlooked the sports field and was ideally situated for summer events as the doors opened directly onto a small patio area affording spectators splendid views over any sports that may be taking place. On the opposite side to where the cadets dined and closest to the main headquarters building there was a specially designated dining room for senior officers where, occasionally, Superintendent Crake would be seen visiting. This was deemed by some as being very elitist and bordering on snobbery. Very occasionally, when Tinkers Hill hosted special events and notable dignitaries were on the guest list, cadets mainly in the female form were chosen to assist as glorified trolley dollies with inane conversation and trays of canapés and drinks.

Access to the amenity block was via a service road, allowing essential supplies to be delivered not only to the canteen but also to the bar. Getting to the service road from the main drive meant vehicles had to drive over the coveted parade square which for some went down like a lead balloon. The gym block was adjacent to the canteen block and this was where cadets spent most of their time in physical training. This building not only housed the gym but also two squash courts, the swimming pool and changing facilities. Most gym and swimming sessions lasted forty to fifty minutes and inevitably there was a quick turn around time between lessons. The swimming pool was twenty-five metres in length and sufficiently wide to have just have four lanes. At the shallow end it was only three feet or so; at the deep end it was just over seven foot, just sufficient to warrant a diving board which, not long after Harry and Ed's commencement at Tinkers Hill, was removed as it was considered dangerous. There were male and female changing rooms for the pool downstairs with additional changing rooms for both sexes upstairs; these were predominantly used when cadets were in the gym training and also by visiting teams who came to play rugby, football, hockey and the like. Initially, the gym seemed massive; it was bigger than the sports hall at Harry's old school, there was a full basketball court, wall-bars on one side with climbing ropes and a wooden beam structure on the opposite side, which could be pulled out into place to form part of an assault course when needed. There was a 'Trojan' horse vaulting box, parallel bars and a huge number of training mats supposedly there to prevent any serious injuries. The gym was also the venue for the twice-yearly boxing tournaments.

Chapter Nine

The Class of Fourteen

Because of their age, Harry and Ed were propelled directly into the second year which raised one or two eyebrows amongst the 'real' second years who had already completed a year in training and knew the practices and protocol inside out. Whist this didn't have any massive or adverse effect on those joining straight into the second year, this delicate situation was managed extremely well by the training administration department. In addition to Harry and Ed, there were twelve other cadets who fell into the same category, meaning that for the next year they would train as one class for academic studies, physical training, swimming and drill. There were three females in this class, which pleased both Harry and Ed although they realised quite quickly that this was neither the time nor the place for fraternising with the opposite sex.

Honky didn't live far from Fordham in the east of the county, having attended the same grammar school as Wings and Doug, the latter joining as a first-year cadet. When Honky was seven his father, who served with the Metropolitan Police, died at a young age leaving his mother to care for him and his younger sister. It may not have been a conscious decision at that point but Honky was more or less destined to follow in his father's footsteps as it seemed, in the circumstances, like a reasonable career path to take. It was either this or the dole as Honky genuinely believed no one else would have him. Academically, he was okay at school passing five O levels, but he was bone idle and lazy and his school reports contained the standard phraseology of "could do better", but Honky seemed much happier just larking around. His real passion lay with computer technology and he had already been head hunted for a role with Barclays Bank, but this meant working permanent nights in London from an early age which he didn't really want to do. He did however persist with computer studies which he continued at college whilst he was a cadet, which later led to him setting up his own business.

Honky was no shrinking violet with a larger than life character which matched his build and, when they met for the first time, he reminded Harry of the cadets from the Mid-shires force with his large barrel chest. Honky was very positive about life in general, had a wicked sense of humour but he was always willing to put others first as he later did in Wales when Denis took a tumble. He liked nothing better than to have a laugh and joke, particularly at someone else's expense, and was the first to point out an indiscretion or a misdemeanour when someone fell out of line. He acquired his nickname when he was later stationed at Fordham where he joined forces with Harry as a senior cadet. A combination of suffering from really bad flatulence coupled with a booming voice prompted colleagues to aptly address him as Honky.

Wings had a very strict upbringing within a small village setting. His brother, who was a couple of years younger, was considered as a bit of a rebel. His father worked on the local farm as a labourer but did lots of other physical tasks in and around the farm, so most mornings he was normally up with the lark. When Wings was ten his mother developed multiple sclerosis meaning that he, as the older of the two siblings, had to take on the role of carer more and more as time went by. Contrary to all expectations, Wings successfully passed his Eleven Plus exam which enabled him to attend the local grammar school some six miles from home. Each morning he would rise at more or less the same time as his father and tend to his mother's needs, ensuring she was washed, dressed and had eaten a healthy breakfast before leaving for school. Special dispensation was allowed by the school which meant that Wings could catch an earlier bus home arriving around five fifteen p.m. when he would again tend to his mother's needs. Whilst Wings was at school, his father returned home from the farm to give Wings' mother some lunch and also help her with any toiletry requirements.

Over the years, this was virtually how Wings spent his days and holidays were virtually non-existent. On many occasions, Wings' father would take the tractor to the local pub before returning home late in a drunken state, taking out his frustrations on Wings for the smallest of reasons. Clearly the fact of having to look after his bedridden wife was taking its toll on his father and, as far as Wings was concerned, the six years between the ages of eleven and seventeen could be summed up in two words, 'Very unhappy'. Being stuck out in a small village meant Wings had limited transport, so he relied on his legs to take him everywhere including late at night when his father had not re-appeared after a day's work and he went to seek him out from the nearest public house. On more than one occasion Wings had to assist his father from a ditch where he had taken refuge after a drinking session. Needless to say Wings did not get on with his father so it was a great relief when, at the age of seventeen, he applied to join the police cadets prompted by his good friend Honky who happened to be in the same class at school. Honky had already been accepted when their discussion ensued. Because of all the additional work at home that Wings was forced to do, he inevitably fell behind with all his coursework and quite unbelievably he left the grammar school without one formal qualification.

As a result of his meagre lifestyle, Wings weighed just over eight and a half stone and was nothing more than skin and bone when he joined the cadets. Other than running, which he considered himself to be quite proficient at, Wings was not an overall sporty type of person and wasn't really a team player as such. He was more than happy to work at his own pace and joined in where he could. Not possessed with a very high level of self-confidence Wings found the cadets very hard, but it was his exceptional grit coupled with a very steely determination that got him through his year and then through his full police service. Wings quickly became friends with Ed and Harry and when he had time between lessons, he liked nothing better than to flick through the horse betting columns in the national papers. He was ably assisted by Ed until the two became quite well versed at picking winners only to dream about what they could have won.

Denis was nicknamed after his Scots international footballer hero who played over 400 times for the majestic Manchester United team of the late sixties and early seventies with Denis showing a particular pride towards his Pict heritage. His parents separated when he was very young; when he was six he was placed into a Scottish boarding school in North West London with his four-year-old brother. Things weren't easy for either boy mainly due to the break-up of their parents' marriage but, with the boarding school fees being fully paid by his Scottish grandfather, Denis and his brother's future at the school where kilts formed part of the uniform were virtually sealed. Denis suffered several initiation events where older and more brutal boarders would inflict torturous punishments on recent newcomers so, by the time he reached sixteen and became a prefect himself, he was fully versed in all the various tricks within the dormitories.

One example of the brutality imposed by prefects to younger scholars was in the gym before meal times, where classes would stand completely motionless and in silence in order to earn the right to a meal. Woe betide any youngster who dared to speak, snigger or even move for those ten minutes; the retribution and punishment was instant in the form of a clenched fist being thrust in a downwards motion with considerable force on the side of the reprobate's head by the nearest prefect. However, when Denis reached the prefect stage he could not bring himself to inflict the same fate upon young, frightened boarders – but he was quite willing to dish out a hundred lines to any young whipper-snapper caught trying to sneak into the girls' dormitories in the middle of the night. Whilst Denis lived in at boarding school, his education was completed at the nearby secondary modern Queens School where he became acquainted with Donbo, a local lad who was a year older. Academically, Denis was not a high achiever although he did gain an English GCE O Level; his main concentration focussed on football and athletics and he spent many a day in the classroom dreaming about his next game or run on the track.

When the time came for Denis to leave boarding school he considered a life in the military; the army was probably the best route in with a view to later joining the Royal Marines as it followed a natural progression, having coped for ten years at boarding school with all the different rules and regulations. One day, whilst out, Denis bumped into Donbo who explained he was now a police cadet with the local force and was thoroughly enjoying it. Donbo recommended this to him as it followed a regimented programme which he was used to. There were ample sporting activities which suited Denis and there was opportunity to further develop on the academic front. He couldn't apply quickly enough and was pleasantly surprised when he was invited for an interview. His mother accompanied him to the headquarters at Tinkers Hill but as she didn't drive they had to catch a series of buses from her home in the far west corner of the county. Arriving a couple of hours before their appointment and with Denis feeling extremely nervous, his mother took him to the nearby lakes where they hired a boat and spent an hour gently paddling round and round amongst the ducks and swans. It was just the tonic, as it eased his tension; he was successful at the interview ultimately joining the class of fourteen and was based in Dotty Street block with Ed under the wing of Section Leader Heinz.

During his first week, the initiation ceremonies started in earnest and Denis could hear the yells and shouts of protestation of unwilling new recruits as the pack of wolves slowly progressed along the corridor towards his room. He was reminded of his time at boarding school. This so-called demeaning ritual was exacted with two aims in mind: firstly it showed the new recruits who actually was in charge and secondly it aimed at toughening up those cissies who were a little homesick. Denis' door flew open and Big Del, a mountain of a man who was a 'senior' but had returned to headquarters for a short while in order to improve his fitness and lose some weight, confronted him. Rod Caves, a second year and Donbo who immediately identified Denis from their days at Queens School accompanied him. Donbo, fearing for his new found friend, suggested to both Big Del and Rod that they should leave him alone as he was an ex-boarding school lad who had experienced every type of initiation imaginable, so anything they did was unlikely to affect him, which Denis thought was a nice gesture at the time. Rod however wasn't convinced and became quite insistent upon inflicting humiliation on Denis by smothering black boot polish across his testicles. Denis, who neither pleaded nor retaliated as he knew both would be futile, stood completely still until Donbo again spoke up in his favour. Much to Rod's frustration it was Big Del's final decision that clinched it with him saying, "We'll leave this one," and the three left the room as quickly as they had entered before choosing their next victim to blacken along the corridor. Denis was a bit of a joker so it came as no surprise that one of his favourite programmes was *The Comedians*. He made a point of rushing back to headquarters on a Sunday night from either his mother or father's to enjoy the comedy provided by Charlie Williams, Ken Goodwin and the like.

Ever since infant school, Polly had wanted to be a police officer. Educationally, she was bright so when the chance presented itself she grabbed the cadet corps with both hands. Whereas the vast majority of cadets predominantly enthused over the physical element at headquarters, most disliked spending time in the classroom being taught by academics that were fortunate to have letters after their names, particularly when Harry knew not one iota of what they stood for. Polly on the other hand was the opposite, she felt more at home in the classroom although she tried her best when it came to physical training and swimming. She hated doing the exercise routines at the nearby lakes as cadets were forced to run through and across the adjoining streams, completing ruining their pristine white plimsolls which took an age to dry out before the white colorant could be re-applied to bring them up to the expected level again. In Harry's eyes, Polly was very mild-mannered, bright and a little shy. Her character was as far removed as you could imagine from the traits shown by a stereotypical police officer at that time and Harry was sure that after a couple of months she would throw the towel in. What did he know? Polly was housed within the girls' block adjacent to Dotty Street with Macca and Rosie from the same class as well as the remaining second-year girls, including Sophie, Marcie and Marilyn. For the purposes of drill and sporting achievements Polly was attached to Buddy Street house under Section Leader Wolfy. She viewed him as an exceptional leader but this did not prevent her turning the fire hose on him one evening as a bit of sport. He stood absolutely still, drenched from head to toe, having to accept a degree of humiliation for having been hosed down by a female. Ultimately, it was Wolfy who had the last laugh as the cadet course leader Ant, despite finding it funny, admonished her with an extra detention.

Macca hailed from Kent, had a happy childhood but with a very strict upbringing which was quite frustrating for a teenager. The opportunity to escape was too appealing, particularly as she was paid for playing sport. She struggled with the amount of discipline but was able to cope mainly due to her naval father's strict regime at home. Macca was a friendly type and enjoyed the camaraderie of the class of fourteen. She was a keen hockey player and went on to represent the force in regional championships. At the time, there was a weekly magazine for girls called *Jackie*, published in Scotland from 1964 until 1993 producing an astonishing total of 1534 issues. It was the best-selling teen magazine in Britain for ten years, publishing a mix of fashion and beauty tips, gossip, short stories and comic strips. The magazine became very popular with teenage girls, not least because of the *Cathy and Claire* problem page, which received 400 letters a week dealing with controversial issues relevant to the readership. However, subjects covered in the column were not reflective of the majority of readers' letters, which focused on sex-related issues. Both the comic and short stories invariably dealt with either romance or family issues and the centre pages usually contained a pull-out poster of a popular band or film star. The best ever selling issue was the 1972 special edition, not because all the female cadets were buying it, but it coincided with American singer David Cassidy's UK tour. The magazine decided to include a short story in the life of a female police cadet which made Macca the centre of attention for a day. She was interviewed and photos were taken for an edition of the magazine which was published later that year. Not only did she feel like a film star for the day, it highlighted the importance of females in society as well as providing some much-valued publicity for the force.

Despite her penchant for a fag or two, Macca was a good swimmer but when the class did lifesaving it always appeared that Roy Rivers wanted the girls to pair with a male for some inexplicable reason. As much as Harry enjoyed being partnered with one of the girls he felt as if he was being punished; being paired with one of the boys seemed much manlier and less girlie, but there was little choice in the matter when Roy was in charge. Shortly after joining, Macca hit it off quite quickly with Wolfy, the section leader from Buddy Street block and as time went on their friendship blossomed into romance, which was not openly encouraged by the regime. It was noticeable that they spent a lot of time together in the cadet lounge talking and Harry thought it quite sweet that something much more was developing. Rules were rules though and male cadets were banned from entering the female block. Wolfy, however, thought differently and occasionally visited Macca in her room. Macca joined Ed as a senior at Tinkers Hill station before joining the regular force in July 1974. It was great when she and Wolfy married before transferring to the Midlands area; sadly the marriage ended after three years when Wolfy went off with his probationer constable.

Tom was a typical seventeen-year-old who didn't want to stay on at school as he wasn't confident at passing his O levels. As luck would have it, he bumped into a former Scout troop member who happened to be wearing full police cadet uniform; he suggested that Tom might like to try the cadets as it was very sport orientated with some academic studies thrown in, and he also had the opportunity to re-sit his O levels if he needed to. At the time of applying for the cadets he had no burning ambition of becoming a police officer. He was a Twatton lad living with his parents and one older, and one younger brother. As a child he suffered from bronchitis which resulted in him regularly missing school, but this seemed to improve when he reached the age of ten; as he took up judo twice weekly, he joined the local Air Scouts at twelve where he enjoyed camping, hill-walking, sailing and other outdoor pursuits. At thirteen, he took up a morning paper round which he did for two years, covering about four miles each day. Undoubtedly all this exercise contributed to his recuperation allowing him to catch up on school work and aided his self-confidence.

Tom was no angel; he had brushes with the law and on one occasion received an informal warning for a misdemeanour. During the police interview, Tom's father let it be known that Tom was thinking of joining the force. On hearing this, the officer quietly closed his notebook and put it away before informing them the incident wouldn't be recorded. Tom's father was an ex-military private and during the Second World War was attached to the Dorset Regiment posted to Malta where he was involved in defending the island from the Germans. Somehow he ended up as part of the D-Day invasion force and his job as a sharpshooter was to fire tracer rounds towards German tanks so that heavy artillery on the ships off-shore could easily locate and fire on them. Sadly for Tom's father the Germans responded to his tracer rounds, resulting in him losing one arm and a large part of his right thigh. After the war his father secured a job with a well-known British aeroplane manufacturer but was later made redundant. This, coupled with his failure to come to terms with his disability, made him prone to outbursts of temper at home.

Tom was always up for a bit of a joke and resided in Buddy Street block and had a lot of time for Wolfy, his section leader who he had great respect for. He also thought highly of Donbo, Albo and Kimbo who also resided in the same block; they were all second years having already completed a year prior to Tom's arrival and most had the respect of all the other cadets.

Trogs was born and raised in the cathedral city of the county. Otherwise known as Cadet Seven he came from a working-class family and was the middle of three brothers. He attended the local boys' school where, academically, he fared quite well. His upbringing reflected his parents' beliefs and although he was a churchgoer, the only reason for him doing so was that it was the only way into the youth centre where he became acquainted with members of the opposite sex. Like many at his age, Trogs was quite naïve but for as long as he could remember had always wanted to be a police officer – so, like many others, he saw joining the cadets as a step in the right direction.

He was based in Lower Street block just a few doors along from Mad Kev. His window overlooked the rear of the female block which was separated only by the flat roof of the cadet lounge. On occasions, mostly at night-time, Trogs would be woken by a gentle tapping on his window by a cadet who had made a hasty retreat via a window from the female block during an unannounced spot inspection by one of the training staff. This was the most direct and safest return to the main block; it gave Trogs a congenial satisfaction knowing he was helping someone find the path to romance and acting as their safety net. As long as this didn't disturb his sleep pattern too often he was more than happy to help.

During his first few months, Trogs found the physical aspect of the regime extremely arduous: he hated the early morning physical training sessions; he hated the gym work and disliked most team sports. He was quite good at swimming which was about the only form of exercise he was happy to take part in. He also hated the 'Bunion run'; during the one time he participated he managed to hitch a lift with a senior cadet who happened to be passing. There were occasions when he felt that he was being picked on, simply because of his lack of ability. By Christmas Trogs felt so disheartened with his cadetship that he considered an alternative career and duly applied for a job at a bank in London. He even attended an interview without the knowledge of the training staff. Trogs was on the verge of jacking it in, but decided that he had come this far so he returned after the Christmas break and never looked back. As a senior, Trogs went on an Outward Bound course to West Wales with Harry and accompanied Ed to a Pontins camp in Suffolk to assist in the care of severely physically impaired pensioners. It was quite astounding that Trogs, who was not a centrefold pin-up in Harry and Ed's eyes, always seemed to have a plentiful bounty of female company around him when he was out, one of which Ed took out several times.

Boris grew up on a council estate in one of the other county New Towns. He was the youngest of three children with a ten-year gap between each of the siblings. His family moved from Southampton as Boris' father had secured a job as an inspector at English Electric, measuring parts for the anti-aircraft air defence missiles, Thunderbird and Rapier, which were manufactured there. Boris was fourteen when his father died suddenly, leaving a void in his life but it also meant his mother had to struggle financially. Boris studied in the sixth form at the local secondary modern school where he was best friends with Cleggy. Boris was halfway through his A levels when it was made clear to him that it was highly unlikely he would achieve his ambition of becoming a vet and the careers co-ordinator was lacking in any alternative advice. His career aim was to follow in the footsteps of James Herriot and becoming a police officer was as far removed from his ambition as having Beef Wellington at a vegetarian conference. One of them, but it is not clear who, decided that joining the cadet corps could prove a bonus for them both, but Boris was an individualist and wasn't really a team player; in joining the cadets he was like a fish out of water and suffered from time to time because of it. The efforts shown by Boris during physical training were regarded by Staff in particular as woefully inadequate by his standards and on many occasion he was called to book. Boris had absolutely no inclination to join in with team games; when the group played British Bulldog in the gym he was more than happy to hand the ball over rather than fight someone for it. He had always been able to swim to a reasonable level and saw himself as reasonably accomplished in the water, but unfortunately that was not the way Roy Rivers viewed it. Boris was also very impressed with Peanuts, not just because of his short hair and strikingly good looks that made him a hit with the girls but also for his phenomenal athleticism and natural élan. Over time Boris and Peanuts went on to become great friends.

Cleggy was the eldest of six children. He was raised in the same New Town and attended the same secondary school as Boris and the two had become good friends. In Harry's eyes, Cleggy was always a bit of an enigma who regularly referred to those who 'messed up' as buffoons. Cleggy had a wonderful way with words which Boris truly admired during their school days as he was exceptional at story-writing. Although a bit of a comedian, Cleggy always was quite opinionated but held views on subjects that most his age had never even thought about. He was the master of sarcasm and could, if required, play the clown to the extent of being very popular, which enabled him to avoid potential bullying situations. One of his favourite party pieces was to recite the 'Friends, Romans and Countrymen' speech from

Shakespeare's *Julius Caesar*. This would be proclaimed deadpan, and in a convincing theatrical manner, whilst stark naked which at least supported the theory that, had his career choice in the cadets not worked out, he could have resorted to work in drama productions instead. No one would question Cleggy's highly intelligent, individualistic and erudite character, and Boris, having known him longer than anyone, believed that having a conversation with Cleggy was always more interesting than with just about anybody else around.

However, Cleggy was not blessed with sporting prowess and, like Boris, when he was required to participate he only put in the minimum amount of effort to avoid getting into trouble. He was always a notoriously bad timekeeper, which was probably the result of him spending a great deal of time lost in his own deep thoughts which some would refer to as daydreaming. Joining the cadets was not motivated by any great desire for a future career in truth and justice, but rather it seemed like a reasonable option, compared to what else was available.

Rosie took a liking to Cleggy; she thought that he was one of the people in the class who stood out from the rest with his comical acts. He was always up to something, which generally meant he was close to breaking the rules. Cleggy started his cadetship a couple of weeks after Ed, Harry and the others in the class as one of his blood/urine test results produced an abnormal result which necessitated a repeat of the process. Cleggy, who was posted to Dotty Street block with Ed and Denis, made his mark during the second trip to Wales when he was sanctioned for having one of those 'daydream' moments.

Not for the first time he was deemed to not be pulling his weight, resulting in the infamous Teflon frying pan incident.

Big Al came from a middle-class family with his father having a 'classified' role within the Ministry of Defence. Together with his elder sister and brother he enjoyed a happy childhood. His decision as to which career path to take after leaving school was a fairly easy one; his older sister married a police officer and his brother, who was two years older than him, also joined the force. Big Al's interview to join Tinkers Hill was notable for two simple reasons: he had failed to get a suitable grade in his English CSE necessitating him in agreeing to and signing up to an English O level course at the local college before being accepted and, secondly, for an unusual 'screwing' activity he performed at his medical. Big Al had a deformity in that when he was almost four years old he lost the top third of his left thumb. It wasn't something he was born with and didn't occur as a result of a major catastrophe. It occurred due to his own stupidity when playing around with his sister's bike which had been turned upside down to spin the wheels round and round as fast as possible. He had been warned repeatedly that this practice was not the wisest but continued regardless, taking some of his mother's precious flowers from a vase and shredding them into a thousand pieces. Unfortunately the tip of his left thumb was no competition against the force of a wheel spinning at several hundred revolutions per minute. As a result Big Al had to get used to holding things again with his left hand.

The administration at Tinkers Hill did not see this necessarily as a problem but they wanted one hundred percent fully fit cadets, so Big Al was given what can be described as a child's wooden tool kit. This was to test strength and dexterity in both hands including the one with the missing tip. Firstly he had to turn the wooden screw into the holder with his right hand and tighten it as hard as he could before unscrewing it with his left hand, which he did without any trouble. He then had to do the reverse, turn and tighten the screw as hard as he could with his left hand before unscrewing it with his right hand. He had no issues tightening it up but, try as he might, he could not unscrew it with his 'good' hand. Believing he had failed the test he finally admitted defeat before handing the object back to the officer conducting the medical, thinking that was the end of his application. Not so, as when the officer tried to remove the screw and extract it from the block he too failed. It seemed that Big Al had tightened the screw with his left hand with so much force that it was stuck. Big Al had proven that his CSE grade and his deformity was no barrier to joining the cadets and he too was placed in Lower Street block with Harry and Trogs under the leadership of Section Leader Guy Roberts, who he had a lot of respect for.

He was a keen rugby player having played it since his school days. Big Al had a lot of time for Roy Rivers who he believed had tremendous grit and determination, although Big Al hated the swimming sessions particularly the sprints where it was virtually every man (and woman) for themselves. In addition to his compulsory English evening course at college Big Al nominated himself for judo once a week as his evening activity, which he thoroughly enjoyed, making it to eighth kyu grade, this in layman's terms is a high orange belt.

Rosie was raised and schooled in the outer borders of North West London. She had a good upbringing and was one of four siblings. Her uncle was a police officer in the northeast of England which may have determined her ultimate career path. She worked at her local Sainsbury's store as a Saturday girl to get some 'life' experience as well as earning some cash. When she was sixteen Rosie genuinely believed that she had finished her schooling and initially thought of a career with the Queen Alexandra Nursing Corps but one thing was certain: she didn't want a mundane nine-to-five secretarial job. In 1971 Rosie applied to Tinkers Hill force for a position as a cadet as she heard they were accepting applications from females for the first time in their history. That year the only stipulation under the acceptance criteria was that female applicants had to reside within the county boundary but, unfortunately for Rosie, she lived approximately three miles outside: a similar predicament to the one Harry had suffered. She found herself back at the same school taking further O levels as well as a shorthand and typing course. The latter course was supposedly a back-up plan but she detested the teacher from the start as, for some inexplicable reason, her tutor was allowed to take her dog into school each day. Rosie felt that she must speak out against this injustice as she believed it smacked of favouritism as well as being a hygiene issue. She told her teacher in no uncertain terms and in a very forthright manner that it was "not appropriate" to bring her dog into school. Whilst not regretting her decision to speak out, the despicable teacher made her life hell for the remainder of the year and Rosie was quite pleased to finally get away.

Rosie re-applied to Tinkers Hill force the following year. Her medical, test and interview happened to be on the same day as Big Al's who she took an instant dislike to because he gave her the 'creeps'. It was for no particular reason; she put it down to his general demeanour. She quietly hoped that if he was accepted he wouldn't end up in her class. Little did she know what was in store. Rosie was housed with the other females and her section leader was Heinz. Rosie was a happy-going person and got on with all her class even though she kept her thoughts about Big Al to herself and knuckled down to a really exhausting year. Rosie would never rock the boat – she could be relied on for everything, particularly her timekeeping, wherever she had to be at a certain time she was there. Rosie went home only one weekend in four, deciding to stay in the headquarters complex where she studied most of the time.

It wasn't until after Christmas that Rosie took a shine to 'Dazza', section leader of Upper Street block. Having helped her during a particularly difficult cross-country run he invited her out to celebrate his eighteenth birthday and slowly things started to develop. Some people saw 'Dazza' as a little straight-laced but Rosie saw him as a committed, focussed and disciplined young man who, in her eyes, obviously had all the necessary credentials as they later married and remained so after nearly forty years.

Minty was young, opinionated and quite a serious young man who definitely knew his own mind. Minty loved playing football and was a proficient swimmer to the extent that Roy Rivers chose Minty to perform evening duties as a lifeguard in the swimming pool, which he didn't mind as it got him out of doing one of the other compulsory activities which he wasn't so keen on. He was equally adept at holding his own with the best at chess which he played in the cadet lounge. He was also not averse to seeking solace at night-time with one of his favourite pastimes: freshwater fishing. Minty would wait until after lights out and the duty officer had finished their checks of the four blocks before collecting his equipment and disappearing off site to go fishing at the nearby lake, which was a short hop, skip and jump over a chain-link fence which separated the lakes from the sports field. He would think nothing of idling two or three hours away into the early hours fishing for chub, roach, bream, pike, trout and carp before returning to bed. He used to hide his fishing equipment in a secret store cupboard to prevent Inspector Broadhurst from seizing it. Minty saw his year out making it to senior cadet status, but became totally disillusioned with it all and saw making tea on a regular basis for officers as a fairly meaningless task and decided that a career in the police was not for him. One day whilst visiting headquarters he took the decision to resign, which resulted in him simply walking out. To prove a point he sanctimoniously walked directly across the parade square right in front of Francis Hardyman who immediately started bawling at him for having the nerve to walk on the haloed ground. Much to Staff's annoyance Minty just glared and walked past him saying, "I'm leaving," before collecting his belongings and taking the long walk down the driveway, never to return.

After Christmas, the class were joined for some studies by Budd, a second-year interloper, which enabled him to crucially catch up on some coursework. Budd epitomised the cadets as he excelled at most things physical. He was great at running, jumping, swimming and football and gave the required one hundred and then percent effort in every case. He also happened to be one of the best boxers in the year as, was Section Leader Guy Roberts, and the two were very good friends to the extent that on occasions they could be seen cavorting and dancing about in nothing but their boxer shorts outside the female block in an effort to attract attention to themselves by showing off their rippling muscular bodies. Budd had fallen behind academically, partly due to his energy and over-confident nature; he never seemed to stop talking and always wanted to have a laugh. Being a slight distraction in his previous class it was decided some stability to get him back on track was required. Harry wondered if that was possible given his highly stimulating and effervescent nature and there were at least two members of the class who felt that his introduction dissected what had been one acceptably friendly group. Budd and Constable Knapweed did not always see eye to eye either, and a few years later following a potentially serious incident had a falling-out over cattle straying onto a main road.

Chapter Ten

Routines

One of the most important features that took place without exception each week was the visit from the barber who was shipped into headquarters from Twatton to coiffure those cadets who had been placed onto the haircut list. This was something that was particularly close to Sergeant Watkin's heart as it always seemed to fall to him to make a note of the cadet's name that required a short back and sides and he was there to ensure that those on the list did not miss such an auspicious occasion. It wasn't so much a punishment or sanction, but cadets became resigned to the fact that long straggly hair did not really compliment an outstandingly well drilled, and highly organised bunch of young men who paraded in pristine uniform. The word 'smart' was part of the regular vocabulary used by all the training staff and was drummed into them from day one, but not all cadets were happy with the barber arrangement with some resenting the number of times that their name appeared on the list.

The actual qualifications of the barber were questionable but one thing he was competent at was a 'short back and sides' which, from a cadet perspective, was probably the easiest and quickest to endure. Extreme designer styles were not permissible even though on odd occasions cadets would chance their arm with something new like a Mohican only to be short-listed the following week for an instant replay. Like many others arriving on their first day, Denis bore a full head of fair-coloured hair which he carefully maintained in a feathered style, popular in the 1970s with both men and women. The hair was grown long on both sides which covered the ears and neck and came with either a side or a centre parting. As with everyone else it didn't take long for Sergeant Watkin to place Denis on the ever-growing list for a short back and sides, but it still came as quite a shock to him when all his hair was lopped off.

It was during his first visit to the barber that Boris acquired his nickname. Upon emerging from his first encounter he was met by Rod Coves, who immediately started laughing uncontrollably at the haircut Boris had just been subjected to. Rod, the same second-year cadet involved with Denis' initiation ceremony and who later went on to join the London Fire Service shouted, "He looks just like Dracula," which had cadets standing nearby in stitches. This quickly evolved into 'Boris' as the agreed consensus, albeit incorrect, that it was Boris Karloff who played the main character in the 1930s film. Had there been some Barry Norman film buffs amongst them, they would have quickly realised that Dracula was played by a Hungarian named Bela Lugosi although, to be perfectly blunt, Boris resembled neither apart from the distinct widow's peak in the centre hairline of the forehead. Sometimes Lady Luck looks down on us; had there been a smarter brain cell between them Boris may have been known as Bela instead, which undoubtedly would have caused even more mockery. The joke passed quite quickly but the name stuck for many years.

Another favourite routine of the training staff were the unannounced ad hoc bedroom inspections. It was not uncommon for those carrying out the inspection to dispose of items that were left out in the rooms. It was a strict policy that the only things on show in a cadet's bedroom were the bed, wardrobe, a small bedside cabinet and maybe a towel hanging to dry from the radiator. The bed frame was made from relatively cheap wood and had slats across from side to side on which the mattress was housed. Everything else belonging to the occupant had to be stored away in the wardrobe or in a case under the bed. Those leaving their room in a state of untidiness, or if they left items scattered willy-nilly around the room when they could have been put away, would receive some form of penalty. This could be serious dependent upon the misdemeanour.

Denis resided in Dotty Street block with a room overlooking the parade square. One morning, during the daily inspection Denis became aware of Inspector Broadhurst in the Dotty Street block. As usual all the cadets, were formed up in their respective houses and standing to attention facing towards the training block, so only a few could really see what was happening to their right. The inspector suddenly leant out of the open window holding a couple of girlie magazines in his hand, probably *Mayfair* or *Penthouse* which seemed to be the favourites of the time. He was waving them with glee, in a manner that suggested he had found the crown jewels and his voice boomed out across the square, "What would your mother think if she saw these?" This caused one of two to ponder over the question before the inspector promptly confiscated them as being of an unpleasant nature and likely to corrupt the young minds of innocent sixteen- and seventeen-year-olds. There was a clear suggestion they might have been lurking in Denis' room; no confirmation was ever forthcoming and no one ever discovered what happened to them afterwards. It wasn't long before Ed laid his hands on some more replacement magazines for light reading at weekends, after which he dispensed them to his old school friend Dudley who would always return them with the pages stuck together.

Cadets inherently had an affinity with water and, coupled with the fact there were fire hoses positioned on each floor of every block, it went without saying that they required regular checks to ensure they were working properly. This task ordinarily would have fallen to the fire brigade during their annual checks but cadets seemed concerned that a fire could break out at any time; therefore it was critical that hoses needed to be in working order. There was only one way to check this and that was to uncurl the hose for a short distance and turn the water on. If it produced a jet of water that reached from one end of the corridor to the other then it was perfectly clear that the system was capable of dealing with any outbreak of fire, should it occur. If a cadet happened to witness this practice first hand by passing along the opposite end of the corridor then they would bear testimony to the hoses being in full and working order. Spider, also known as 'Hosepipe Harry' because of his excessive use of the fire hoses was a first-year cadet based in Buddy Street block. It went without saying that he looked up to his Section Leader Wolfie but also had great admiration for Donbo and Albo, who always had time for the younger cadets. Born in London, Spider was placed into care at Holyfield Square at the age of four months, so he was quite used to institutionalisation by the time he turned sixteen. The site previously featured a print works, a converted carpenter's shop, and a farm where boys undertook apprenticeships. Girls were mainly trained in domestic service with some achieving sewing and office skills. In the nineteenth century the town was renowned for its straw weaving, mainly carried out by women who produced trendy bonnets or boaters for the local farmers' markets.

Academically, Spider struggled during his early years at school before going to the local secondary modern school where he sat his CSEs. He quickly became accustomed to all sorts of personalities and odd behaviour that took over people's lives but never did drugs and never smoked; he couldn't quite understand the appeal. Similarly with skinheads who were quite popular at the time, he never quite got what they were all about. From an early age he realised that joining the police might be a good job prospect as deep down he always sought to do good and saw joining the cadets as a way in. Spider was very impressed with Inspector Broadhurst, who the young cadet believed exuded an exceptional level of authority accompanied by a great sense of humour which, as far as Spider was concerned, made him a 'great'. When it came to sport, Spider was no team player but loved cross country and was at one stage elevated to the county team. During the year he was also awarded a certificate for the most improved cadet although he was at a complete loss as to why he was the beneficiary given he was part of the badly behaved, infamous Class 13. Clearly someone recognised something in Spider that would see him go on to have a long and successful career.

Another favourite pastime involved filling condoms with water. The lubricated item was held out one of the bedroom windows on the middle floor of Upper Street block. As water was poured into the condom it gradually expanded in size. As it extended in length and size, cadets could be seen leaning out of the tilting window hanging on to the open end for all their worth until such time that the condom touched the ground floor below. It could mean two or three cadets stretching out for all their worth before the condom could no longer compete with the law of physics and would burst, sending what seemed like gallons of water all over the rear of the Lower Street block.

Inspector Broadhurst seemed to take great pleasure from carrying out the bedroom inspections as on one occasion he entered a middle-floor room of Upper Street block and, much to his irritation, found what can only be described as a brown smeared stain in the middle of the sheet covering the mattress. It was about two thirds of the way down the bed and it didn't need a genius to work out what had caused it. The occupant of this room was not known for the fullest personal hygiene and additionally had a distinct problem with their feet. This had not gone unnoticed by many of the other residents of this block and, more importantly, Inspector Broadhurst, to coin a phrase had got wind of the problem.

Suddenly and without notice, part of the bed frame including the mattress and bedding flew from the window of Monty's room. There was no warning or signals and the bed fell to the ground with a distinct splintering sound. Inspector Broadhurst was quite disgruntled saying, "You owe the Constabulary for a new bed," and promptly set about arranging repayment for the damage directly from Monty's wages. For those who witnessed the event it was most amusing but at the end of the month Monty's wages were deducted the princely sum of seventeen pounds for a new bed, which he was unsurprisingly quite miffed about. As far as the authors of this book are concerned, Monty learnt his lesson and never repeated his mishap with nature. Because of the expected high standards of dress and deportment, shaving became a necessity on a daily basis. Cadets could probably get away with not shaving for the early morning PT sessions but once the more formal parade process got underway every inch of the face was closely scrutinised. Any hint of recent furry facial growth was frowned upon with the poor cadet being sent "off parade" with a flea in their ear and an instruction to review their facial features and to shave properly. This was followed by an extra duty dependent upon whether they were a repeat offender. It was a routine that soon became second nature to Harry and Ed.

Cadets were paid on a monthly basis; Harry and Ed were over the moon to receive their first pay cheque at the end of September. A grand sum of £31.14: it would have been more but for Tinkers Hill deducting nine pounds for board and lodgings. What a nerve; nine whole pounds for providing three full meals a day for a month as well as providing heating, lighting, bedding and as many hot showers as were required. Cheques were issued to each cadet at the end of the month and generally around lunchtime a cashier from a local bank would turn up, accompanied by a consignment of cash and a rather antiquated system would follow whereby each cadet would present their cheque to the said cashier in exchange for money. In later years this system stopped as salaries were paid directly into cadets' bank accounts.

Generally, each weekend for cadets began at twelve thirty p.m. on a Saturday; officially they had to be back by ten thirty p.m. on the Sunday night although some decided to sneak back ultra early on a Monday morning before the early session of physical training commenced. This relatively short weekend made it extremely difficult for those who lived further afield to get home easily, including Harry and Ed, so they ended up staying at headquarters which was the real start to their friendship. However, once a month there was a long weekend break starting at twelve thirty p.m. on the Friday. This was even better for those who lived within spitting distance of headquarters but it still remained nigh on impossible for those living further away to return home and have quality time before having to catch a return train back to Tinkers Hill. Harry returned home once or twice on long weekends but even they seemed short-lived. Logistically, the practicalities of catching two or three different trains made it really difficult for Harry; even then he would be reliant on his mother collecting him from the nearest station. The one thing he was guaranteed was a huge welcome and plenty of lovely home cooking.

Whenever cadets left for a short or long weekend break it was customary for a cadet inspection to ensure they maintained a degree of decorum even when wearing their own civilian clothing; they were still expected to maintain high standards through being associated with the force. Harry noticed that time and time again, the task of inspecting ranks of cadets dressed in weird and wonderful clothing fell to none other than Inspector Broadhurst. Harry was positive that the inspector must have had a secret desire in checking the dress code before finally letting them loose into the wilds of general society. Jeans and T-shirts were not an option and occasionally there was a new trendy item that appeared before him. One of the female cadets had clearly forked out a fortune on the latest fashion in clothing; it was a rather slinky number, which had those around her talking. The cadets lined up in drill formation in three ranks with the inspector walking slowly up and down the ranks occasionally stopping to check the suitability of clothing on show. The inspector approached, stopped in his tracks and stared at the female for a while; this ultimately caused some wry smiles to appear on the faces of those nearest to her. Not being one stuck for words he uttered in his unmistakeable deep stern voice, "Excuse me, Miss, will this fashion catch on?" to which she and those immediately around her fell about laughing.

In the early seventies groups such as the Bay City Rollers had a penchant for very wide flared trousers with huge turn-ups and, typically, Harry was one of the first to embark on this new fashion trend and wore a pale green pair of these new and interesting garments and stood in the front rank as left marker. Honky, also in the front rank and standing two places along from Harry, could clearly hear the conversation that was to follow. As was usual, Inspector Broadhurst appeared from the training department to ensure cadets were dressed appropriately to mix with the general population. He walked along the front rank, walked around Harry and appeared to carry on before suddenly stopping in his tracks and returning to further examine Harry's attire. He looked at Harry's trousers from just about every angle possible and, by this time, there was much mirth and sniggering in the ranks. Then Inspector Broadhurst uttered those immortal words in his own special way, "What's that you've got on your legs, Cadet?" There then followed a conversation between the officer and Harry concerning his tailor, whether or not there were any shoes under said trousers, and whether he kept his bus or train tickets in the turn-ups.

Similarly, Cleggy was involved in a contretemps with Sergeant Watkin who carried out the spot inspection. Cleggy was dressed in the appropriate contemporary garb, including a magnificent pair of, quite expensive, brogue shoes with an antiquated leather finish. This finish was much admired and in vogue at the time and consisted of an artificial distressing of the leather to create a highly fashionable patina. Upon casting his eyes down on Cleggy's footwear, the illustrious sergeant let forth a stream of vile expletives and instructed him that he was going nowhere until the shoes had been properly polished. Cleggy's protestations that the shoes were brand new and "meant to look like that" carried no weight whatsoever and poor Cleggy, was quite late getting home having had his subsequent polishing efforts rejected several times. Sergeant Watkin, clearly not up with the latest in fashion accessories was finally happy after Cleggy produced his new shoes with the antiquated leather effect having been completely replaced with 'parade bull' boot polish. Unfortunately the shoes were never the same again.

In the main, Harry and Ed would stay at weekends. This was soon noticed by Inspector Broadhurst who was quick to enrol Harry into some extra-curricular football on a Saturday afternoon. This saw him playing alongside more seasoned police officers who made an instant impression on the youngster, notably for their typical crunching leg-breaking tackles and their no-nonsense approach to a game where they were quick to exploit any weakness shown by a referee, which they immediately turned to their advantage. It was after one of these games that Harry committed the cardinal sin of walking on the parade square.

If Harry was not playing football he and Ed would go into London by train and explore the vibrant shops of Oxford Street or visit the small monkeys at the BT tower. Having been brought up in a small town by the coast, this was a big experience for Harry in particular to see the bright lights of the capital. They would normally be back in time for an evening meal and afterwards they would wait until dark, creep out of the back door of Upper Street block and past the oak tree before scaling the chain-link fence that separated the sports fields from the nearby lakes. There was a distinct area in the corner of the field where the top of the chain-link fence seemed decidedly lower than the rest, giving a clear indication that this was a regular access point from and into the complex. Harry and Ed made their way through the railway arch, along a track before reaching the Jolly Roger pub where, feeling relatively safe from prying eyes, they secreted themselves in the corner of the public bar and enjoyed one or two pints. Although they knew it was a disciplinary matter they felt it was worth the risk as it was just nice to get away from that humdrum institutionalised feeling. Occasionally, Ed and Harry were joined by one or two others who stayed, but they made a point of doing this only at weekends; it seemed safer that way and less chance of one of the cadet training staff team stumbling upon them.

The evening duty squad was made up of two cadets specially selected to work after evening meal in uniform to assist with security on site and, at nine thirty p.m., they were expected to make a sweep of the gymnasium block to ensure any visitors weren't still lurking in the swimming pool, gym, squash courts or any of the changing rooms. It was in effect cheap labour as it negated the need to employ any sort of security officers, but it gave cadets experience that came from the added responsibility that they would need in years to come. The complex was fairly expansive so cadets had to be quite fleet of foot in order to lock up. Being part of the duty squad also meant taking it in turns to man the front barrier and check identities of those entering the site. It was during one of Ed's stints at the barrier that he made a bit of a name for himself. Generally, those visiting headquarters during the evening were there to participate in some sporting activity or to just simply meet a colleague for a quiet drink in the bar. In most cases visitors to the site were more than happy to identify themselves by showing their warrant card or something similar. Cadets were under strict instructions, which had been drummed into them that if anyone could not ably identify themselves then they should be denied access, which under the circumstances was more than reasonable.

One evening saw Ed and one other perform the duty squad and Ed was manning the front barrier when an elderly gent pulled up in his relatively new Mini Cooper sports car. Never having seen this man before, Ed politely asked to see a form of identification. The man immediately said that he didn't have his warrant card but identified himself as the assistant chief constable which would have meant squeaky bum time for many a cadet. Ed remained calm and again politely pointed out that he was under instructions not to allow anyone access without correct identification. The gent huffed and puffed and was quite indignant about Ed's refusal to allow him access. He duly turned his sports car round and left the complex. Thinking nothing more of it, Ed was summoned to the training department who informed him that he had done the right thing even though he had declined access to the assistant chief constable. It was a lesson learned, not only for Ed but to all other cadets just in case they succumbed to any feeling of intimidation. Ed had followed protocol by doing the right thing, but probably had not endeared himself to the assistant chief constable who now had Ed's name firmly embedded on his brain. Whether or not that was a good thing only time would tell.

There is a saying that an army marches on its stomach; the same applied to life in the cadets. The canteen staff supplied three full meals each day to the eighty or so cadets in addition to the multitude of lunches they provided to police officers who were attending various courses as well as the other staff working at headquarters.

The whole process was very well drilled with a small but dedicated bunch of hard-working individuals who did their best to produce a wholesome meal. Whilst not of a gourmet quality the food was plentiful for the needs of hungry, growing cadets and was sufficient to see them through to the next meal. If their appetite was still deficient after tea, a large tray of sandwiches was prepared which the evening duty squad would collect from the kitchen and deliver to the cadet lounge for around eight p.m., but not before some of the gannet second years had hijacked the said tray en route and pillaged the more popular choice of sandwich generally leaving the corned beef and cheese ones with the turned up corners behind. As well as the wife of Roy Rivers, one of the most identifiable characters toiling away in the kitchen to feed the ever-hungry cadets, was Violet, a something thirties local resident who was part of the permanent staff. Poor Violet was not in the best of health; she had difficulty with mobility due to her legs being like small tree trunks, which Harry and Ed attributed to some kind of oedema condition. She usually started the morning by getting a lift in with the ever obliging Mick Green, but Violet's days would rapidly fall apart in the heat of the kitchen. This wasn't helped by her lengthy hair which had to be tied up for health and safety reasons. It seemed to be a cause of constant irritation as she was forever putting it back into place. She insisted on having it long but the clips that held it in place endlessly came loose, causing much of her hair to fall in front of her face, giving the impression that she had been dragged through a hedge backwards. Violet wasn't the brightest star in the sky but she warmed to the politeness that was granted to her even though there was a small amount of ribbing received from certain quarters.

Harry and Ed saw Violet as an asset as she worked tirelessly during the week and at weekends. This was when they showered Violet with praise in an attempt to get an extra helping of whatever was on the menu.

Undoubtedly, one of the more popular routines outside of the work environment featured the Sunday night disco at the Berry Bush pub in Tinkers Hill which attracted most cadets who had not gone home for the weekend. Even those that had been home sometimes returned early so they could swing their hips into action on the dance floor. Attending these functions inevitably caused a bit of a stir with the locals, who seemed to take pleasure in goading the cadets. Whilst there was no illegality in paying a visit on a Sunday evening to the Berry Bush there was likelihood that cadets under age would be tempted to try half a shandy or something similar. In any walk of life temptations are sometimes too great; occasionally cadets returned in an inebriated state only to find themselves being stuck into a cold shower by their section leader and others in a kind-hearted way to try and sober them up. The Berry Bush pub was also a convenient meeting place for cadets and their girlfriends where they could spend some quality time with each other. This was also Harry and Ed's first ever introduction to a wet T-shirt competition where the local girls vied for an up-front position. Both Ed and Harry could never work out why none of the female cadets entered this uninhibiting glamorous gladiatorial event.

Chapter Eleven

Parade Square

The Parade Square was the one place fundamental to the whole regime of training. It followed a military style which turned young immature boys into determined young men using all sorts of practices from shouting and bawling to insulting and intimidating, as well as cajoling and praising although Harry did not see much evidence of the latter. One lasting memory that all cadets from 1972 had of Sergeant Watkin would be the pace stick that he carried dutifully every morning when inspecting the parade or when he was taking a class of cadets for drill. To avoid any embarrassment about where the pace stick originated from, it would be fair to say it was borrowed from a local Territorial Army base not far from headquarters. The circumstances of how it came into the possession of Sergeant Watkin was a bit of a mystery but it certainly did the trick, as every cadet genuinely believed he was totally empowered to use it.

The idea of the pace stick was twofold: firstly it was an indicator of rank as it is supposedly only ever carried by the regimental sergeant major in the military, something which, funnily enough, Sergeant Watkin had never been. Secondly, it was a tool for measuring the pace taken during a marching step on a parade ground so that all soldiers were trained to march at the same pace.

If there was anyone who could carry off this small deception, it was undoubtedly Sergeant Watkin, as he was a stickler for perfection whilst cadets were undertaking drill exercises.

The parade square was the place which started the day off. This was the regulatory meeting place for all cadets where they would commence their early morning physical training. Unless it was an exceptionally freezing cold icy morning this is where cadets would be made to run on the spot or complete mandatory press-ups, sit-ups, star jumps and any other silly exercises such as piggy back or wheelbarrow races which training staff thought up as they went along. If a particular cadet was not performing well or if one of them still appeared sleepy eyed, the early morning trainer would send them all for a sprint past the Buddy Street block, down the embankment, across the rugby pitch to the fence at the far side and back again. The last person back would endure more pain with further exercises on the parade square. This was also the starting and finishing point for any lengthy runs that the instructor might choose if they decided to let them run out of the headquarters complex, which happened occasionally particularly if Constable Knapweed was the morning trainer. He very rarely ran with them so was at a loss as to whether or not cadets fully completed the course he had set before returning to headquarters.

Sometimes, accidents and other mishaps occurred during these early morning physical sessions. It wasn't long into Harry and Ed's appointment but it was a bitterly cold morning and the cadets had been lined up in their regulation white singlet, black shorts, white socks and white plimsolls and had been ready to start for a few minutes. Charlie, a first-year cadet from Buddy Street block, was standing two places away from Kenny, another first year from the same block. The whole group were given the order to stand to attention which they did. About twenty seconds later and for no apparent reason Kenny fell forward hitting his head on the parade square, causing an almighty crack which stunned those around him. There was a momentary pause as Kenny lay there before he started shaking uncontrollably as if he was having a fit of some kind. Mick Green immediately sent everyone back to their rooms and an ambulance was called before carting him off to hospital. Kenny had only been a cadet for a short while; he was a nice enough lad but it was clearly not known by anyone, perhaps even him, that he suffered from epilepsy, something which neither he mentioned at his medical and which never showed up during any of tests that were made as a matter of routine. Sadly, Kenny did not return to the cadets and was never seen again; it was something that affected Charlie for some time to come.

After breakfast at nine a.m. the cadets would be back on the parade square fully dressed in their pristine uniforms ready for inspection by Superintendent Crake or his deputy. When the superintendent or the chief inspector were engaged on other matters this task fell to Inspector Broadhurst who was probably more rigorous with his inspection than his senior officers and there was absolutely nothing which got past him. This daily event resembled something from the monkey world as cadets formed in little groups brushing their uniforms with a stiff brush to eradicate any particles of wool, dust or other dirt that would likely give rise to an adverse comment or two from whoever was carrying out the inspection. There were huddles of twos or threes, inside and outside the four main blocks with each taking turns to brush the back of a buddy.

Each house would line up on the parade square with Upper Street nearest to the training block in three ranks. Behind them was Lower Street followed by Dotty Street and finally, propping up the rear, was Buddy Street. Their section leaders stood in front of the first rank ready to receive the inspecting officer. Each house in turn would receive the first command shouted by their section leader at the top of their voice: "Squad!" This indicated that a second command would follow very shortly afterwards. ATTEN-TION! The object of the exercise at this point was for everyone in the house to raise their left foot in unison to at least knee height and stamp it down hard next to their standing foot. Simultaneously, they would bring their straight arms close into their sides with their hands tightly clenched and thumbs pointing down towards the ground. The order to stand to attention was normally given just prior to their house being inspected. For one or two cadets this simple movement of the leg left much to be desired and caused some hilarity within the ranks when someone over-egged the movement, resulting in them either toppling to one side or causing a wobble of major proportion. The front rank would then take their bearings from the person standing at the very end on the right-hand side and were referred to as the "right marker". Each person in the front rank would look to their right and throw their right arm up so it just touched the left-hand shoulder of the person to their right. A short shuffle of the feet ensured they were stable and then the two ranks behind would simultaneously check that they were in line with the person in front. Once the inspecting officer had thoroughly examined the cadets at close quarters for any imperfections, he would move on to the next house allowing their section leader to give an order for them to stand at ease, meaning they could stand with less tension in the body.

Like other numerous cadets Boris and Harry had little expertise in the art of ironing so, on joining in 1972, they were expected to wash their clothes, iron shirts, tunics and trousers to an instantly high standard, but as neither had done this before things became a little unpredictable. Soon after joining Boris stood on parade with a tunic that he had spent an age trying to get right but had overdone it a touch, causing a scorch to the shoulder area. For some reason, Boris thought it may not be noticed but during one morning inspection the trite Chief Inspector Broome noted the said burn and demanded that young Boris complete what was commonly known as a G30 form, which he duly wrote out with some guidance from a more seasoned cadet with experience in this field. It mattered not that the scorch was a complete accident caused by an ironing novice as, exactly one month later on receiving his monthly payslip, Boris duly noted a deduction of ten pounds for the damaged tunic and he was therefore able to obtain a new one from the headquarters stores.

Similarly, Harry had the same experience again with the unsympathetic Chief Inspector Broome but this time it was trousers which had suffered a scorch mark, if not an actual burn. Harry did not have the common sense to mention it to anyone beforehand – if he had done so he may have avoided such a public dressing down from the normally reserved chief inspector. Soon after starting, Harry had been advised by his section leader that the creases in his trousers needed to be as sharp as a razor which, to a complete greenhorn, seemed easier said than done. Harry had managed to lay his hands on a heavy-duty iron on one of his rare visits home. Whereas, normal irons have varying heat settings, this particular one just had the one – very hot. It was generally okay providing a damp cloth was used over the top of the trousers to prevent direct contact between the iron and the woollen fabric. Again, with anything in life advice was freely available from those who seemed to know it all and shouted the loudest, as Harry was told that brown paper would also assist with producing an excellent crease as an end product.

Perhaps, due to his zealous nature, he tried too hard on one occasion causing the extreme heat from the iron to penetrate the brown paper, resulting in a burn on the crease of his right trouser leg just above the knee. It was pretty obvious that Harry was not going to elude the inspection and was prepared for a rollicking. Even before the inspection commenced Guy Roberts, who did a cursory walk round the Lower Street contingent, noticed the burn which stood out like a sore thumb. His advice to Harry was to accept whatever was coming. Eventually, the chief inspector walked slowly round the cadets one by one, looking them up and down. He arrived in front of Harry pointing at the mark which was clearly obvious a burn. The senior officer was in no mood for any malarkey and wanted a straight answer from Harry as to why he had cause a burn to his trousers. The only defence Harry could raise was that "The iron was too hot, sir" in a veiled attempt to pass the blame onto an inanimate object. Sadly, his attempt at passing the buck failed and Harry was stung with having to pay for another pair of uniform trousers, something which hurt at the time and which he never ever repeated.

The wearing of boots as part of a parade was part and parcel of the pomp and ceremony ritual and they came in for some very close scrutiny during parade inspections. The toecaps of each boots had to resemble a mirror and the only acceptable way of producing this was constant fingering of the area with a cloth in a small circular motion using a combination of boot polish and a small amount of clean water. This process would gradually build up the level of polish resulting in a pristine glistening effect. This art of polishing the boots was commonly known as 'bulling' and cadets would spend hours sitting with a cloth in one hand and the boot in the other nurturing it towards their goal. Somehow, Denis discovered that a good deal of work and 'bulling' could be saved in preparing one's best boots for parade by the use of a 'Damp Start' spray normally intended for damp or cold engines. A series of short sprays, applied to the toecap, bought the boot up with a remarkable gloss that was barely distinguishable from the real thing. This wonderful invention took hours off the traditional method so a number of others started using the same process, until one day Sergeant Watkin walked on parade with his pace stick. Clearly having been informed of this illicit habit, he slowly and carefully inspected every boot in front of him. When he arrived in front of Denis he took particular interest in his brilliantly shining toecaps so gave it a light tap with his pace stick. The gloss, which was of an artificial texture, cracked and broke away from the boot. As a consequence, Denis spent the rest of the afternoon running around the parade square as a reminder of his feeble attempt at deception.

The parade square was without question sacred turf and no one was allowed onto it unless with the express direction of one of the training staff and only then to perform drill exercises. It is almost certain that over the years many a cadet fell foul of this, as did Harry on one occasion when leaving the gym block on a Saturday afternoon. He had just finished a game of football and instead of going straight back to his room on Upper Street he decided to shower in the male changing room. By the time he had finished and changed into his weekend clothes it was almost six p.m. It was dark outside apart from the street lamps that were positioned around the parade square. Harry stepped up the slight rise to the footpath which adjoined the 'no-go' area. It was deadly hush and no one was about. Harry cast a glance towards the training block where he noticed a solitary light on in the office. He stood for a moment scanning the whole area including the cadet blocks opposite which were, in the main, empty as most cadets had gone home for the weekend. Not a peep from anywhere. He checked again towards the training block before making a dash straight across the middle of the parade square towards Dotty Street block. He ran in through the double doors, reaching the cadet lounge in double quick time.

Harry thought he had successfully made it but as he entered the lounge the phone was ringing, so he answered it thinking it would be for one of the cadets who couldn't be bothered to get up from watching television. The unmistakable voice of Sergeant Watkin bellowed down the phone, "Who is the cadet in the white jumper that has just run into the lounge?" Harry, who just happened to be the only one present, wearing a white woolly polo neck jumper, admitted his indiscretion immediately knowing full well it was futile to try and deny it.

The following Monday evening Harry reported in his PT kit at six thirty p.m. to Sergeant Watkin, who duly informed the young cadet that absolutely no one was allowed on the holy parade square even if it was a weekend. To see the error of his ways Harry had to run around the perimeter of the said square fifty times which was a lesson learnt as Harry never contemplated it ever again.

On another occasion Sergeant De-Bris was taking another class for drill who were lined up outside the training block. Whether he was having a bad day or whether he became over enthusiastic in getting the young sprogs to energise themselves, he commenced the session with a shrilled voice shouting, "Squad!" which was the precursor to the group he was addressing to be ready to stand to attention as that would normally have been the next command. Unfortunately, as he shouted, his false teeth fell from his mouth onto the tarmac which promptly sent the class into hysterics. Unable to utter the word *attention* the poor sergeant had the unenviable and embarrassing task of collecting his teeth from the floor, replacing them and starting the process all over again.

Chapter Twelve
Girls' School Disco

Each year an open invitation was sent to the cadet corps requesting their company at the Twatton girls' school disco, which generally occurred during the first week of November and was an event that caused some consternation amongst the whole regime. Tom was always up for a night out and as Twatton was his home ground he felt it was obligatory that he showed some of the new cadets the welcoming nature of this New Town. Tom, as it turned out, was centre to everything that happened that night, he was never one for backing down; he had an ingrained sense of determination and dug his heels in when it was required, which stood him in great stead when he started playing rugby.

This self-determination became more evident following the disco at the girls' school where Gwen Trelawney the headmistress had a reputation for being a hardliner and her sole purpose was in protecting the welfare of her charges; she also happened to be quite capable at spotting a drunk when she saw one. She was fully aware of how alcohol affected a male's perception of a female. It was word of mouth that drew Harry's attention to the fact this annual event was on at the girls' school and as a newcomer he felt it only right to support his fellow classmate. Harry had only known Tom for about ten weeks but he liked him and trusted his judgement, so when Tom announced that he was going and the evening's entertainment involved girls, Harry and a few others nailed their flags to the mast. They headed off early evening for Twatton with the sole objective of gaining entry relatively unnoticed into the disco. That was partly where the plan failed as Tom thought it a good idea to have a few alcoholic drinks in the Black Swan beforehand. The pub was in the centre of the town and had certain notoriety as the locals disliked anything to do with the 'Old Bill' so it was imperative that Tom and co kept things under wraps to avoid a full scale riot. The Black Swan was nothing like the pubs Harry had visited with Ernie back home and he felt an underlying tension in the air. Unbeknown to Harry, Tom had managed to obtain a half bottle of whisky from an off-licence which he used for supplementing drinks he had in the Black Swan. The bottle size meant it would easily fit into his jacket pocket and would be hardly noticeable when they finally reached the girls' school.

Harry had no idea of time when he, Tom and the others finally bowled up to the disco. Getting in was the easy bit but by now the effects of having drunk quite a few pints of beer, topped up with almost half a bottle of whisky, was taking its toll on Tom. He sat at the edge of the dance floor sneaking the odd sips of whisky. It went all blurry on him and, as opposed to having an evening of dance with some pleasant Twatton young ladies, he began to lose control of his faculties, falling over and slurring his words. Needless to say some attention was being drawn to the small group of males in an inebriated state, so it came as no great surprise when a teacher who was chaperone at the disco came forward insisting that Tom was taken to the headmistress's office. Oblivious to knowing what was happening, Tom, much to his incredulity, was half carried up some stairs to the office of Ms Trelawney. Yet as soon as he arrived, the call of nature descended and it was imperative that he answered it before it was too late. The only available place to go was behind the headmistress's cupboard which he promptly did.

Soon afterwards, Ms Trelawney appeared and suggested in no uncertain terms that the group should leave forthwith saying, "I know who you lot are and I shall be speaking to the chief constable in the morning." Harry was well miffed as he was expecting a dance or two from the sixth formers, but soon found himself staggering with the others down the drive back towards Twatton town centre. The events of the remainder of the evening became a little blurry as Harry and Tom became separated but it ended for Tom when he was slung into the back of a police dog van before being driven back to headquarters. Fortunately for Tom he was placed in the empty compartment next to the dog rather than in the same side. Harry and the others managed to get back relatively unscathed by taxi before lights out.

Everyone, except Tom, was up and raring to go for the early morning physical training session, although there were one or two who were still feeling the effects of too much alcohol including Harry. Constable Mick Green took the PT session that morning and as was usual before any physical exercise, he did a short roll call of the four different houses to see who was absent and, more importantly, why. If cadets were genuinely ill it usually fell to their section leader to explain the reason for their absence to the instructor. Constable Green asked the question, "Where's Tom?"

The answer came back, "He's not well, Constable." On this noteworthy occasion Tom's non-appearance was identified, but no real justification as to why he was absent was given by Wolfy, his section leader, and Mick Green, apparently oblivious to the previous night's excursion, insisted on some cadets from Buddy Street extracting Tom from his bed and bringing him to the parade square to join in the fun – and moreover, everyone would stand still until he arrived.

After a short while, Tom appeared from the entrance of Buddy Street block ably assisted by two cadets who were holding him up under his armpits. *At least he was wearing his PT kit,* thought Harry, even if it did look as if it was inside out. He was helped the twenty or so paces to the edge of the parade square where the remaining eighty other cadets were standing and beginning to get cold. Harry, out of the corner of his eye, thought Tom looked as white as a sheet and wondered if he resembled that colour himself. Mick Green walked purposely across to where Tom was standing, and took one look at him, before ordering the two cadets to take Tom back to his room which they did. Constable Green had instantly identified the problem and decided that some one-to-one treatment was necessary, so he started a very brisk session of PT with the group which, it was noted, only lasted about twenty minutes instead of the normal forty-five. What the constable wasn't aware of was the state of Tom's room as on several occasions during the night Tom had urinated in his own cupboard and had also been sick, making things fairly undesirable within the confines of his own space. Mick Green soon had Tom out of bed and promptly had him jogging around the rugby field for what seemed an eternity in an attempt to get some feeling back into his alcoholic, stained body. This was followed by copious amounts of coffee at the back of the canteen before being returned to his room to clear it up and get ready for the morning parade.

What followed during the next few days was a concerted effort to have Tom removed from the cadet corps via the back door route and he was consistently cajoled by staff and cadets alike. Although he had done wrong and broken all sorts of rules, resigning as was being suggested was furthest from his mind. Tom was one to respect morals and high principles but was not one to succumb easily to bullying or threats of violence, and the more pressure put upon him made him even more determined to fight his corner. It transpired that the chief constable had received a phone call, as had been intimated, which in turn sent a resounding message around the whole of the training department. Surely it was inevitable that Tom's days were numbered. He was formally disciplined and served with regulation papers and he could look forward to his hearing in a week's time when it was almost a foregone conclusion that he would be packing his bags and going down the drive. It was testament to Tom's resolve that he withstood some pretty nasty provocation during that week, with threats of violence from cadets who felt he had besmirched the good name of the cadet corps as well as having soiled their civilian clobber.

Tom's disciplinary hearing was heard in front of the assistant chief constable and Superintendent Crake. The whole proceedings were hanging by a thread and it appeared on the face of things that he was going to be walking down the slope to the main road. Suddenly, Tom produced what can only be described as a 'Paul Daniels' moment when he called his father, who had been waiting patiently outside, into the arena to act as a character witness. It was an absolute masterstroke as in walked the ex-military officer who only had one arm with an indomitable look in his eye. He was going to give it straight to them with both barrels. Tom was asked to leave the room so it is not known exactly what was said, but it is thought Tom's father pleaded to their better nature and promised his son would never perform such a stunt again. Being an ex-military man himself Superintendent Crake relented to this stroke of genius and Tom was subsequently let off with a severe reprimand.

This, sadly, was not the end of the debacle as almost a week to the day later two female cadets, Sophie and Marcie, found themselves packing their bags and walking down the main drive on their way out of the cadets after fourteen months of hard graft, sweat and tears. Sophie and Marcie commenced their second year as cadets in the September 1972 at the same time as Ed, Harry and Tom. They were part of an historic intake in 1971 of ten female cadets; it was the first time females had been accepted since the cadet scheme started in 1957. It was seen as somewhat of a victory for feminism as up to that point it was positively a male-dominated arena. Sophie's reason for joining was simple: her elder sister had joined the regular police where she picked up some interesting information from others about the cadet process and, although Sophie considered furthering her education it was equally inviting because of outward-bound courses, and on top of all that the Constabulary paid them. She firmly envisaged the experience would be similar to boarding school but was not expecting the physical side to be so demanding. She was the spitting image of her elder sister, so much so that one day Inspector Broadhurst took exception to Sophie wearing a normal regular police hat and uniform rather than the regulatory cadet uniform with the blue band around the cap. He was quite expressive in his demands saying, "Why are you dressed like that, Miss?"

Her sister, guessing he had not twigged she was not Sophie simply said, "It's normal, this is my uniform." The inspector began to lose patience before it suddenly dawned on him that instead of questioning Sophie he was actually speaking to her sister. Marcie was a really beautiful girl and good friends with Sophie, but was slightly non-conformist and Rosie for one believed that she seemed like a fish out of water and wondered why she was even there. Marcie didn't like the rules or regulations and she was never ready on time for the early morning PT sessions. During morning parade, Inspector Broadhurst would constantly berate her for her untidiness and occasionally question whether she was obtaining money under false pretences.

The newly integrated females were ably assisted by the matron on site, but their responsibility was also overseen by a woman superintendent who was highly charged on the discipline front and on one occasion had to speak to them as a group about a female matter. It was early evening and the girls were getting ready to go out. Sophie was in the middle of applying mascara in her room when the 'super' arrived, delivered her speech and left. Sophie thought nothing of it until the following day when she was hauled in front of the same senior officer to be castigated for her insolence. Her apparent crime was that she had continued to apply her make-up whilst the superintendent was speaking. This was not the first encounter that Sophie would have with this woman.

Sophie and Marcie had signed up each Tuesday evening for a typing course at Tinkers Hill College which they intended to see through as it would add to their skills list. They missed the last session in November but were intent in making the following week. Unfortunately, they were running behind time leaving headquarters en route to college, so were offered a lift by a senior cadet who had been visiting headquarters that day. His car wasn't the best and when it came to starting the engine it would hardly turn over, so they asked for a helping hand from the training officer on duty who, reluctantly, assisted in giving them a jump start from the car park down the driveway. In was clearly evident that Sophie and Marcie would miss part of the typing class so they decided to give it a complete miss and ended up in the Berry Bush pub in town. The three of them spent some time talking and both girls consumed no more than half a pint of lager each before returning to headquarters before their curfew ended. They were literally only five minutes late getting back which was sufficient for the duty officer to start asking questions. Given the unfortunate incident involving Tom the week before, it was believed that the regime had tightened the belt with regards to latecomers, so the girls were informed that a report would be made.

Sophie pointed out they had been late because of the car problem, but this appeared to make no difference and the duty officer then asked if they had been drinking. Sophie immediately denied having had anything but the duty officer, looking her straight in the eye, slowly and deliberately repeated his question, "Have you been drinking?" They both admitted to having had one half of lager. They pleaded for him not to report them but this admission fell on deaf ears as it effectively sealed the deal and they both gingerly walked back to their rooms, clearly upset by the whole episode.

Within a couple of days Sophie and Marcie were up before the fateful female superintendent. She had her job to do and what she was about to deliver undoubtedly came in the wake of Tom's incident the week before at the girls' school in Twatton. It is probably conjecture as to whether or not the decision to dismiss the two girls was based on that incident alone. It is unlikely the truth will ever be known but in hindsight it seemed like an over-reaction; but at the end of the day, rules were rules. The twist in the tail came after their dismissal; they were both informed that if they wished to re-apply when they were nineteen they would be considered for the regular force. Marcie chose a different career path but Sophie re-applied and re-joined the regulars in March 1974. It was soon after joining she was approached by a senior officer and asked a question, "Would she consider a role in training future cadet courses?" With her demise still fresh in her mind, she politely refused the offer.

Chapter Thirteen

Sports

Team sports played a pivotal role in the cadets' training regime as it was perceived, whether rightly or wrongly that bonding in sporting competition was more likely to help them later in their careers as police officers forging a closer working relationship on shift. For some of the trainers, the whole meaning of camaraderie was aimed at everyone pulling together as a team irrespective of whether they played football, rugby, or hockey or if they formed part of the lifesaving, swimming or athletics teams. Ed loved his sports and was naturally good at sprinting and gymnastics. As a team sport, it followed that he participated in the hockey sessions and as a compulsory evening activity he joined the fencing club which was overseen by Chief Inspector Broome.

Boris too had chosen fencing as his compulsory activity as he disliked other team sports, but this was one of the very few activities that he was happy to participate in. He viewed fencing as more like an art or science and one which he could reap some enjoyment from, as it was one versus one with each competitor requiring a degree of skill. Boris viewed Roy Rivers as an angry man who possessed little finesse and this was evident during a fencing lesson that the chief inspector was taking one evening. Not renowned for his poise and refinement, Roy decided to try his hand at fencing, but before long it was all huffs and puffs and he soon began ranting and raving at everyone when things didn't go his own way. Had Roy been in a tournament situation, Boris believed that he would have been issued with a black card by the *directeur* disqualifying him from continuing simply because of his bad temperament.

Ed was naturally gifted and excelled at gymnastics so immediately became a fan of Staff, who used him to demonstrate to others how a particular vault or routine should be perfected. Some in the class found somersaulting over a wooden vaulting horse too much to bear including Harry, who attempted the manoeuvre on several occasions without success only to be rebuked by Staff who placed him in the useless category. Harry was more than happy to compete in the indoor circuit training which involved rope climbing, sit-ups, squats, star-jumps and bench presses, but the gymnastics session which involved forward rolls over the vaulting horse had him quaking in his pristine clean plimsolls. Once he tried too hard, almost breaking his neck, which resulted in Staff immediately banning him from further involvement in anything to do with turning himself topsy-turvy in mid-air in an effort to clear the stationary horse and land in any sort of position on the mats on the other side. Whilst Ed was soundly proficient at this, Harry knew at that precise moment that his chances of joining the gymnastics team for the end of year display was in serious jeopardy, which pleased him greatly. Staff was always on hand to give encouragement with his "Harder yet!" rallying call and nothing pleased him more than cadets giving one hundred and ten percent effort.

Because of his skinny appearance, Wings was constantly under the eye of Staff who thought it quite funny to repeatedly remark as he passed him with, "I've seen more fat on a chip," which made Wings conscious about his weight and, the more it continued, the more Wings would fret about it. He considered it a form of psychological annoyance and it constantly preyed on his mind.

Staff also seemed to reap fulfilment and enjoyment at dropping a medicine ball onto the stomachs of male cadets when performing gym work; strangely he never reciprocated this on female cadets but always seemed to be on hand if they were having difficulty in negotiating the horse in the gymnasium.

Running formed a large part of their daily exercise regime and Harry and Ed soon became accustomed to regular visits to the nearby lakes where they would run round both the sailing and boating lakes, which were joined by a small river in the middle which was tailor-made to ensure cadets soaked their plimsolls on a regular basis. The yearly cross-country event consisted of a figure of eight round both lakes and was hotly contested between Denis, Section Leader Roberts and Budd with Denis ultimately winning the trophy. Ed did very well whilst Harry was just happy to finish as cross-country was not his strong point. The run always started from outside the training block, meaning running down the driveway was the easy bit. Unfortunately at the end everyone had to return up the dreaded slope, meaning more sapping of energy and increase in pain.

Probably, one of the hardest disciplines of the year was the Bunion run, a ten-mile slog wearing training kit and boots making it even tougher than normal. It was

•

named such as it was inevitable that most would have sores on their feet at the finish line, if indeed they finished at all. Such was the distance and intensity that the group were followed by Staff in the training van, who would follow at the rear collecting the tail-end stragglers providing he was satisfied they were hopelessly exhausted before allowing them aboard. Before doing so, he would attempt one last rallying call with his usual "Harder yet!" This was more likely to have the opposite effect as on hearing his voice it seemed so much easier to capitulate and hitch a ride in the van.

This was a demanding run to sort the men from the boys and the distance was alien to Harry who, although having experienced cross-country at school, was mindful of the fact that this definitely was a notch up and he struggled. Harry tried to take in the countryside in an effort to take his mind off the pain. He reached a point where he passed a nice country pub and thought how nice it would be to stop and pop in for a swift half. Ed, meantime, was flying ahead without due consideration for those behind as he was fully aware that, when he finished, time thereafter was all his own so he pushed on with greater determination and resolve. Not long after the pub Harry was so tired that he resorted to walking, which would inevitably attract some loud and vitriolic abuse from any of the training staff who discovered him taking this easy option.

He had already developed bunions on both his left and right pinkies and could feel the skin chaffing on the inside of his boots. As much as he tried he could not find the strength or air to start running again. After what seemed like seconds at walking pace the unmistakable sound of the training van engine could be heard approaching from behind him. Harry made a quick check as it appeared round the corner with Staff in the driver's seat. "Harder yet!" he shouted, as he drew level with Harry. "This is a run – not a walk," he continued. Too frightened to look or speak, Harry burst into life and began jogging again but it didn't last long. No sooner had Staff driven past he resorted to walking again. This went on for about another mile before Staff reappeared from the rear again, presumably having done a whole circuit in the van. This time it was curtains for Harry who was identified as being at the back of the pack with little or no chance of progressing further up the field. He was ordered into the back of the van where he joined several other equally weary-looking, burnt-out cadets. This process carried on with Staff barking orders at the tail-end runners before scooping them up like sprats at Billingsgate market. This run separated the elite from the ordinary; although Harry felt partially aggrieved at not being able to complete this run he understood he needed to work on his stamina and fitness and promised himself an improvement for the next time. Sadly, this was the one and only time he completed the Bunion run; in some small way it was a huge relief.

Rosie became part of the cadet lifesaving team; this was partly by default as she was a half decent swimmer and any female who could give the males a run for their money was signed up quickly by Roy Rivers. Rosie suffered greatly during her year at Tinkers Hill and any running or swimming caused great consternation as it seemed that excessive exercise caused a shortness of breath and her face turned a funny pinkie-red colour, which gave the impression that she blushed a lot. On one occasion Rosie was running the figure of eight cross-country course round the lakes and was struggling for breath. She had passed Staff once who was positioned near the bridge to ensure cadets didn't try and miss the compulsory river crossing. Rosie was clearly not on the same wavelength as everyone else with her short run followed by a walk routine. Having seen enough, Staff gave the order for Rosie to be accompanied back to headquarters at walking pace. Unsurprisingly, this onerous task fell to none other than 'Dazza', who had already completed his run.

Another occasion where Rosie suffered with severe breathing difficulties was during a swimming session. One of the requirements at the end of an eight or ten lengths' session was for cadets to extract themselves from the pool without using the steps, and this required quite a bit of upper body strength. It was the females who had most difficulty with this, but one of Roy's strictest rules was to refuse cadets already out and on the side to assist those still languishing in the pool. Clearly, Rosie had given her all and just couldn't manage to pull herself out to the point where the remainder of the class stood for some time strumming their fingers. Roy Rivers was not very complimentary and it didn't take long before he started shouting at Rosie. "Get out of the pool, Miss!" he screeched. She was struggling for breath and either Roy did not understand or chose to ignore her plight. Eventually, two male cadets were instructed to pull her from the pool, at which point she doubled up gasping for air. Rosie being Rosie was embarrassed at letting the others down. Having suffered for ages with a breathing problem during any intense exercise, she finally discovered many years later that she actually suffered from asthma, an ailment that could have easily been treated at the time. Peanuts and Joey had no such problem with swimming and Peanuts was captain of the lifesaving team, of which Joey was an integral part and a superb swimmer. As a 'senior', Joey won a men's individual lifesaving championship in a strenuous competition with representatives from many clubs within the county. Unfortunately, despite his natural talent and ability, he was unable to make it to the national finals but in Harry and Ed's eyes he was still a superb swimmer.

Wings was another who disliked swimming intensely as he was little able to complete any formal stroke other than doggy paddle for the eight or so lengths instructed by Roy Rivers who he didn't really like. Wings persevered with the doggy paddle when the rest of the group did front crawl, backstroke, butterfly or breaststroke; but as Wings did with everything, he tried exceedingly hard to improve. It was during a training session for the bronze medallion award at lifesaving that what confidence Wings had in the pool was completely shot to pieces. Cadets had to retrieve a black brick from the floor of the deep end. This was generally commenced from the shallow end where cadets would enter the water; swim the twenty or so metres to the far end before performing a pike-type dive to the bottom of the pool to retrieve the brick. Try as he might Wings was unable to perform this task and Roy became a little annoyed at his inability to perform this simple undertaking. To give him a helping hand Roy gave Wings a short push in the back whilst he was standing at the side watching others complete their mission. Wings hit the water like a sack of spuds, simultaneously receiving a mouthful of water. Once he had composed himself, Roy commanded him to retrieve the brick as, in his own words, "He was halfway there." Wings tried and tried but slowly began to lose the will and failed the task, ultimately failing the lifesaving award. Years later, this episode came back to haunt him when, as a rural officer he was involved in the search for an eighteen-month-old girl who was reported missing. Wings made enquiries at a neighbour's house only to discover the toddler had, unknowingly to anyone, fallen into their swimming pool but due to the cover in place no one had seen or heard her. Despite valiant attempts to revive her, she sadly died, but the whole incident of his failing the lifesaving test came flooding back in a flash. As a consequence since that fateful day Wings has never set foot in a swimming pool or in the sea.

Harry had experienced a tinge of boxing when he was in the scouts which resulted in him getting a bloody nose from one of the scout leaders. It therefore was complete stupidity as to why, for his evening activity he chose to learn the art of boxing from the no-nonsense Sergeant De-Bris, who would work the group really hard during a two-hour session. In his own mind Harry felt that he had something to prove and wanted to show that he could stand up for himself and give as good as he got. Unfortunately, Harry did not have quick hands which he soon realised was a fairly important attribute in a boxing match, as well as being able to duck and dive when necessary. The twice-yearly boxing tournaments attracted quite a few spectators; senior officers from headquarters and around the force as well as the parents of cadets who lived within travelling distance came for an evening of brutality. Each cadet was supposedly matched against someone of a similar ability.

Boris, like all truly cultured people, possessed an inherent sense of dignity when it came to boxing with him being more inclined towards poise and posture, rather than outright speed. This noble trait occasionally handicapped him in respect of many sports, particularly so in matters gladiatorial. When Boris was compelled to enter the ring he would always act like a true gentleman, refusing to strike the first blow but would manfully accept the inevitably resultant blow to the point of his nose. However, when he tried to return the compliment, his opponent would inevitably jump out of the way. Not content with having thus revealed to the world his perfidious nature, his opponent would then compound the contemptible act by stinging Boris repeatedly about the ears, before he had time to compose himself from having punched the thin air around them. Poor Boris felt these bouts were always appallingly badly refereed, as not once did he recall any of his opponents receiving the slightest reprimand, let alone being forced to stand still and take their turn at being punched. He felt particularly aggrieved during his first tournament, believing he was the victim of an extraordinary poor piece of refereeing by Sergeant De-Bris. The three, two-minute rounds allowed Peanuts to deliver a volley of jabs, upper-cuts, left hooks and at least one below the belt thump without reply. The fact he was able to get away with it in excess of forty consecutive times showed the bout to be totally one-sided.

For his first tournament Harry fought Butch, another second year in a much benign affair. During the first round there was a great deal of weighing his opponent up and, although the two had not really spoken beforehand, it seemed that neither really wanted to inflict serious harm to the other. During the minute break between rounds Harry was coached by Roy Rivers, who seemed totally disinterested with the proceedings; he threw some cold water over Harry's neck and face and provided some words of encouragement. "Just hit him as hard as you can," he whispered in Harry's ear before pushing Harry out into the centre of the ring for another two minutes. Harry tried his best during the next two rounds but it was to no avail, with Butch being hailed as the winner. Harry didn't seem to mind as neither opponent was seriously injured, but the loss was noted by Section Leader Roberts who had a severe warning. He felt that Harry had not tried sufficiently hard and had let Lower Street down with his half-hearted attempt against Butch. His words echoed in his ears so when Harry fought his next match he tried so much harder against the mighty Heinz, who also happened to be the cadet rugby captain. Harry approached this match with a totally different outlook; Heinz was a much respected member as well as being a section leader and it was clear to all that he would go on to greater things in his police career. Harry put all the tips he had learnt from his evening classes into practice.

The theory was simple – get in close, fire a quick left-right jab and get out again. Moving was quite key to the whole principle but Heinz was no slouch and was very well prepared for the onslaught. Harry managed to get in and out, unleashing a couple of jabs, but the roles suddenly became reversed with Heinz doing exactly the same to Harry who thought to himself, *This isn't in the script.* And so it went on: Harry tried very hard and was encouraged during the brief breaks by Staff who was his corner-man on this occasion. It ended with a victory for Heinz. Harry took it badly – he wasn't so much battered and bruised but his pride had taken a massive dent. He sulked off to the changing rooms where he cried, mainly through sheer frustration and disappointment. Mick Green appeared moments later giving support and reassurance to the youngster, telling him that he had put on a good spectacle and it was no disgrace to lose to Heinz. The words gave little comfort to Harry, but he was grateful for the time spent by Constable Green in trying to cheer him up.

One of the funniest matches of the year involved Spider and Streetman, both first-year cadets who happened to be in the infamous class thirteen, who were notorious for their misbehaviour. Neither cadet was particularly gifted with the attributes of a Sugar Ray Leonard or Barry McGuigan but this match was one of the highlights of the year simply for its entertainment value. Both cadets gave it their all for the three rounds; it was full on with hardly an opportunity for a gasp of breath. Both were like a whirling dervish; there was no subtlety, no quick jabs, no upper cuts and no full-on knockouts. Spider adopted the theory that it was hit or be hit and, rather avoid the situation and dilly-dally round the ring for a few minutes on his toes, he decided the meet his opponent full-on. It seems that Streetman had the same idea and the audience was entertained thoroughly with both boxers exchanging blows to the head, neck, chest, body, arms and legs; it was that untidy with Spider using not only his fists but his elbows, forearms and even took to standing on Streetman's feet on occasions. Forty years on and this fight is still talked about – not as a sensational boxing classic but in terms of hilarity, fun and sheer entertainment value.

Harry had always loved football and soon became a regular in the cadet side which took part annually in a national championship. This started as a regional competition with the winners moving on to play further rounds at a national level. The tactical brain behind the cadet team was Inspector Broadhurst, who was not particularly interested in flair or flamboyance from his players. He was a much more long-ball enthusiast coupled with a no-nonsense 'if in doubt kick it out' mentality. He wanted all his eleven players to be one hundred and ten percent fit, be able to run for ninety minutes plus and show full commitment, passion and endeavour for the whole of the game. If he felt that any individual was slacking he would make it known and then, in his own generous way, would make the whole team perform extra physical training before playing the next game, which acted as a gentle reminder. Course Leader Ant was a favourite with Inspector Broadhurst and captained the team and was present during one of the momentous occasions in cadet history. The team had played a couple of preliminary matches but, in the next round, had been drawn against one of their fiercest rivals and one of the big favourites for the competition. They also happened to be the largest and most metropolitan of areas just a short trip away. It was an afternoon game and Inspector Broadhurst rallied his team at lunchtime for the short journey down the road, with Roy Rivers driving the force bus. Harry noticed there were a few senior officers from headquarters who he had never seen before, so he realised the importance of this game; also there were some 'volunteers' who were press-ganged into attending as supporters including Ed, Macca and Rosie. He was also happy that Budd was playing, as whenever he was in the team there was every chance of getting a result. Harry was asked to play at left back, a position that did not really suit him as he was right footed and only used his left for standing on. Nevertheless he was happy to be in the team, which was full of players willing to give their all.

The first ten minutes was a tight affair, without many chances from either side, and without much room being afforded to strikers and Denis was having a torrid time up front trying to run the channels and beat the offside trap. Then calamity struck when the home team scored, which sent their supporters into rapture and willed them on at every opportunity. Yet Inspector Broadhurst was a fine tactician and ensured the home team did not get any room in which to play their fast attacking football. Out of nowhere the home team scored again and it now seemed like curtains with half-time fast approaching. Harry was up against a nippy winger who was much shorter and more agile than him. Several times at the start he was beaten for pace only to be helped out by one of his centre backs, so he needed to drop off a little rather than clatter into the back of him and risk giving a free kick away in a dangerous area. Minty played in midfield but was substituted after a little while after receiving a really bad knee injury.

In the second half Harry noticed that even more support had been mustered for the home team with approximately fifty people booing every time the away team touched the ball. All was not lost as the team from Tinkers Hill scored a goal and, within five minutes, drew level thanks to another goal from Heinz which, for a while, subdued the noisy nature of the home crowd. Again, it was tight all over the pitch and Harry was still trying to get to grips with the number seven. At one, point the winger received the ball and turned as Harry had backed off, waiting for him to come onto to him. He foolishly thought that this tactic may be his best chance of tackling for the ball but the winger, who was like lightning, played the ball between Harry's legs – commonly known as a 'nutmeg' – before nimbly collecting the ball, much to the amusement of the home supporters who were on their feet cheering and whooping at the tops of their voices. Harry's mind was buzzing; this immediately attracted some sound advice from all corners of the pitch, particularly from Inspector Broadhurst on the touchline. "Not again," Harry quietly said to himself making a very conscious decision to place much closer attention to this cocky young individual. No sooner had this embarrassing 'nutmeg' occurred when Harry's team went down the other end and Budd scored what turned out to be the winner somewhat against the run of play. The crowd weren't cheering now but for the last ten minutes it was all backs to the wall stuff with the home team coming close on several occasions, only to be denied by some last ditched goal line clearances. It was a glorious and very hard fought win and afterwards in the changing room Inspector Broadhurst appeared congratulating all the players for their monumental victory and surreptitiously handed them a small can of beer with which to celebrate.

Although he couldn't be sure, Harry thought that the win had brought a tear to the eye of their coach for, as they were leaving, he noticed the inspector wipe something from his eyes with a handkerchief. The victory was short lived as in the next round they played a cadet team from the Midlands only to lose 5-1. That historic match was the first and only time that Harry was beaten by someone performing a 'nutmeg' in a match.

Mick Green was sometimes press-ganged into helping as the 'bucket man' at football matches; in today's sporting age such a person would be referred to as the trainer with a whole host of qualifications before being let loose on a field to treat the injured. Apart from his bucket of cold water and sponge he had a dubious spray can which cadets were told was an instant pain relief in the form of a deep heat-type treatment. When this was duly sprayed to the affected area cadets would instantly rise like Lazarus from the turf jumping about in no time at all. It transpired that the tin, which was covered with a plain wrapper, was no other than a tin of fly-spray, although on occasions the inspector was known to swap it for a simple can of tap water. Both, it appears, had the same resounding effect.

Denis, during his year in training, experienced severe ongoing problems with his knees, in particular both cartilages and at times he was in great pain, so it was quite extraordinary how he managed to win the end of season cross-country race. This was probably as a result of all the stress and pounding to his knees from the extraneous physical activities that cadets had to undertake. In later life Denis had both knees replaced with prosthetic ones. His predicament was assessed sympathetically during the year by Sergeant Watkin who advised him to take it easy wherever he could, which was much easier said than done. Denis, like Ed, had a lot of time for Staff as they both believed he was a real motivator. Denis excelled at athletics, in particular the 100-metre sprint and was chosen alongside Ed and two others to represent Tinkers Hill in the 4 x 100 metre relay team firstly at a Pre-Services Athletic Championship at the beginning of June. This was the start of an intensive three-week period during which the athletics team competed in no less than four separate meetings, three at regional level with the last culminating in a national inter-force event. The Pre-Services meeting was usually a foregone conclusion as police cadets were generally trained to a much higher level than their counterparts in the army, army training corps or sea cadets. The sprint relay team won in a time of 47.3 seconds and Ed made it a hat trick with wins in the long jump and 110-metre hurdles.

Their meeting ten days later met with stiffer opposition at the South East Region Championships; yet again the sprint relay team were victorious, retaining the cup with another stunning performance of 47.1 seconds. In the next meeting the relay team could only muster second place with a disappointing time of 47.8 seconds with Ed also coming second in the long jump and the hurdles. The final meeting in June 1973 saw Tinkers Hill compete in the Midlands at a national championship. Again, the team of Ed, Denis and others showed pure grit and determination by winning the meeting overall by ninety-seven points with another pulsating 47.1 second display in the sprint relay, a new record from Peanuts in the high jump, Denis winning the 400 metres and Ed winning yet another hurdles race equalling the record with a time of 16.4 seconds. This was relatively unprecedented for such a small force to win such a prestigious event. Superintendent Crake was so ecstatic that he allowed each one of the team members to have some champagne in the post competition celebrations. Ed and Denis attributed their success over this short twenty-one day period to one man: Staff had insisted on extra training for the athletics team above and beyond their normal training regime. Denis particularly remembers an extraordinary motivational speech that he delivered just before their southeast region competition. Staff on the whole was not an emotional man but this was one of those seminal moments in the life of a cadet when he urged them to give everything. He believed in them, knew they were something very special and he wanted them to show it in the best way possible. Of course, to ensure the message got through, Staff had to place a certain emphasis to his team with his usual rendition of "Harder yet!"

Towards the end of their second year Harry noticed that Peanuts seemed slightly unhappy and word had it that Marilyn was seeing more of Guy Roberts as they lived in the same town. This clearly upset Peanuts who could not contain his anger, making it known to all and sundry. As a consequence, this dastardly imposition had reached the ears of the senior officers who couldn't allow any continuance of the volatile situation that had arisen between the two males, deciding that the only way to resolve their differences as lovesick puppies was not through dialogue or negotiation but from a much older and combatant approach. The second boxing tournament of the year was fast approaching and it wasn't long before names were drawn from the hat; unsurprisingly one of the first names on the fight list was Peanuts who, unsurprisingly, found himself matched against Guy Roberts. Even worse for him was that the boxing tournament fell on the evening after a lifesaving competition in Kent that Tinkers Hill were competing at. Peanuts was not happy; he was expected to captain the team during the day, return and then take on one of the best boxers in the year. Peanuts complained to Roy Rivers quoting the fact that he would already be knackered from the lifesaving and all the travelling. Roy Rivers told him not to worry and there was no question of him losing to Guy Roberts. Peanuts wished he had the same level of confidence. On the day, Peanuts returned from a very tough competition in Kent to find that his bout against Guy Roberts had been scheduled for just prior to the mid-interval break. Peanuts went to the gym block changing room to find it empty apart from his opponent, who was practising some last-minute shadow boxing in the mirror. There was no conversation and a short while later Guy left to go down to the gym. No sooner had he left than Roy appeared with a pair of boxing gloves which he threw down on the floor in front of Peanuts. He then promptly started jumping up and down on them like a madman to flatten any protection within the glove itself. After a fairly heated first round Roy whispered that the next round would be the showstopper. Miraculously, and against all the odds, Peanuts came out for the second and floored Guy Roberts to the point where he was counted out. Peanuts felt fully vindicated, having sorted out the bloke who had designs on his girl. Of course, there was a downside: with Peanuts as the victor, he automatically booked himself a place in the boxing team to represent Tinkers Hill against the Met cadets a few weeks later. Was this any sort of reward for such chivalrous behaviour?

Chapter Fourteen
North Wales

The class of fourteen second-year recruits were introduced to the natural beauty of North Wales on two occasions during their year at headquarters. For some unknown reason Macca, Polly and Rosie did not accompany their male classmates during either trip; they made their acquaintance with this area of outstanding beauty the following Easter when they went with the other females and a small group of first year cadets.

Harry's experience with the scouts had given him an insight to the art of camping so at least he had some idea of what to expect. Their first visit was over a weekend in the November and was meant as an introduction to the basics; unfortunately Tom was a no-show due to his impending disciplinary hearing as a result of his exploits at the girls' school. Roy Rivers drove the old work horse of a coach; he was clearly against the clock as he drove like a lunatic for the last twenty miles or so taking out one or two renegade sheep that happened to stroll passively alongside the winding narrow lanes. When they arrived it was raining heavily, blowing a gale and became a race against time to find a suitable spot to pitch their tents before getting soaked to the skin.

To prepare themselves for this first visit and to introduce those who had not camped before, one or two sessions were held on the grass area alongside the training block in the fortnight leading up to their departure. Tent-wise, Harry was paired off with Honky who also had some prior experience of camping; Boris was paired with his ex-school buddy Cleggy, but the two of them soon started clowning around and failed to pay adequate attention to the pre-expedition 'tent erection' practical provided by Mick Green and Francis Hardyman who tried their best to show the group of ten the most efficient and quickest way to pitch a tent and encouraged everyone to listen. Clearly, whatever Boris and Cleggy took from that session did not register fully, if at all, as when they arrived in North Wales it came as no particular surprise when they got into a terrible fix when pitching their tent. They managed to get it up amidst much arguing and commotion, long after Harry and Honky were safely tucked up warm and dry in their sleeping bags. However, given the extraordinary weather conditions the tent was not properly secured and had also been erected on an unsheltered ridge.

At around one a.m. Harry was woken by the wind and what seemed like muffled screams. He rose from his warm sleeping bag and peeked out through the tent flaps, before taking immense pleasure in waking Honky from his snoring by drawing his attention to the utter scene of devastation that was happening in front of them. Both Boris and Cleggy were still half in their sleeping bags and were desperately trying to contain their tent that had, inevitably, come adrift and was being held to the ground in very high winds only by themselves and one remaining tent peg. After some time and with Harry and Honky in hysterics the two clueless cadets managed to maintain control over the tent and, by some magical process, were able to secure it enough to prevent it from totally blowing away. When the group woke in the morning everyone was surprised to be met with about two foot of snow surrounding them with a smallish stream partially running through the centre of Ed's tent. This visit was simply a taster session, but there was a much more strenuous test to come.

Some most noteworthy moments of cadet life came during the Easter trip to North Wales. Harry and Ed's class of eleven were accompanied by Sergeant Watkin, Constable Green and Francis Hardyman as well as Roy Rivers who had driven the coach, again narrowly missing one or two sheep en route. Their base was a brick-built hut owned by the county council, which had bunk beds, a small kitchen, toilet and staff accommodation. The whole week was spent putting cadets through their paces to see how far they could push themselves, both physically and mentally. There was a constant, "Harder yet!" in the background from Staff on most days except when the class was split into two groups for a separate trek and orienteering challenge where they spent two nights away from the base. The first and most notable incident involved Boris, who hated team sports at the best of times. The group of eleven cadets and three instructors had spent most of the morning climbing some fairly minor peaks in the Snowdonia mountain range. Eating half-frozen cheese sandwiches and lukewarm tea boiled in a billycan was no fun particularly in unpleasant weather conditions. The day had started with the usual run down to the main road which ran alongside a very cold and sometimes fast-flowing river. Unsurprisingly, the cadets' objective was to get into the river and swim to the bridge and back, which was probably no more than about forty metres. The cold of the water was extreme and took everyone's breath away. This was a difficult task at the best of times but was made greater by the force of the current. On at least one occasion a cadet would struggle and get carried away with the current only for Staff to leap like a gazelle along the embankment and hold out a branch for the weary cadet to catch hold of. Once this routine was over and done with, it was a hard sprint back to the hut for some well-earned breakfast and hot tea. Boris gained no pleasure from this exercise and viewed this particular activity as building esprit de corps through shared adversity, an apt phrase for such a warped exercise.

For some, getting over the early morning river adventure took longer than others and it had a draining effect for the remainder of the day. Clearly, the instructors were less than impressed with the efforts of the group, deciding that additional training in the form of a quick hike at double time was required up the highest mountain in the area. The route followed a notorious path up the back end of the mountain which was an alternative steeper route up rather than the easier trail that followed the small mountain railway. It is fair to say that most cadets were already flagging due to the morning hikes but with Staff amongst them encouraging them with his "Harder yet!" rallying calls they started with real enthusiasm and romped up the first half of the route. The group took a breather before setting off on the next step. No one had noticed any deterioration in the health of any of the youngsters but Harry was feeling extremely tired and was sweating profusely and Boris was beginning to wilt. The weather was starting to draw in and it was getting much colder as they neared the summit. Around the two-thirds mark, Sergeant Watkin decided to let the group have another short break. There was little time to catch their breath before he had them back on his feet and ready to go. Boris, at this stage, was beginning to have the onset of hypothermia as he was dehydrated, really wet and physically exhausted. What anyone had failed to realise was that his body functions were slowly closing down. Whilst the rest forced themselves to their feet ready to continue at a formidable unrelenting pace, Boris sat staring aimlessly at nothing. Sergeant Watkin called for Boris to get to his feet but by now his brain was finding it difficult to register and he was experiencing a shocking pain in his stomach. He was cold and getting colder by the minute. The sergeant moved closer to him, repeating his request to get to his feet. Boris then let loose with a short expletive, "Fuck off!" telling the somewhat surprised sergeant in no uncertain terms where to go. This was totally out of character for Boris and all the other cadets in earshot were utterly aghast at this unprovoked response from the normally well-mannered, amiable cadet.

Fortunately, the brusque sergeant identified immediately that poor Boris was suffering from the onset of hypothermia and immediately got him behind some rocks, which kept him out of the freezing wind and placed him into a sleeping bag in an effort to increase his core body temperature. Staff was on hand to administer some coffee from a special container which happened to be laced with rum or something similar. This had the desired effect; Boris began to be more coherent but his final assault on the peak of Snowden was halted abruptly as he was led back down the mountain with Constable Green in attendance. The remainder of the group soldiered on, not knowing the extent of the situation that had almost befallen them. They managed to reach the peak but nothing was visible due to the appalling weather conditions. They took another very welcome but short break and a quick bite before making the descent which, for Harry and one or two others, could not have come soon enough.

The instructors would lead you to believe that this was a prime example of being prepared for all kinds of conditions and having the right equipment for the occasion although Boris might have something to say about that. It was questionable as to the foolhardiness of commencing such a trek given the level of physical endurance they had already endured in the morning sessions. It certainly tested the mettle of them all and at seventeen years of age, but it was something they had all signed up to; additionally they would not have dared to question the integrity or the rationale of such well-respected and experienced trainers.

On day four of the trip, and with Boris having made a full recovery, the group were split into two smaller teams and set a challenge of trekking out on their own and camping overnight at a specified location before returning to another prearranged destination for one final night under canvas. They would then return to the base camp and clear up before making what was certainly going to be a long and bumpy return trip home with Roy Rivers at the wheel.

Denis was nominated leader of one team with Harry, Honky, Wings, Minty and Boris. Ed led the other group with Trogs, Cleggy, Tom and Big Al. Apart from their camping essentials and food they were supplied with a map and compass and dropped off at separate points. The weather was reasonable: it was a typical April day, the sun was out, and it wasn't too hot or cold. It was perfect for hiking and without the training staff to push them Harry saw it as a bit of a stroll amongst the Welsh hills. Their destination for the first night was a small hamlet somewhere in the middle of nowhere, but fortunately there just happened to be a pub within 100 metres of their prearranged pitch. However, both groups were warned in advance by Sergeant Watkin not to enter licensed premises as they were all under age and it would be a disciplinary matter if they were discovered.

It was the first time in Harry's life that he had visited Wales; he and others were confused with many of the names which started with the letters 'll' in the name but sounded completely different. The two groups spent several hours following tracks and footpaths taking in different terrain. Occasionally, there were differences of opinion as to which route to take. Finally, as the light started to fail, both groups arrived at Llanmachi, the prearranged site where they set up camp for the night. Similarly to the November trip, Harry was doubled up with Honky and in no time at all they had the tents up and the primus fired up ready to cook the evening meal.

As both groups were indulging themselves on their dried food pouch, talk turned to whether they should visit the pub later that evening. There had been rumours of cadets from previous years being caught in the same pub as each intake followed exactly the same training regime and, having been set the same routes, it went without saying that the landlord knew these short-haired, snotty nosed teenagers with North London accents were likely to be police cadets and it was his prerogative as to whether he reported them or not. The eleven had all received the verbal warning so they were fully aware of the consequences. It was a group decision that if they were caught inside then they would have no excuse. They were a few miles from base camp and the general consensus was that if the training staff bothered to drive out all that way just to check a boozer, then they were sadder than anyone thought. "We mustn't give the landlord any reason to complain about us," suggested Ed.

So it was that both teams descended on the little hamlet pub after all the cooking materials had been cleaned and stored away. It wasn't the best pub Harry had been in but it was certainly upmarket from the Black Swan at Twatton where Tom had instigated his last downfall. The pub had a rather unusual male toilet; most, if not all the walls were covered in mirrors causing much amusement when visiting the little boy's room. Tom was reminded of his mistake from the previous November; he vowed not to drink to excess and resolutely he stuck to his word. Instantly after the group had ambled into the pub both the landlord and locals knew all too well who they were; but regardless of this a darts challenge was set between locals and cadets which started off quite friendly, but after a couple of hours and a few drinks later deteriorated rapidly into a bit of a slanging match, culminating in a local lad inviting a cadet outside to 'sort things out'. Supposedly it was over a girl, so without wishing to antagonise either the locals or the landlord it was felt that the cadets should retire to their tents, only to find them in a state of disarray with some of the pegs having been removed. You didn't need to be Sherlock to work out who may have been responsible. Whilst it was a good night rather than a great one, some cadets were relieved to have got back without a fight having erupted, but equally happy they had not been subjected to a surprise visit from the training staff to catch them out.

After a good night's sleep the two teams woke to find a distinct change in the weather; it was much colder than the previous day and the mist was really low making visibility a problem. They hoped this would clear as the day progressed as they knew a difficult trek lay ahead of their final destination. Ultimately this was a competition between the two groups and both teams started off as they had ended the previous day, irrespective of them having had a drink together the night before. Neither wanted to be last back to the rendezvous point where they would spend their last night under canvas, so Ed and Denis were keen to get their teams up and running as quickly as possible after breakfast. Neither wanted to be the first to make a move as undoubtedly the group that left second would follow the trail of the first team; there was only one realistic path to follow initially but, as Denis studied the map, he identified several different alternative routes about two miles in. Strategically, Denis felt he had the upper hand so imparted this information to the rest of his group allowing Ed's team to set of first followed about ten minutes later by Denis, Harry and company.

Each person was carrying a large rucksack on his back, some had a heavier load simply because of the tent but this evened out over time as rucksacks were interchanged. After about half a mile, the trail entered an old disused slate mine; cadets had been pre-warned about this place which was not only dangerous if you ventured into the wrong areas, but even the trails shown on the map weren't easy to follow and some were not even shown at all. There were stories of previous teams entering this huge area and walking round and round in circles for hours not knowing where they were. The additional problem was that everything looked the same; there were no landmarks to pick out, it was all very grey, dank, wet and dreary and the mist which lingered showed no sign of lifting. There was a lot of debate in Denis' group as to the most appropriate route and for Harry this part of the trek was taking an absolute age; it seemed to him that they may have been going round in circles but no one seemed too sure. After what seemed like hours, the group finally hit the edge of a forest, which was clearly identified on the map, cheering everyone up. With all good intentions Denis decided that time was of the essence and, as it was likely that Ed's group were still ahead, he suggested that the pace was increased which the remainder were happy to go along with. The group was marching purposefully down through the forest towards a clearing which led to a main road. The walk down was not particularly steep but the grass was still damp from the overnight mist which, at that point, was starting to clear.

Without warning Denis appeared alongside Harry slipping, sliding and eventually toppling over and rolling several times down the grassy knoll in between some rocks which were in very close proximity. Initially Harry thought he was playing the fool but, when the remainder reached Denis who was lying on his side, it was clear that he had suffered some sort of 'slip and trip' due to fatigue or even a mild case of hyperthermia. Although not unconscious he was extremely groggy; he had difficulty in comprehending where he was but, most importantly, he didn't appear to have any fractures. The group removed his rucksack and Denis was moved to an area where he was placed into the recovery position and kept warm by clothing from their rucksacks. Harry and Honky walked down to the main road to try and summon help. As luck would have it there was a phone box just further along the road, so they rang base camp and spoke to Sergeant Watkin. This was no time for heroics, it wasn't fully clear whether Denis had hit his head whilst rolling so it was decided that he should stay where he was with another cadet in attendance and the training staff would drive out and collect him in the training van, which was at base camp.

Sergeant Watkin promoted Harry as leader of the group; he made an instant decision and one that overall he felt was best for the whole team. Harry asked Honky to remain with Denis until they were collected. He suspected that Denis would not need hospitalisation and gambled on Denis and Honky being taken directly to the final rendezvous point where they would camp that night. If Honky remained, it meant Harry could leave the tent they would share that night in the hope that, when he reached the destination, Honky may just have had time to pitch it. This also applied to the tent that Denis shared with Minty but thought it a step too far if they left the third tent that Boris and Wings shared as well. Now, as a team of four, they had to re-group and work harder to keep one another motivated for the remainder of the hike. The group didn't wait for the instructors to arrive; leaving Denis in Honky's capable hands they plodded on regardless. Honky managed to get a tent up on his own and placed Denis into a sleeping bag to keep him warm. Like the stalwart he was, Honky fired up a primus and made some tea laced with plenty of sugar for the patient.

Having taken close scrutiny of the map Harry noted that most of the remainder of the hike was across boggy land which had to be negotiated with care. Harry's group of four set off along the main road for a short distance of no more than 200 metres before they came to the point where they joined a track leading to a vast expanse of bog. As they reached a stile in the fence-line the four could see Ed's group well ahead; they had clearly taken a different path through the forest, missing the area where Denis had fallen and were ahead by some considerable distance. "So what if we lose?" said Harry to the others. This was a downbeat moment and some heads went down as it was clear that the four were in no physical shape to catch Ed's team. It was agreed that they should try and attract their attention with a view to the groups amalgamating with each other and, if Ed had known of the situation, he would have surely stopped and waited. The group of four started shouting as loudly as they could and were waving furiously. At one point Ed's team stopped and looked back only for the five of them to all start waving back. They had no idea what had happened to Denis but later apologised for not stopping and waiting. It was just a case of plodding on in the knowledge that Ed's team would be victorious and accepting defeat graciously. Funny as it was, the four decided to laugh in the face of adversity; as they half walked and half staggered they sang and hummed some songs but, every so often, someone would add the immortal words "Harder yet!" to inject some humour to their increasingly weary bog-land hike.

After what seemed like an absolute age, the four managed to make the rendezvous point just as light was beginning to fade. As they reached the top of what was to be their last ridge of the day, Harry was cheered at the sight of two tents having been erected to one side of the camp, where he just make out the figures of Denis and Honky. *Relief,* he thought and what was even better was the news that Denis was okay and Honky had already started to cook the evening meal. When they arrived on site all the four had to do was to erect the tent belonging to Wings and Boris and they all mucked in. Needless to say Ed's group had a semi-muted sense of victory given the calamity with Denis, but overall it was a tremendous two days with lots of support being shown to one another along the way. In hindsight, Harry believed that Honky was the right person to leave with Denis; the fact that it saved having to put up the tent when he arrived had nothing to do with the decision.

The final day saw both groups pack up and return to base camp where a final clearing session took place. Whilst cadets spent most of their time under canvas, the staff had the luxury of the cabin with relative mod cons for the time. Cadets had a rota to assist the training staff with their domestic chores that included washing up all utensils including those belonging to the staff. This included an expensive, then new technology: Teflon-coated frying pan brought along by Sergeant Watkin. It became customary for the duty squad that performed this task to take the dirty utensils and wash them in the nearby river. Cleggy, being particularly anxious to please the sergeant, mistook the Teflon coating for burnt-on grease and dirt and accordingly attacked the pan with several Brillo pads, completely removing the entire non-stick coating. Pleased with his work, Cleggy returned to the cabin handing the spotless, gleaming frying pan to Sergeant Watkin – who was not best pleased as this brand new technological kitchen utensil belonged to his wife. Cleggy's punishment for this misdemeanour was to be given a filthy galvanised dustbin that stood in the yard of the staff quarters, together with a whole box of Brillo pads, and was sent back to the river under instruction not to return until the bin looked as new. Cleggy certainly made notoriety from that trip and it forever remains a question as to whether this was the result of his typical 'buffoonish' behaviour which he regularly displayed or whether this was some kind of revengeful act for the brogue shoes incident and he knew exactly what he was doing when cleaning the pan.

Before everyone left North Wales they all had one last piece of cake which had been specially baked by the wife of the deputy chief constable; this was something they had done for many years driving it all the way to North Wales themselves to personally deliver it to the base camp. It was very well received by everyone and, in a funny way, it gave a very small indication that maybe, after all, senior officers had a heart.

Over the years the pub at Llanmachi featured in subsequent visits by other groups of cadets from Tinkers

Hill. One occasion involved Honky's ex school buddy Doug who had been in the pub with others which included amongst their ranks one or two female cadets. Doug had laid the seeds for a bit of hanky panky with one of the females and was hoping to make a closer acquaintance in his tent only to be dashed at the crucial point by his fellow tent mate who was quite insistent on him taking his place for a good night's kip rather than letting Doug have his fun. This was the same trip whereby a disagreement had taken place between cadets and the locals in the pub; this had reached the ears of the instructors which included Chief Inspector Broome who decided he would make examples of those involved, particularly if they were found to have consumed alcohol. The chief inspector appeared early on the scene the next day and ushered the landlord from the pub. He then formed up all the cadets as if they were on a 'line-up' asking the landlord to walk along to see if he could identify who had been drinking in his pub the previous night. The landlord walked very slowly looking each cadet in the eye before reaching the end and then walking back. Showing a degree of excitement the chief inspector asked the landlord, "Were any of these people in your pub last night?"

The landlord faced him and with a straight face said, "No, I have never seen them in my life," and turned and walked back into his pub.

Another incident involved the infamous Class 13 whereby Spider and his classmates were visiting a hostelry for a few alcoholic drinks during one of their Welsh trips. The next thing they knew was they were being busted by the local North Wales Police for underage drinking. Details were taken and they were informed a report would follow to Tinkers Hill. When they returned, each miscreant was given a severe warning and told that if it happened again they would be packing their bags and walking down the drive. This was a very low moment for Spider, as he believed he had blown his chances of becoming a police officer. Although he was a mischief at heart Spider had very few vices compared to others; his happened to be one of drinking alcohol but he wasn't an alcoholic and it didn't cause him too many problems over the years.

Chapter Fifteen

End of Year One

The year flew by, mainly due to the intensive nature of the combined physical and academic studies taking place continuously. By now Harry had mastered the art of ironing his uniform without scorching it as well as 'bulling' his boots to a high standard and, whilst he was enjoying most of the academia, he was still having problems with his mathematics.

It was around this time that Harry caught a bug which affected every muscle and limb in his body. Sickness was something not easily accepted within the cadets as it was perceived by some as being feeble rather than having the mind and heart of an ox. Harry woke one morning at the usual time but instead of leaping out of bed to change into his PT kit, he found himself feeling nauseous with a severe headache, shivering and he was sweating buckets from head to toe. Every bone in his body ached which suggested he was suffering flu-like symptoms; he knew that he wouldn't be able to take part in the morning physical. He immediately informed Mad Kev who in turn told Guy Roberts. Unbeknown to Harry, he was not the only cadet as several others had been stricken by the same so-called bug. Harry remained in bed for about a couple of hours when Matron suddenly appeared at his door. *Perhaps she had come to give him a bed bath*, he thought to himself. No such luck: he was ordered to get some toiletries and nightclothes together as he was moving to a room in Buddy Street block which was set up as a temporary sickbay for those suffering from the same ailment. This had been implemented for those referred to by the training staff as sick, lame and lazy and housing them in the same block made it easier for Matron to monitor their welfare.

This was the first time during the year that Harry had felt alone and he wished that his mum was there to give him some TLC, which he knew full well would not come from any other quarter. Harry trudged slowly down the stairs and through the cadet lounge which was empty; he assumed that everyone was in their respective classes as it had gone ten a.m. There was a clean room with a freshly made bed which Harry settled into falling asleep almost straight away. He wasn't sure exactly who else had been shipped into the block but was aware that Donbo was in the room next door as he heard him talking to Inspector Broadhurst, who came round to check that everyone was actually ill rather than trying to pull a fast one. At teatime a tray was brought over from the canteen and deposited at Harry's door with a short tap on the door to indicate its delivery. Harry was unsure why they couldn't bring it into the room; perhaps they thought he had the plague or something more contagious. He managed to eat the bread and soup which made him feel a little better before leaving the tray outside and returning to bed. Later that evening Matron visited to check the patients and gave a pill to Harry to take.

The next morning Harry woke forgetting he was in a different room. He was feeling better and was just about to open the curtains when he realised his error. All the cadets were on the parade square participating in early morning PT. Had he inadvertently pulled the curtains back they would have seen him in all his glory and undoubtedly poked ridicule in his direction, so he discretely watched as they were put through their paces. Again, as he had done the day before, Inspector Broadhurst made a grand tour of the temporary sickbay about lunchtime, suggesting to all who were languishing in their beds that a spot of fresh air might aid their recovery. Harry thought he might spin it out for a little longer, so he pretended to still be ill, but soon realised that those in the rooms next to him were slowly returning to their own blocks, meaning that the normal residents would return soon. That night, after having something else to eat, Harry felt a lot better and made his way back to his own room. He felt weak for the next couple of days but soon was the road to recovery and fully participating in all physical activity.

By the time July came round, everything was centred on the final passing-out parade where a highly respected local dignitary in the form of the Private Secretary and Equerry to the Queen Mother was invited to inspect the cadet corps. They put on a display of foot-drill, physical training in the form of gymnastics and a lifesaving display in the pool to around 300 visitors, including senior officers from around the force, members of the police committee, academic and training staff as well as the parents of cadets who came along to see their precious children.

On the academic front it was time for final examinations; second years completed their Final

Certificate of Academic Studies whilst first-year cadets completed the slightly less arduous Intermediate Certificate. Whilst the results would not define any one cadet's life thereafter, it was another goal to be achieved in the whole spectrum of the year's demanding training schedule. As with anything to do with mathematics Harry was just pleased to scrape through with a pass in the statistics exam, whereas Boris achieved a merit in the same paper; this was partly due to the question being based on gaming and in particular racehorse permutations. What the establishment did not realise at the time was that Boris worked as a 'boardman' at Ward-Hill bookmakers. On joining the cadets he gave it up but, during holiday periods and some weekends, he would return to earn a little more cash in hand. The boardman's role was to write up the starting prices of horses and greyhounds onto a board prior to a race. His mind was therefore focussed on figures for most of the day so, when it came to one of the exam questions, worth 25% of the overall mark, he was extremely confident of the result. Only a handful of people knew that Boris was moonlighting. Yet occasionally things in life fall nicely into place and this was one of those times when he could not have asked for a better exam question. Perhaps this kind of luck was some recompense for all the unpleasant moments he had suffered during the year.

As with most students in any school, college or university, exam times are a fairly tense time and there was quite a bit of pressure placed upon cadets to reach the required pass mark in each of the subjects. Inherently, most cadets were honest and approached the exams with a degree of the *je ne regret rien* mentality. Peanuts and

Rod Caves shared the same class and during one of their exams Peanuts, who was sitting two places and at a slight angle behind Rod, noticed that he seemed to be looking at some unsolicited material and formed the opinion that he was cheating. This was not to be tolerated or expected from anyone, but no one else seemed to have noticed this blatant attempt to obtain a better grade. Peanuts had a lot of respect for Rod as they had been through their first year together and Rod was one of the top boxers in the year, but Peanuts felt this was a step too far. He continued to watch before vocally objecting on principle to Rod's behaviour and made his feelings known to the class as well as to the presiding invigilator. Clearly, Rod took exception to this ultra piece of honesty and launched himself across the desks towards Peanuts, which ended with the two grappling on the floor before Rod gave Peanuts a pasting, knocking him unconscious.

As a result of this ferocious attack poor Peanuts ended up in the local hospital with bruising, five or six chipped teeth and a sore head. Despite not wishing to press charges, the establishment had no alternative but to instantly dismiss Rod for the unwarranted level of violence shown towards a fellow cadet, simply for doing the right thing. Rod was marched to his room; he packed his bags and he was escorted down the drive and off the complex. Whilst he was no angel, Peanuts had sufficient backbone to stand up and be counted whilst others acquiesced.

It was also the time of year when the more senior of cadets became a little bolder and braver as their time at headquarters was slowing coming to an end and they needed to get rid of all their pent-up aggression from the exams that were taking place. On one particular unfortunate day in July Constable Knapweed was prepared for the worst. He had just finished the early morning physical exercise outside when some of the more 'bullish' cadets including Peanuts decided to move what was left of their training into the swimming pool area rather than continue outside in the torrential rain. The reason for this was that a decision had been made to throw Knapweed into the pool as a gesture of the cadets' appreciation for everything that he had done or not done throughout the year. It was one of those times when he lacked the necessary authority and things got quickly out of control. One of the cadets had the foresight to release the lock on one of the pool doors in advance, making the process of getting him into the pool so much easier. It was fairly inevitable that something would happen to Knapweed either before, during or after one of the early morning physical training sessions. He half expected something to happen so, when he was lifted by a number of cadets, he knew he was going to receive a dunking so had the forethought to wear more appropriate attire under his tracksuit. He went in with a huge splash followed closely behind by some even braver cadets who believed that simply throwing him in was not insult enough. Somewhat unfairly, Knapweed received a severe reprimand from Superintendent Crake for leaving his soaking wet clothes on a radiator to dry in the training department. The poor bloke just couldn't win!

The final passing-out parade was the last thing on the cadet calendar before breaking for a well-earned summer vacation. Visitors were entertained to a display of drill, gym work and lifesaving. Practice for the final passing-out parade was virtually non-stop for several weeks leading up to the big day. Everything had to be spick and span; everyone had to be singing from the same hymn sheet but not literally. To prepare the whole cadet corps for this notable occasion, a large tannoy system was erected adjacent to the parade square to assist with the co-ordination required when marching. 'Mouldy Old Dough' was a 1972 favourite hit for Lieutenant Pigeon and featured a piano-playing mother in a boogie-woogie, honky-tonk, ragtime, toe-tapping style which was ideal for marching purposes as it had a steady and regular beat that even the most disorientated, uncoordinated cadet could follow. The music blared out whenever a cadet class was practising their manoeuvres. Occasionally, Inspector Broadhurst would speed things up just to avoid any monotony; marching at double time not only increased the heart rate, it also increased the chances of mistakes which is what the inspector was really trying to avoid. If you could avoid making mistakes whilst marching at double time then it went without saying that marching at normal time would be a stroll in the park.

"Harder yet!" Staff would yell as their little legs were moving at ten to the dozen. After five to ten minutes of vigorous double time, things would grind to a halt where cadet chests would heave up and down gasping for some well-earned oxygen.

Additional to the larger formal passing-out parade, a very small number of twelve hand-chosen cadets were formed into a 'silent' drill squad which Honky was a member of. Their task was to march together in unison without any orders or to music. Honky was specially chosen because of his meek voice and would act as the lynchpin in the middle of the group and, if any words had to be uttered, he was one that the responsibility fell to. The remainder would instinctively react to orders given by Honky as quietly as possible, giving the impression to the viewing public that the five-to-ten-minute performance was impeccably rehearsed without any prompts from any quarter. Those chosen were known for their natural marching rhythm and could maintain the grace and poise of a gazelle. Practice was the key to this success which the group did every day, come rain or shine.

Occasionally things went a little awry, particularly when Constable Knapweed was asked to stand in as a last-minute replacement for either Inspector Broadhurst or Sergeant Watkin. Knapweed never used the expression 'Harder yet', probably as he did everything at one pace. The 'silent squad' as they became known saw this as an opportunity to rib the unfortunate officer and would often perform the opposite to directions he gave. The group were marching down the parade square; as they neared the bottom corner Knapweed gave the order to right wheel: in basic terms this means the group would turn a right-hand corner in a dignified and specially choreographed manner. Unfortunately, at that point the whole group suffered a hearing defect and marched in a straight line between the section blocks heading for the rugby field. Knapweed, who was standing outside the training department, started shouting louder and louder for the group to halt, but this too fell on deaf ears. At a normal and leisurely pace the group descended the short embankment, walking across the long-jump pit and onto the rugby field. By this time Knapweed, fuming and irate, proceeded to chase the group across the sports field where they were finally halted. They saw it as nothing but a bit of light-hearted fun but were thoroughly rebuked by Inspector Broadhurst who gave them a severe dressing-down. Come the day of the finale, the demonstration went according to plan and the whole thing was an entire success, with Honky orchestrating things from the middle.

Both Harry and Ed's parents attended on what was a very sunny day and were extremely proud of their son's achievements. This was the first time that Harry's mother had seen his newly acquired stack-heeled shoes which he had purchased quite recently from London. She too was slightly taken aback by his fashion sense.

Ed and Harry and all the others from the Class of Fourteen were extremely chuffed with their achievement of having made it through their first year; they could now look forward to being senior cadets, but more importantly Ed, Harry, Wings and Honky could now look forward to a nice and relaxing break in Shakespeare's county, which would see Harry reunited with the wonder of Warwick.

Chapter Sixteen

Shakespeare's Revenge

Throughout the year Harry remained in regular contact with Lena, the wonder of Warwick who had turned his head whilst holidaying at his home seaside resort. They had agreed to stay in touch and in the days before the introduction of smartphones or the Internet, a system with letters was the more considered method of communication between people wishing to express themselves but who lived significant distances from one another. At headquarters there was the communal telephone situated in the foyer of Dolly Street block just below the stairwell that led up to the female block, but invariably it was in regular use of an evening. In most cases cadets were phoning their parents, friends or loved ones and, in some cases of the latter, were even attempting to hold intimate conversations in what was essentially a busy thoroughfare. Harry thought that having just the one phone within the block was a little thoughtless as no sooner had one cadet managed to commandeer the handset and began their conversation than another would appear in an agitated state, beckoning and making signs indicating that their call was much more urgent.

There was an additional problem in that Lena did not have a phone at home so any calls had to be made to the neighbour who, although happy with the arrangement, then seemed to spend an age fetching her from next door. Harry referred to Lena as his pen pal, but secretly hoped that she might have feelings for him above and beyond the monthly letter. Each morning after the post had arrived Harry was like a little child in a toyshop, anxiously checking the pigeonholes outside the admin office during the morning break in the hope that Lena had remembered him. Without fail, she stuck to her end of the bargain even though Harry may have forgotten to reply to one or two of her letters. Reading her letters was reassuring and comforting and Harry yearned for the next time they could meet in the hope of rekindling any fire. By the time June approached, the theme of the letters had changed slightly and Harry was concerned that Lena may have found alternative attention and possible romance from someone closer to home. Perhaps the negative thoughts he was having were all in his mind as he had a tendency to over-analyse things, so he suggested that he and some pals visit her during the impending summer holiday. Lena, in her reply, was all for it; even suggesting that she had some friends who could buddy up with any mates that Harry brought along. It sounded like a perfect idea except that Harry had not discussed this plan with anyone, so now had the difficult task of selling the scheme to anyone who might have sufficient cash for a week at Shakespeare's birthplace.

Harry mentioned this proposal to Ed, Honky and Wings who all signed up to the venture as long as Lena had 'friends' and preferably ones with 'benefits'. As the three shy, retiring and naive stalwarts had not previously met their arranged partners it was decided that they too should enter into corresponding by mail prior to embarking on this cultural trip. This meant, letters heavily soaked in Brut aftershave together with a malapropos acronym written on the rear of the envelope which was sure to impress, being sent to the lucky recipients. So the scene was set and the four were booked into the Valeta Hotel on the New Road for one week at the beginning of August.

It was an agonising time between their final passing-out parade and when they eventually set off to explore the heritage area of Warwickshire, making the intervening three weeks really drag. Harry in particular was desperately counting the days before he would see the lovely Lena again. What would he say? More importantly, what would he do and how would she feel on seeing him again?

The four adventurers met up at Euston Station before taking the two-hour train journey north. It was late afternoon by the time they arrived and booked into the Valeta Hotel, which Harry likened to a bed and breakfast rather than a hotel. He made this comparison based on the hotel where his father worked which had about fifty rooms whilst the Valeta only had about eight rooms and the residents' lounge was a tad bigger than his front room at home. Nevertheless, it was clean and warm and he and Ed shared a twin room whilst Wings and Honky shared another down the corridor.

Their unpacking was interrupted by the arrival of Lena and her best friend Jules who had come to meet their holidaymaking visitors. This was the first opportunity for Ed, Wings and Honky to meet Lena who made an instant impression on them; even Harry was beginning to feel butterflies in his stomach at seeing Lena again. The girls insisted that the cadets accompany them back to Lena's house where her parents had laid on some refreshments. Food and cadets always seemed to have a natural infinity between them and Ed applied the principle that it was rude to refuse, so the six of them caught a bus from outside the hotel to Lena's home, which was a short distance away. Harry had previously met Lena's parents before during their holiday visit to his home town and there was an air of nostalgia when they brought up their previous holiday in conversation. Harry loved nothing better than talking about his roots and the various incidents on the beach and along the coast that had occurred over the years. The lads spent several hours at Lena's before saying their farewells and making the short trip back to the hotel. There was plenty of discussion in Harry and Ed's room that night about how they rated Lena and Jules in the 'character and good looks' test. Harry hoped their visit wouldn't turn into the proverbial cattle market where the four cadets would exert 'bullish' behaviour over one another in an effort to pull the best from the bunch. Tomorrow would definitely be another day.

Breakfast at the Valeta was interesting to say the least. This was clearly where Honky would draw experience from, for his career in later life as an hotelier. Most of it was self-service with a glass jug containing milk which looked as if it had been there for several days. There was a small choice of cereal with little or no fruit on offer but there were the usual small plastic pots of jam and marmalade to accompany the toast. On the plus side, there was ample selection from the cooked menu as long as you had a liking for eggs as they seemed to come with anything and everything. Eggs and beans, eggs and bacon, eggs and sausage, eggs and mushrooms, fried eggs, scrambled eggs, poached eggs or boiled eggs. If you were that way inclined you could even just have egg on toast as long as you didn't mind having the toast burnt, hard or cold. If you were really unlucky it might be all three. The food was average but plentiful and as the cadets had not booked on a half-board basis they had a long day ahead before eating again.

The group decided on a historical visit to Coventry to see the medieval St Michael's Church which dated back to the late fourteenth to early fifteenth century. Being one of the largest parish churches in England it was given cathedral status in 1918 but was bombed almost to destruction during the Coventry blitz in November 1940 and now stood as a ruin, but remained hallowed ground. The new cathedral was built next to the old one. Jules and Lena accompanied the plucky four who found the whole visit inspiring. It was during the climb to the top of the tower that Harry got closer to Lena as she was complaining of the cold; he placed his arm around her shoulder and pulled her closer towards him. She didn't object or pull back so it seemed fairly clear she was happy to have close contact with him. *Things might just develop,* he thought to himself. The group had lunch and then explored some more before heading back to the Valeta.

An evening meal beckoned at the infamous Breakdown Restaurant close to where Jules lived and the girls had booked a table for four as Honky and Wings had arranged to do their own thing. Besides, they didn't want to be gooseberries for Ed and Harry. After showering, the pair got suited and booted wearing their newly acquired bow ties before their visit to the Breakdown, which was an olde-worlde pub-cum-restaurant where the food was exquisite but not beyond their relatively meagre salary. Harry and Ed paid many compliments to Lena and Jules during the meal in the hope that things might begin to hot up. At the end of the meal the four went back to Jules' house where they talked before giving the girls a polite goodnight kiss on the cheek.

By this time Harry and Ed were making good headway with Lena and Jules, but Honky meanwhile was beginning to feel left out; he was particularly peeved as Ed was already showing interest in Isabelle, another friend of Lena and Jules who Honky had been corresponding with for several weeks and was yet to make an appearance. He knew Ed well and could see that Ed was not content with just one female in tow and was showing signs of muscling in on his girl.

The following day, Jules' sister Helen turned up to join in the festivities. Helen was a couple of years older than Jules and really didn't have much time for any of the four cadets. She was there to chaperone her younger sister and to ensure that no hanky panky occurred, but she joined in with all the conversations and banter. She seemed a much more sensible person and less gregarious than her younger sibling.

The next day the four cadets went swimming but Ed found the pool too warm so only stayed for a short time before disappearing with Isabelle, who had appeared on the scene that day. As Honky had suspected, Ed took an immediate fancy to Izzy as she was known, which caused much consternation as Honky thought that sending letters soaked in tacky aftershave signalled an automatic entitlement to have first refusal on Izzy's booty. Ed spent the rest of the lunchtime and into the afternoon eating sandwiches and talking with Izzy, who he found more refined and self-confident than Jules which he found more endearing. He later confided in Harry that he fancied Izzy more than Jules but was stuck between a rock and a hard place as he didn't want to offend Honky, who would consider him a blaggard and a scoundrel if he took the prize from under Honky's nose. Ed soon shook himself out of it when Jules and Lena turned up at the hotel.

Both girls seemed to want to get to know Ed and Harry on a more informal and intimate footing, so they spent the next few hours in very close contact. Harry and Lena had the relative comfort of the bed whilst Ed and Jules got cosy together on the floor next to Ed's bed. This was where Harry learnt to perfect the French kiss and he had plenty of opportunity to practise. Before anything too heavy could happen Honky was banging on their door telling them it was time for dinner. *Who could eat at a time like this,* thought Harry to himself. The four young playmates decided to adjourn for some food but agreed to reconvene the next day which almost sent Ed and Harry into a state of delirium. "Harder yet!" they joked as both got ready for dinner. Strangely, the following morning was spent playing cards before the group headed off to the cinema to watch a rendition of *Steptoe and Son* which bored the pants off Ed. Then it was time for round two and this time Ed and Jules had the bed whilst Harry and Lena cavorted on the floor. It was during this head to head that Jules told Ed that she was utterly jealous of him and Izzy. She had noticed he had been spending more time with Izzy but, given his current position, it wasn't the most appropriate time for his philandering with her friend to be raised onto the agenda. Needless to say, Ed managed to talk his way out of it which he became quite accomplished at doing. Everything was going quite well until Honky yet again interrupted proceedings with what was becoming his favourite pastime: banging away at Ed and Harry's door to announce that he was going out. This behaviour was beginning to slightly annoy Harry who came to the conclusion that Honky was out to sabotage any fun that might have been on the cards with the girls. Despite Harry and Ed being prepared with the right equipment for a good time, in the end both Lena and Jules were not quite ready to lose their dignity in a dingy bed and breakfast to a couple of young stud muffins regardless of how many Mates they had in their wallets.

The next couple of days saw Ed in particular make a play for both Jules and Izzy although he strenuously denied that he was trying to 'make out' with either and suggested it was time the boys got down to some serious drinking. Ed, Harry and Wings decided it was time to impress Lena and her friends with their ability to drink copious amounts of alcohol and, as they were midway through the holiday, there was no better time. For some inexplicable reason which didn't become clearer until later Honky and Izzy decided to stay behind at the Valeta; Harry genuinely considered that the two wanted to play another game of cribbage or pontoon. The others headed off to the Angel's Reply which was less than half a mile away. It was not clear whether Honky and Izzy being left behind had anything to do with Ed's behaviour that night, but his mind seemed to be elsewhere as all he wanted to do was drink. It may have also been to do with the fact that ten days previously he had turned eighteen so he felt totally at liberty to drink as much alcohol as he could possibly manage. Harry and Wings were the sensible ones along with the girls that evening and tried to remain conservative with their consumption, but within a very short space of time Ed had downed two vodka and limes, closely followed by two stout and ciders. Harry and Wings attempted to persuade him to slow down but it seemed as if he was on a mission. By the end of the night Ed had consumed a further seven rum and blackcurrants. No one was in any state for any funny business so it was back to the hotel for some well-deserved shuteye only to find that the room being shared by Wings and Honky was locked. Whilst Wings went off to reception to track down a duplicate key Harry and Ed listened intently at the door as there seemed to be muffled sounds coming from within. Harry was sure he could hear giggling and was able to decipher words such as Wasps, Stings, Tongues and Tails. Ed and Harry exchanged quizzical glances and wondered whether Honky and Izzy were engaged in some sort of new fetish. Wings returned with the spare key which was placed carefully into the lock in readiness for them to spring a surprise on the loved-up couple. The three cadets were totally taken aback as they stormed into the room; both Honky and Izzy were full clothed and standing facing each other on either side of the bed in a theatrical pose. The two had been doing nothing other than reciting exerts from The Taming of the Shrew. The boozed up cadets were convinced that Honky had been engaged in some slap and tickle and in some ways, it was a relief not to have found them in a compromising position. The question did remain as to which one was the wild animal.

The following morning Ed unbelievably woke with no headache at all. His protestations claiming that he was completely fine fell on deaf ears at breakfast as no one believed him. Their plans for the day were to visit the home of the Bard's wife: Anne Hathaway's cottage by the River Avon in Stratford. Joining all four boys were Lena, Jules, her sister Helen and Izzy, so it was a full house. Although Harry was supposed to be hitting it off with Lena, he also found Helen very attractive and during one quiet moment he told her so. She had a very nice smile and her bob-styled blonde hair extenuated her beautiful facial lines. Instead of being suitably impressed with his compliments she almost smacked Harry; she was a little older but much wiser and was clearly only there to protect her younger sister and made it perfectly clear she had no liking for any of them. Meanwhile, Ed's fancy for both Izzy and Jules was building up a head of steam and, during the day, his attention seemed to settle more on Izzy than Jules as he was flirting and paying her much more attention. That evening, after dinner Harry, Jules and Lena returned to the Angel's Reply for some more drinks but not to the same extent of the night before, leaving Honky, Wings and Ed at the Valeta. Harry and Lena spoke at some length about their relationship; both hoped it would continue with Lena agreeing to carry on writing to him at his new address at Fordham.

The penultimate day was a bit of an anticlimax. Harry managed to entice Lena onto the river for a short trip in a rowing boat. Unfortunately, Honky had offered to take the helm and the expression up a creek without a paddle curtailed any chance of the two lovebirds reflecting on their time together. The holiday was coming to an end and all four had made new friends and, perhaps with the exception of Wings, all had become a lot closer and overcame hurdles relating to the female sex. During the morning Ed wrote a fairly long and detailed letter to Izzy which he later delivered personally to her place of work. He was quite open about his feelings for her and although not wishing to extinguish any fire that may have been smouldering in the direction of Jules, he had clearly decided that Izzy was the better option. He also had a long conversation about her relationship with Honky and whether it was going anywhere. That night, the four had dinner together before Honky disappeared to go and watch a live bout of wrestling at the local club. He was a true fan having watched it regularly on the television and which, naively at his tender age, believed was actually real. Everyone thought it was a rather bizarre way to spend a last night particularly when there were four fantastic females to spend time with. That night, Harry and Ed had many a deliberation over what might have been with the girls; their conclusion was that there was always a next time.

The final morning saw Harry knock over the jug of milk in the restaurant; purely accidental of course but subconsciously he felt it was about time for a refill of fresh milk. The moment they had been dreading had arrived and the four friends checked out of the Valeta and headed for home. Lena came to the hotel and accompanied them into town where they met with Jules and Izzy before going to the railway station. Lena and Harry had a final smooch on the platform before boarding the train, not realising it would be their last and Ed played a French kissing game with both Jules and Izzy. As the train pulled out of the station Harry was still hugging Lena through the open carriage window until they got to a point where he had to let go. He noticed the tears in her eyes and at that point he knew he really meant something to her. Feeling quite emotional, he thought quietly to himself, *It's like something from a bloody Shakespeare play.*

In no time at all, Ed had settled down for the return journey only to be planning his next conquest: a meeting with one of Trogs' old flames as soon as he got back to Tinkers Hill.

Chapter Seventeen
Senior Cadets

Just before the summer recess and before their trip to Shakespeare country, all second-year cadets including Harry and Ed were informed where they would be stationed as senior cadets. Reaching the dizzy heights of a 'senior' meant either achieving the age of eighteen and/or having completed one or two years in the cadet training programme. Occasionally, senior cadets were employed directly into that position because of their age but they were in a relatively small minority. Being a 'senior' was seen as one step away from being a proper bobby on the beat but without having the requisite powers afforded to a constable. Additionally, it still required a presence weekly at headquarters to continue with physical training, swimming and drill; this also gave the training staff an opportunity to ensure that the high standards of the cadet corps were being upheld. Apart from the kudos that went with being a 'senior' there was an additional entitlement; allowing them to wear a shiny silver braid on the edge of each epaulette indicating their 'senior' status.

Harry was being posted to Fordham in the far east of the county and he would stay in lodgings, or 'digs' as they were commonly known, something he was quite excited about. The downside was this necessitated a fairly lengthy journey by public transport to headquarters although on occasions he was lucky to cadge a lift from someone. Ed too would be in lodgings but was based in the New Town of Tinkers Hill meaning he was a lot closer to headquarters. Both Harry and Ed saw being in digs as a step upwards and was another small, yet critical phase to feeling more grown up. It was totally different from being in the hostel blocks where there was something always going on and optimistically, no one to tip you out of bed in the early hours of the morning. It also did away with the soakings from a fire hose and the unscheduled room inspections carried out by the proverbial Inspector Broadhurst. Harry envisaged it would be more tranquil, he would have more time to himself and he would be waited on hand and foot. How wrong could he be?

Fortunately for Harry, his parents had travelled the hundred or so miles down to attend the annual passing-out presentation and awards ceremony at headquarters, so it made perfect sense and an opportune time to pay a visit to his lodgings on their return to meet his landlady and to check the conditions.

Beryl Blackett was a widow in her early seventies and had an arrangement with the constabulary to take in police cadets as and when they were posted to Fordham. As she had done this before, she was used to the unpredictable timetable that Harry had to follow. Incredibly upbeat and very sprightly for her age, Beryl did not stand on ceremony and was very direct with anything she had to say. Her son, who lived in the town, visited regularly, took her out shopping and helped with any general handiwork around the house as and when required.

The house was a 1930s semi-detached in a small cul-de-sac and, after initial introductions, Beryl showed Harry to his room on the first floor. Initial impressions were that it was quite dark and dank as if it had not been lived in for some while. One of her first comments to Harry was her ruling on visitors not being allowed in the bedrooms; this was followed promptly by a request for Harry to check when she would receive her first payment from the force. Clearly, it was quite obvious to Harry that Beryl had her priorities sorted, as well as being quite strict about who was in her house at any given time.

Harry would be eighteen years old in a few weeks' time and always respected his elders, but he felt it a liberty that this old biddy was already telling him what he could and couldn't do even before he had formally moved in. The room had all the necessary accompaniments such as a bed with sheets, blankets and an eiderdown. There was also a bedside table, a wardrobe and a small chair. There was one window on the side which directly overlooked the window of the semi next door. This pokey room with what seemed like only a twenty-watt bulb in the light fitting would be his base for the next year, as in addition to working shifts at Fordham station Harry would be completing numerous attachments away from, as well as in the local area. The bathroom with toilet but minus any shower was on the first floor along the corridor. This was probably the one factor which Harry would miss the most, as at headquarters showering became second nature and there was always one available somewhere within the complex.

After their epic trip to Leamington Spa, Harry and Ed returned to their respective home towns. Clearly in need of further relaxation Ed was whisked away by his parents for another fortnight's holiday to the North West Highlands of Scotland. Meanwhile, Harry was back at home which meant celebrating his eighteenth birthday at a nice restaurant with his family before hooking back up with Mrs Blackett at the beginning of September for what would be a highly enjoyable and interesting twelve months. During his time at home, Harry managed to catch up with Ernie and they continued their friendship almost from where they had left off by lazing about on the beach by day and playing darts, bar billiards and the occasional drink by night. It was remarkable how Ernie's experiences varied from Harry's and how each force differed in their approach to the cadet regime. Harry was very determined not to lose any of the fitness he had built up over the past twelve months, so most days he would take a short run of a mile or so just to keep things ticking over.

Chapter Eighteen
Fordham

Harry and Ed reported to their respective police stations at nine a.m. on Monday 3rd September 1973. They were both looking forward to an exciting year and no one could have predicted what lay ahead. Ed's first week at Tinkers Hill turned out to be nice and short as he only had to work for four days before he had the weekend off. There were soon to follow the delights of shift work; the sheer thought of staying awake in the middle of the night was a real eye-opener, or not as the case may be.

Also starting at Fordham was Honky who was assigned to a different shift to Harry although from time to time they crossed paths, including returning to headquarters weekly to maintain the peak of fitness they had achieved from the year before. It was the first time that Harry had seen Honky since their infamous escapades at the Valeta Hotel and they shared a joke about being 'seniors'. Referring to the shiny silver braid on his epaulette, Honky went further, almost teasing Harry by saying, "That'll be the only time you wear something shiny like that during your service." Knowing Honky as he did, Harry didn't take this off the cuff comment to heart, he secretly hoped he was messing about and having one of his many 'jokey' moments.

On arrival at the front desk at Fordham that morning Honky was met by Mac, a constable with a considerable amount of service behind him and a no-nonsense type of guy. He was Yorkshire through and through so when Honky appeared at the front counter fully dressed in a smart cadet uniform with senior braids, Mac looked him up and down noting the neatly pressed trousers, the spotlessly clean tunic and the regulation short hair. In his strongest Yorkshire accent, Mac delivered the following welcoming words of inspiration and encouragement: "What the bloody hell is a good-looking lad like you want to join an outfit like this for?"

Mac was one of many experienced officers at Fordham at that time and both Harry and Honky were introduced to a whole host of different characters who were individuals in their own right but, when together, they worked as a well-oiled machine. Looking back over thirty years it was here that Harry thought that the groups at Fordham were not only extremely hard working but also enjoyed one another's company both on and off duty. This may also have been due to the fact that the majority of officers stationed there were in the twilight of their service and were more than content to just plod along at their own pace. It was inevitable that Harry would be singled out for less exciting tasks and invariably his first job of the day was to make tea for the shift. Overall, the station was under the command of Chief Inspector Don although it seemed as if he was away at meetings a lot of the time and whenever Harry passed his office it always seemed to be empty. On a day-to-day basis the station and policing of the town was the responsibility of a sergeant and four or five constables with an occasional flying visit from an inspector. The station even had their own Criminal Investigation Department in the form of a detective sergeant and two constables. If the need arose, they were supported by other officers from the divisional station some twelve miles away. Apart from the odd talk or two from plain-clothes officers during his year at headquarters, Harry had never met a real life detective before, so to be amongst them at Fordham really was inspirational and for most of the time he felt in complete awe.

The building was an old place, also housing the magistrates' court which was upstairs but which Harry seldom visited. The cell block was where the 'baddies' were kept overnight to sober up before being released in the morning. Most of the operational side was all on one floor with the front office being the main point of contact for members of the public who wished to report anything that might be police-related. It was Harry's second day when he arrived for work about twenty minutes early. From Beryl's house it was a brisk fifteen-minute walk across the railway line and the meads which brought Harry out on the edge of the town centre. A short stomp up the hill took him to the station where normally he would head for the small kitchen area to make a brew. Before he could get his coat off Harry was met by one of the most colourful characters at Fordham. There were one or two grumpy officers at Fordham but in the main Harry felt everyone was so helpful and supportive.

Sergeant Stan Phipps was one of the stalwarts at Fordham and very well respected; Harry thought he was quite a serious type of person but with a wicked sense of humour which endeared him to the young impressionable cadet. Stan knew all about cadets: his son, who was a few years older than Harry, had been through the same process, so had a very good idea what made cadets tick. It was Stan that taught the eighteen-year-old a very valuable and important lesson. He had a job that required Harry's immediate attention, but totally innocently and quite politely Harry said to the sergeant, "I don't start until 9 o'clock." For the next five minutes Stan had his face as close to Harry's as was physically possible. There was no shouting and no swearing, but what Stan had to say made an indelible impression upon Harry for the rest of his life. Time was just a number and, as far as Stan was concerned, Harry was already at work as he was in the building. If he wasn't in the building then he wasn't at work, it was as simple as that. But it was the manner in which Stan delivered his statement that stuck in the youngster's mind. Today, had a union representative been present, they may have taken a different view on the whole episode but on this occasion Stan was the sergeant: he was God and he was in charge. Harry felt extremely small and slightly intimidated, so quickly disappeared into the changing room where he removed his 'civvie' coat, collected his tunic and cap and returned to the parade room where Stan was waiting. "Come with me," said Stan abruptly, grabbing his patrol cap from the desk. Harry followed like a little lamb still reeling from the admonishment he had just received and not knowing how Stan was going to treat him for the rest of what probably would be a very long day. They walked to the rear yard where they both got into the sergeant's patrol car.

Stan explained in a forthright fashion that all police officers had to expect the unexpected and that included anything that may befall them as they walked in through the front door. There was a saying at that time that police officers were never off duty, meaning that if anything happened in front of them they would be expected to deal with it accordingly. Stan drove the car out of the yard but never mentioned where they were going. Harry sat pensively trying to absorb the last ten minutes of his life. He was still thinking about what Stan had said when they pulled up outside a house on the edge of Fordham. There was another patrol car already outside and Harry followed the sergeant into the house. As he entered, Harry heard the other police officer say, "Thanks, Doctor," and an elderly looking man carrying a small leather bag passed them on his way out without saying anything. Stan was already talking to the other officer.

Harry seemed to be in his own little world when all of a sudden the sergeant's voice was calling. "This way, Cadet," as Stan started to climb the stairs. Harry still had no idea of what was happening and he was desperately trying to put the pieces together in his mind. *What was so urgent in the first place that warranted Stan insisting in Harry getting his uniform on before he had even started work,* he thought.

He was soon to get his answer because as Harry neared the top of the stairs he was met by an unusual smell but could not work out whether it was a dead animal, perhaps a rat, as he knew they gave off a rather unpleasant odour when their corpse started to rot. That, however did not really explain why the doctor had been there. As Harry followed Stan into a bedroom he noticed the smell intensified and was becoming increasingly nauseous. "Your first sudden death?" asked Stan. There was a sombre tone to his voice but at the same time Harry thought there might have been a hint of ridicule. Stan knew full well that Harry had never been to an incident like this before, given this was only Harry's second day as a 'senior' and it was highly improbable that he had seen a dead body before whilst based at headquarters. It dawned on Harry that his attendance was perhaps no coincidence as he discovered later that the other officer had been called to the house at seven a.m., almost two hours before Harry was even due to start work.

Stan briefly explained that where someone died unexpectedly, a doctor had to certify the death; if they were satisfied with the cause they could issue a certificate which allowed for a funeral to take place relatively quickly. If there was no certificate issued it usually meant an investigation by police followed by a coroner's inquest into how that person died. Depending on the circumstances, this could take some time. Here was an eighty-year-old male who had not been seen for a few days; the last person to have seen him was the same doctor on a home visit. The gent had been suffering for some while with angina and atherosclerosis and had suffered a heart attack the year before. The GP who certified death was satisfied with the cause of death and issued a certificate for the funeral directors. *Why then was there a need for police attendance,* thought Harry asking this aloud. Stan fully explained the reasons to Harry who was rather expecting an early exit from the house, but Stan had other ideas and wanted to run through the whole procedure for the benefit of the 'senior'.

First of all they had to check for any unusual marks or wounds which necessitated rolling the person over onto their side so a complete inspection could be made of their back. Surprisingly, there was nothing that might indicate foul play so Harry thought again about a quick exit. No, Stan was having none of it and clearly was extracting some pleasure from seeing Harry turn a unusual pale colour; by now the funeral directors had arrived in their dark coloured van with blacked-out windows and it was Harry's job, under immediate supervision from Stan, to assist them in removing the body from the bedroom, down the stairs and from the house into their van. Unfortunately, the poor deceased gent was quite portly and it took great effort to lift him from the bed and into a special plastic zipped bag. From there, the bag had to be physically lifted and carried downstairs and placed on a metal trolley which the funeral directors had placed just inside the hallway. Harry thought he was quite fit, but soon realised that running a few miles or playing football for ninety minutes was nothing compared to this sort of physical endeavour. By the time they reached the ground floor and had placed the body on the trolley Harry was sweating profusely and breathing quite heavily. Meanwhile, he had noticed Stan talking quietly with one of the funeral directors in the corner of the lounge. It was not uncommon during this era for funeral directors to make small donations to the police benevolent fund particularly when they were flying solo or if they had a 'difficult' corpse to deal with; therefore any assistance in the form of lifting and carrying from a police officer was always greatly appreciated.

After the funeral directors had left, Stan explained that the next of kin had already been informed by the other officer so it just left the matter of securing the property and returning to Fordham station to complete the rest of the paperwork. It was on their return to the station that Stan let it slip that he had specifically been waiting for Harry to arrive at work that morning and had deliberately delayed his attendance at the scene, as he believed this would demonstrate to the young impressionable cadet that not all policing just involved chasing bad guys around. Stan was as good as gold after that event and Harry learnt an extremely valuable lesson. Whilst their introduction to each other could be referred to as extremely brusque, Harry had the utmost respect for Stan and was particularly upset when, a few years later, he learnt of his own premature death.

Fordham nick enjoyed any excuse for a good old knees-up. The social committee would knock up a few posters and flyers which hopefully would raise some money for a good cause as well as put some brass into the meagre social fund. Harry particularly remembers one around Christmas time. Inspector Barry was well known within the station and he always had plenty to say for himself. Harry was certainly wary of him and would avoid him where possible as he knew that, given any little opportunity, the inspector would have Harry carrying out little chores here and there. It wasn't that Harry was not prepared to help; it was just that others at Fordham had warned him to give him a wide berth where possible. If the inspector was particularly annoyed about something he would let it be known with a tirade of four-letter words.

One of the reasons for Harry going to this disco was due to speculation that the daughter of the head of the special constabulary would be there. Harry believed he had a chance of something with her having had a sniff of her perfume during the briefest of dances at a previous disco. On Harry's arrival, Inspector Barry was already in attendance, as he was at most of these events and was clearly in the middle of a tiff with his wife. The bar at Fordham wasn't particularly big; the inspector was at one end of the bar and his wife was at the other end. Harry wanted a drink, so had no alternative but to step into the middle of the bar between the two of them. Immediately on doing so he felt a tension in the air which made him slightly uncomfortable, mainly because he had no idea of what was happening. Cynically, Mrs Barry mentioned something about her husband's drinking habits, which were not entirely decipherable by Harry who later discovered that her husband liked a tipple or three. Harry wondered if Inspector Barry was somehow related to Superintendent Crake.

The inspector was holding his spirit glass close to his face and appeared to be staring through it at his wife with a vacant look in his eyes. Harry glanced in the direction of the officer who seemed to have trouble focussing on the senior cadet. The inspector, who Harry guessed was either drunk or well on his way spoke very slowly, "Listen, son; whatever you do in life don't ever get fucking married!" He delivered this extraordinary piece of advice with complete conviction in a loud enough voice that could have been heard in the room next door. His wife, a very polite, pretty and well-dressed woman said nothing but just stared in his direction. She was clearly embarrassed at her husband's outburst. *If looks could kill,* thought Harry, who was now in a slight predicament. The inspector had spoken to him and the one thing that Harry had learnt from all his training was that if a senior officer spoke directly to you, you were expected to give some sort of reply. The alternatives were to ignore the inspector altogether, which would probably incur his wrath, or become embroiled in a domestic tangle which ultimately would do him no favours either. Harry could think of nothing that might smooth over this delicate situation so all he could say was, "Yes, sir," before grabbing his drink and moving away from the bar as fast as possible to the other side of the room where he felt more at ease. Apparently, this behaviour from Inspector Barry was not unfamiliar to others that knew the couple.

Whilst at Fordham, Harry was introduced to other various aspects of policing, some of which included manning the front desk, answering the phones, walking the beat, getting used to all the different radio jargon and most importantly making the tea for the sergeant and his troops. He was also introduced by the trilby-wearing detective sergeant to the pros and cons of the wonderful crime-recording system in at that time.

Chapter Nineteen
Fordham Hospital

Cadets were expected to perform various attachments during their senior year but how many they actually completed depended entirely on when their nineteenth birthday fell as the age determined their entry into the regular police force. Harry knew that he would be at Fordham for almost a whole year so one of his first attachments was at the local hospital, where he spent two weeks working in the A&E department followed by a further fortnight working on a surgical ward. One can only imagine the reasons for putting seniors through this process; presumably it was to test their mettle and resolve and Harry felt this assessment was similar to making cadets climb mountains in torrential weather conditions in North Wales. Whereas the latter was purely physical, the former was psychological to see how someone could cope with any given emotional situation.

Fordham Hospital was formerly a workhouse but took on a new and important role at the beginning of the Second World War. Its size was less than adequate to cope with the number of expected injured servicemen returning from Europe. It meant that rows of huts were rapidly built to act as wards and these were added to as the War progressed in time. Additionally, the new buildings were supplemented by operating theatres, X-ray facilities; a dispensary and a hut where servicemen could be entertained. With the introduction of the National Health Service in 1948 Fordham was designated as a general hospital and at one stage provided 1,900 beds. Sadly, today as a result of changes in the political and economic climate the site is predominantly a new housing estate, but also provides a local community hospital for the townsfolk.

Harry began his two weeks in the Accident Unit working alongside, nurses, doctors and orderlies, also known as auxiliaries. Harry witnessed several events which to any ordinary person would have seemed very stressful and traumatic; they certainly did to Harry with some particular incidents remaining vivid in his memory.

Whatever, they throw at me, I will do my best, was one of Harry's thoughts as he duly reported for duty on his first day at A&E. This determination was not something that came naturally, but had stuck with him since his days in the scout movement when a sense of perseverance was at the forefront of any adventure. To get off on the right footing, Harry, having learnt the lesson from the infamous meeting with Sergeant Phipps, turned up just before nine a.m. Things started swimmingly as the sister in charge was actually expecting him.

She explained some basic health and safety rules before politely telling him that if lifesaving operations were on the agenda, Harry would not be at the forefront of performing them. Harry was visibly thankful for this advice until he learnt that it was her way of trying to be funny. His role was mainly an observational one but where possible he was expected to help out anyone in the department who asked for his assistance. Funnily enough, Harry had exactly the same thought when he was introduced to a couple of the single younger nurses on the shift.

One of his first tasks was to prepare Eric, a forty-year-old male, for a hernia operation. The man was being triaged by Anna, one of the younger nurses who Harry had taken an instant shine to. Eric had been experiencing some pains on and off for quite a while and had developed a prominent lump in his groin area. He had been diagnosed as having an acute hernia and the consultant had decided that he should undergo a relatively simple surgical procedure to remove it. Having only qualified a year before, Anna was not entirely experienced at preparing someone for this type of surgery, but at least she was no novice like Harry.

She led the young naïve cadet to an equipment cupboard where she handed him a number of disposable razors, a pair of scissors and a plastic bag. Harry, believing that Anna simply wanted him to carry the items for her, got quite a shock when they returned to the cubicle where Eric was lying with nothing except a white hospital gown tied up at the back to hide his modesty. Anna explained that for this operation to be successful the patient had to be 'shaven' but it wasn't his face she was referring to. Politely, and trying not to show any sense of nervousness, Harry asked the one burning question on his mind: "Why?" Anna clarified that it would allow easier access to the area and less hair would reduce the chances of any post-op infection. "I'll give you twenty minutes," said Anna as she brushed aside the cubicle curtains leaving the two males alone.

Once she had departed, Harry dropped the facade that he had been displaying in front of Anna and apprehensively explained to Eric that this was the first time he had performed any procedure like this, at which point Eric retorted, "Funny that – it's my first time too," before shuffling onto a paper sheet that Anna had handed through the curtains. Harry was uncertain where to start, he certainly didn't want to be responsible for damaging this gent's manhood so decided to start shaving at a point about one inch below Eric's naval, which seemed like a relatively 'safe' area. Things were going quite well and Harry was stuffing the plastic bag as full as he could with pubic hair, but it was noticeable how quickly the razors became blunted and occasionally little nicks to the skin would appear. Harry took his time, believing that Eric would get bored and maybe decide to shave himself.

After what seemed like a lifetime, Anna returned to save the day, taking over the procedure as she made it perfectly clear to Harry that he was taking too long. On reflection, Harry felt extremely embarrassed with having another man's bits in his hands especially as this was an age of pre-surgical gloves. Following his venture, Harry spent a considerable amount of time washing and re-washing his hands for fear of catching some sexually transmitted disease even though he knew deep down that Eric didn't seem to be the type to have one. On the plus side, Harry was utterly impressed with Anna's professionalism and how she had handled the whole procedure even though this was part of her job. Given the right setting, Harry made a mental note to speak to her about the prospect of a possible action replay minus the actual razors.

As well as the hernia incident, two other notable events occurred during Harry's attachment to the accident and emergency department. The first was a couple of days after the hernia patient when an elderly gent was rushed in having suffered a heart attack. Sadly the man died but not before losing control of his bowels, which Harry later discovered was not uncommon in instances of this nature. The smell was indescribable and choked half of the staff on duty at that time. Nurses and orderlies were heading for the exits and the sluice room to be sick as was Harry, who succumbed to the stench. Despite all the windows in the unit being opened he could not control the violent attack of sickness which brought water to his eyes and heaving to his throat and chest. Unfortunately, Harry felt totally helpless but amongst adversity there was courage and spirit in the form of the casualty sister and a doctor who battled through the nauseating conditions, carrying out cardiopulmonary resuscitation and doing what they could for the poor soul. Harry had never witnessed a smell like it and has never since. Afterwards, the unflustered sister explained quite vividly how this could happen in cases of cardiac arrest. Harry, already a great admirer of the National Health Service, had his views reinforced ten-fold that day.

The second incident involved a little bit of skulduggery on behalf of the accident and emergency staff and occurred late one afternoon. Harry was quite busy assisting nurses in their roles of suturing patients' wounds and plastering minor cases when the duty doctor came in to advise that the ambulance was bringing in a case from a road traffic accident and he thought it might be useful for Harry to see what sort of injuries he was likely to encounter when he finally joined the force. Significantly, at the time the doctor made no reference to the injuries sustained by the patient and Harry thought nothing of asking further questions, having accepted it at face value that it would simply give him valuable experience.

About twenty minutes later Harry was aware that the ambulance had arrived and was fully expecting to be called into one of the resuscitation bays. He curiously noted that a few staff members were congregated by the ambulance bay entrance and the paramedics, also part of this little ensemble, did not seem in any rush to transfer the patient into the hospital. A short while later, Harry was approached by the casualty doctor who explained that the patient had sadly died en route to the hospital and that he, as the doctor on duty, would have to certify the death which he was intending to do in the back of the ambulance. Harry noticed that the doctor expressed little emotion in either, his voice or in his body language. The doctor asked Harry if he would like to accompany him into the rear of the ambulance to witness the process. Harry considered for a moment, thinking this may have been some sort of prank, having heard of similar stories where cadets were sent to a mortuary only to encounter a 'live' corpse in the form of the hospital practical joker. Harry agreed, and followed the doctor past the two paramedics into the rear of the ambulance and the rear door was shut, leaving Harry and the doctor alone.

What happened next was quite surreal. The doctor peeled back the top half of what can only be described as a large sleeping bag. Harry took a deep breath expecting someone to jump up at any second but what he suddenly realised was that this was no joke. The patient was clearly dead as pointed out abruptly by the doctor. Harry noticed the man's head had become partially detached from the rest of his body. The doctor explained that he would normally check the carotid artery for a pulse that lay to the side of the neck but, as most of this was missing, he had to revert to check for a pulse in the groin and in the foot. Harry, studying the image of the head which lay to one side of the sleeping bag, thought it an utterly pointless exercise for the doctor to undertake as it was as clear as day to the 'senior' that there was absolutely no possibility that the male could still be alive, but the doctor diligently carried out the necessary checks as he needed to be one hundred percent sure. Harry stood rooted in a slight daze, still half expecting a surprise before being asked if he was okay by the doctor.

It was quite a shock and probably more so than if someone had played a practical joke on Harry. It transpired the male had been driving a sports car with a convertible top and had driven straight underneath a heavy goods vehicle at speed sheering off the top third of the car. It was another one of those moments in Harry's life which left him reflecting on whether this was the right arena for him and this particular moment would stay with him for a very long while.

Harry moved on to working on a surgical ward for the remainder of his month's attachment. He found this more mundane and slightly boring compared to the hustle, bustle and excitement of the accident and emergency department and more importantly all the nurses were either older, married or male which did little for his love life. Nevertheless, he threw everything into it and tried his best but there were only so many bedpans and catheters that he could empty in one day. The only incident of note during this part of the attachment involved a very elderly gentleman who only had one leg which he lost during the Second World War. The patient, who Harry had warmed to because of his sense of humour and of the way he handled his disability, had been admitted for a minor complaint which resulted in him having an operation from which, sadly, he did not recover from.

He passed away in his sleep one night and Harry learnt of his sad demise the following morning when he came on duty to the ward. Because of the circumstances, there was to be a post mortem and the duty sister asked Harry if he would like to attend. She phrased it in such a way that it would have been rude for him to refuse. The post mortem was booked for that afternoon so on the advice of the ward sister he took a very light lunch before going along to the mortuary, where he met the pathologist who would carry out the procedure. This was the first time in Harry's life that he witnessed such a thought-provoking and upsetting challenge, but the weird thing was not so much the smell that exuded from the body but the attitude of the pathologist, who went about his work in a macabre manner. The pathologist seemed more interested in the hypothesis of how the patient had lost his leg during the War rather than establishing how he had actually died. During the medical procedure Harry took a moment to reflect on the deceased's life, wondering about his encounters during the War and the sort of life he had afterwards. The pathologist, albeit slightly odd, outlined the whole process from start to finish to Harry, who had trouble keeping up with all the anatomical terms. The resulting conclusion was that a post-operative blood clot was probably the most likely cause of death with other contributory factors such as old age.

Not everything at Fordham Hospital was so dull and boring and Harry had completed his attachment around the Christmas period, so there were quite a few parties for patients and staff alike. Carol singers came onto the ward which briefly cheered patients up and more importantly Harry had been asked by Anna from the A&E department whether he would like to attend the annual Christmas social club bash. Luckily, he was free and wild horses would not have prevented him from getting closer to Anna and if there was an appropriate opportunity he would raise the issue of her 'shaving' technique. Arriving at eight o'clock just as the disco was getting underway Harry got a drink from the bar and joined a small group of other A&E nurses and doctors who had bagged a table midway between the bar area and where the disc jockey was strutting his stuff. He recognised most of those present but most importantly Anna was missing. Harry thought he would play it cool; not showing too much interest in her whereabouts. About an hour passed and things were beginning to warm up and the drink was flowing freely. Still no sign of Anna and no mention of her by anyone when, suddenly, she wandered into the club dressed in an Elf's costume with a very short skirt.

Wow, thought Harry, he felt as if Christmas had come a week or two early. Harry's attention was fully focussed on Anna so had failed to notice the little fellow behind her dressed as a goblin. Anna was making her way around the table saying hello to everyone; when she reached Harry she gave him a small peck on the cheek, wished him a Happy Christmas and introduced the goblin who was behind her as her boyfriend Gary. Harry's face was a picture, as were most of those present who knew that Anna and Gary were an item, something which none of the A&E staff had chosen to mention. Harry discovered that Gary was a trainee investment banker working in London so naturally jumped to every conclusion possible about why they were together. He wore spectacles and had big ears so what did he have that Harry didn't? He felt such an idiot; there was only one thing to do and it involved alcohol. Traditionally, at these social events there was a 'Yard of Ale' contest between hospital departments. At least two volunteers from each department were teamed together and their aggregate time for consuming the 'yard' was taken as the department score. Harry was nominated but, as he had never drunk a yard of ale in his life, he quickly offered the role to Gary as he thought he might make a fool of himself in front of Anna. Gary was having none of it so it was left to Harry and one other to represent the A&E unit.

Time was getting on and it seemed as if this contest had come at the wrong time of the night, particularly for Harry as he was beginning to feel the effects of the beers he had drunk already. He was trying to listen to the rules as best he could but, between the noise of the disco and the distraction of Anna's legs, he was left with some advice from a drunken hospital doctor which was to down it as fast as possible without dripping it everywhere. He was reassured by the same person that if anything went wrong he was in the right place to receive the best medical treatment. It soon became Harry's turn and his teammate had managed to drink the 'yard' in two minutes and forty seconds; a very reasonable time considering the opposition. Harry picked up the long glass with both hands which someone had just informed him held three pints of the best bitter. That in itself was a negative as Harry very seldom drank bitter and was more at home with a pint of lager. The rules apparently meant that everyone had to drink the same beer, something which had failed to reach Harry during the reading of the rules ceremony. The clock was set, and Harry started the very slow process of trying to maintain drinking whilst steadying the long and cumbersome yard glass. He was very conscious of well-wishers turned know-it-alls who seemed to be locked onto his ears. They were whispering pockets of encouragement and advice, which differed depending on which side of Harry they were standing.

The time was shouted out at intervals; Harry reached the minute mark but the glass looked as full as it did at the start, but he felt as if he had drunk at least half the glass. "Two minutes," was then called and Harry was beginning to feel the pressure. He didn't want to let anyone down so started to push a bit more. "Harder yet!" he said to himself quietly, thinking that was what Staff would have shouted. Despite continuing to drink slowly Harry did not seem to be making any ground up. He started to tilt the glass a little higher which caused an air bubble in the middle of the tube. Unbeknown to Harry this could cause problems; taking in too much air could make the stomach feel bloated sending a signal to the brain that you've had your fill. He had now reached the three-minute mark and it looked as if he would not even equal his teammate's time.

"Slowly, slowly does it," said someone in Harry's ear. By this time Harry had got over the bitter taste in his mouth and was actually semi enjoying the taste of the beer, although some was beginning to drip down the sides of his mouth and onto the floor. The adjudicator was there to ensure fair play and that if too much missed the target, then Harry would be disqualified.

"Four minutes!" was the call and Harry felt he was doomed to failure. Now someone different was whispering in his ear, saying that the A&E team couldn't win and he should give up trying. Harry was still determined to finish, if only to prove to Anna that he was good at something. Finally, when five minutes was called, Harry decided to throw in the towel; he took the glass away from his mouth and stood the yard glass on the bar. To his absolute astonishment he had only drunk about a third of the contents which caused quite a bit of ribbing from the A&E contingent. Needless to say they did not win and, even worse, this was to be the last time that Harry saw Anna; he hoped that she would have a wonderful life with Gary the goblin if that was what she chose. The only regret he had was the missed opportunity to speak to her about a 'shave'.

Chapter Twenty
Honesty and Integrity

One of Ed's attachments during the early part of his senior cadetship was at Pontins holiday camp in East Anglia where he was accompanied by Trogs and a couple of other senior cadets for a fortnight of frivolity where they were 'assigned' a particular elderly person to sit with, spend time with and engage in idle chit-chat to keep them entertained when the Hi-de-Hi staff were not around. Sadly, this was to be the only attachment that Ed completed during his senior role although others had been arranged in advance for the new year namely a month at the Ullswater Outward Bound Education Centre in the Lake District which was set in eighteen acres of woodland at the heart of Wordsworth country. In addition, Ed also had an attachment to the Cheshire Homes pencilled in the diary as well as a taster driving course, which cadets were eligible for and which Ed was really looking forward to. The driving course was designed to give cadets an insight into the Highway Code as well as practical aspects including the infamous system of mirror, signal, manoeuvre. Ed's course was due to precede his Outward Bound and Cheshire Home attachments.

His senior days at playing a real policeman flew past really quickly with Ed throwing himself into the role which he was thoroughly enjoying day by day. Unfortunately, this soon came to an abrupt end as after eight weeks or so the Tinkers Hill force was placed onto a high-level security alert footing due to a suspected national terrorist attack. Subsequently, a shortlist of senior cadets was drawn up to return to headquarters to undertake security guard duties on the front gates. It could be said that due to Ed's previous encounter with the assistant chief constable he was considered as the right man for the job. Needless to say Ed considered this as drawing the short straw in what would ultimately turn out to be a life-changing experience.

Fortunately, with Harry being posted at Fordham and several miles away from Tinkers Hill saw him overlooked from this potentially dangerous task. It also meant Ed leaving his digs temporarily and moving back into residence again at headquarters. At this particular time the weather was bitterly cold, making their security patrols of the main gate, where they stopped every vehicle diligently, thoroughly miserable.

The female sex had always been of interest to Ed having grown up in an environment where they were given the utmost respect. However, here was a red-hot blooded male and curiosity was eating away at him where many young, slim and demure young ladies were waltzing around headquarters in their short miniskirts. Some, as in the case of Chief Inspector Broome's daughter, visited to use the swimming pool on a weekly basis, others were personal assistants to the senior executive and others simply wore a uniform. Whatever it was, Ed's hormones were working overtime and beginning to have an effect on him.

Having been fortunate enough to have befriended Trogs, Ed was, occasionally, invited back to his parents' house, where Trogs always seemed to have an abundance of female friends. It therefore followed that where Trogs went Ed would follow in the heady belief that romance was in the air. Actually it was more like the young at heart, but nevertheless much fun was had by all with the odd kiss here and there, coupled with periods of intense gazing! The eyes gave so much away, at least that is what Ed thought, but where would this lead?

At the end of November security duties had continued throughout the week. On completion of their shift Ed and his counterparts would take their refreshments in the canteen, where the exchange of banter was prevalent with the females remaining at headquarters.

Fully aware of the rules and regulations, Ed, Big Al and others decided to meet up later with the same girls to continue their conversations within the female block. Without considering any real consequences, off they strode to the 'out of bounds' block where they engaged in nothing other than mere conversation deep into the night. This was no almighty orgy, not even a little one and certainly no drink and no drugs were exchanged. It was pure unadulterated conversation between males and females together with good old-fashioned laughter but with the odd suggestive comment thrown in for good measure. There may have been wanton desire in some people's eyes and perhaps even a smacker on the lips, but generally speaking hormones were kept in check and this was as far as it went. After much exchange deep into the night, Ed and the others decided it was time to leave. They wandered off back to their rooms without a care in the world, only to bump into Constable Knapweed! It may not have been too bad had it not been for Big Al being caught deep in the throes of an intense kiss, tongues a wagging one could say and this time the game was definitely up.

During breakfast the following morning Ed was told to report to Superintendent Crake's office at 0930 hours. Knowing the superintendent as he did from all the athletics triumphs six months before, he knew he was a very fair man but nevertheless was still considered as 'old school', having served as an army officer. His conversation would be slow, his demeanour powerful, yet still Ed had absolutely no idea as to what might happen or how much they actually knew. Ed duly attended as instructed where the interrogation began in earnest, so Ed thought. Superintendent Crake asked one simple question; Ed, having been brought up to always tell the truth couldn't prevent himself from spouting forth and the full goings-on from the previous night were laid bare before the man in charge. Ed's explanation was non-stop similar to water flowing from a tap, except in this case it was words from his mouth. A phrase continually presented itself into poor Ed's mind: *Tell the Truth and Shame the Devil!*

Superintendent Crake deliberated before telling Ed to resume his security duties. At that precise moment he was none the wiser, but believing that honesty was the best policy he happily wandered off to the front gate to continue his work. He later discovered that Gibbo, a second-year cadet, had also recited the same story line to the superintendent. It was therefore clear that those involved appeared to be singing from the same hymn sheet, which convinced Ed that things were going in their favour.

Just after lunch, with other senior cadets in attendance on their weekly training day, a larger group including those involved in the clandestine visit the night before, were assembled in the admin office where they were addressed by Inspector Broadhurst. He told his audience that it had come to notice that male cadets had been witnessed entering the female block which was clearly marked 'out of bounds' to male cadets, which was in direct contravention of the rules. What followed was a bit surreal in that the inspector asked for complete honesty in any reply the cadets made, requesting that anyone present who had ever visited the female block should take a step forward. Naturally, Ed, Big Al and a couple more who had already been quizzed by Superintendent Crake shuffled one pace towards the stern-looking Inspector.

Harry, considering all his options in a flash, decided to stay put; not necessarily because he was a devious liar but more to do with self-preservation as he got the distinct impression that something unpleasant was about to befall them. Besides, he may have visited the female block on a different occasion but it was not as if he had done anything untoward with a member of the opposite sex, so he had absolutely nothing to feel guilty about. Harry was trying to justify his decision for keeping quiet, but the only person he was kidding was himself.

Ed genuinely believed that he was joining a profession where everyone told the truth, after all a police officer's word was accepted as gospel, but clearly during this gathering this was not to be the case. Ed could see his fellow friends – well, what he thought were friends –

remain tight-lipped and silent whilst Big Al and Ed owned up to their misdemeanour.

In the minds of most people the question of honesty and integrity is twofold; is it something which we are born with and therefore already in our genes, or is it something that is instilled into us by our parents from an early age, remaining with us during our adult life? There are frequent situations that test our resolve to be entirely honest; this tendency begins when we are children and want to avoid punishment. Fear gets the better of us and we say or do something in an effort to avoid the consequences of whatever it was that we did. If it works, then it suggests that lying is less painful and requires less courage than honesty. It is true to say that some people are naively honest in admitting to the most minor of rule breaking because it is the way they were raised, yet others who were raised in an equally truthful environment will justify distorting the truth in only the simplest of situations where they believe it is for the better good. For others, lying becomes their strategy of choice and, as long as they don't get caught, they feel no guilt or remorse.

For Ed and Big Al the worse news was to come as those who denied any involvement or kept quiet simply walked from the room. Within the hour both seniors had been summoned to the main headquarters building where they met their fate. They were faced with a stark choice, resign or be sacked for a discipline matter. In effect, Ed tendered his resignation from a job that he loved for simply telling the truth. He was utterly inconsolable with the shame of having to leave the cadets and even more upset knowing the embarrassment he had caused to his parents, who were summoned to collect him. "You have ruined your career," said his mother, who was deeply ashamed that her son could have done such a thing. But what really had he done other than tell the truth?

Being honest may not always be the easiest or most convenient course; that is why courage was required from Ed and Big Al who showed it in abundance that day. With honesty comes integrity and regardless of the prevalence of dishonesty, we all have the freedom to choose to live by a higher standard. This was not to be the end for Ed, as his father discovered that by taking the resignation route, nothing detrimental would be shown on his personal record leaving the way open to re-join the 'regular' force at nineteen. This virtually guaranteed him a place back at Tinkers Hill but was no real consolation given all the hard work they had put in for sixteen months. Despite such reassurances, Ed still had to live out the next eight months and considering the close proximity of the Christmas festivities when people were celebrating, the only thought in Ed's mind was one of complete ignominy and doom.

After leaving, Big Al went off and joined the Civil Service before moving on after ten years. He was stalked by his manager, an older married woman in her forties; something that most young men could only dream of but which, for Big Al caused much grief and ended unceremoniously… with him leaving.

Meanwhile, upon returning home a job search commenced for Ed and, within a week, another job had been secured working for BUPA within their accounts department. Christmas, as it turned out, was fine after all and it was during this time that Ed began to realise just who his 'true' friends really were. There followed the requisite applications being made during 1974 when Ed returned to Tinkers Hill where he met up again with Harry. Ed went on to complete twenty years in the Police Service before retiring on medical grounds.

Without feeling totally unsympathetic for Ed and Big Al's plight, Harry, not wanting to appear disingenuous, never mentioned his lack of honesty for many years to come; not through any feeling of triumph but more one of embarrassment. It was something that Ed would never let him forget.

Equally, the same principle could have applied to the situation involving Peanuts which saw him end up in hospital. Cheating by anyone during an examination should never be tolerated, but it seemed that no one else other than Peanuts was prepared to speak out. Clearly, it was not acceptable for one person to cheat whilst others had studiously revised for that moment. Given his own level of misdemeanours it has to be said that it showed Peanuts in a good light, particularly given the appalling retribution shown towards him.

Chapter Twenty-One
Outward Bound

Between early February and early March 1974 Harry went to Aberdovey Outward Bound Centre in West Wales for a month, travelling together with Trogs by train via the infamous Crewe station which acts as a gateway to the North-West of England and Scotland. The Outward Bound Trust is an educational charity that utilised the outdoors to help develop young people from all walks of life. They run adventurous and challenging outdoor programmes that equip young people with valuable skills to help them become more confident, more effective and ultimately more capable in education, work and life.

This was a fantastic opportunity and it really taught Harry a lot about himself. Even though he had gained valuable experience from the North Wales trips in his first year at headquarters, it was nothing compared with a whole month as a 'Bounder' doing various sporting activities, mainly on and sometimes in the water. After arriving at the nearby railway station Harry and Trogs were driven with other visitors in an old army wagon which had clearly seen better times as it appeared to have lost all sense of suspension as every little pothole it found threw the passengers in all directions. Harry saw very little of Trogs during the month who was placed into a different section. Each group was placed into a wooden barracks named after an intrepid explorer. Harry was in Shackleton barracks with a dozen other expectant and nervous volunteers who were under the command of a group instructor named Andy. The group was made up predominantly of police cadets from other forces. There were also teenagers from a diverse background including one Army cadet and white collar professionals such as bankers. There was also a lad known as 'Nozzer' who it seemed had been nominated to undergo the course by a borstal training facility or something similar. Harry discovered that he came from a deprived background and had been in trouble with the law and it soon became apparent that 'Nozzer' was not going to play by the rules of the centre and was constantly having one to ones with Andy. For some reason, whenever they were out on an expedition 'Nozzer' only seemed content when he was moaning and groaning about the wet, cold or lack of food. The days were very long as it was up at six a.m. and the nights were cold as the barracks had very little heating and, coincidentally, it just happened to be the middle of winter.

According to the Outward Bound literature, the aim of the charity was to change how young people think and feel about themselves and their lives, by building their personal, social and emotional skills at critical times in their education before their transition into employment. Their goal was to foster a sense that anything is possible, where 'bounders' left the centre after one month with renewed optimism, raised aspirations and improved self-esteem. Harry wondered if that aim was supposed to include people like 'Nozzer' as he appeared to be the exception to the rule.

Most days during the month started in exactly the same way. At precisely the same time every morning everybody had to slip into a pair of swimming trunks, put their plimsolls on and carry their towel from the barracks to the swimming pool, which was a short walk or jog down a tarmac driveway. On many occasions the trunks were still wet from the day before as there was little opportunity for them to dry. The pool was about twenty-five yards in length by about ten yards wide. On the signal of an instructor's whistle three volunteers would step up onto the end of the pool and, once the instructor was happy there were two arm lengths between them, he would blow the whistle a second time. This command meant the three had to jump into the pool in a synchronised fashion. As long as they went under the water getting their heads wet the instructor would allow them out to return to their barracks. If they failed to complete the manoeuvre in unison or if one person did not go under, the three would have to do it again and again until the instructor was satisfied. On occasions this took some time as there were approximately eighty 'bounders' all queuing patiently in the freezing cold for their turn. Everybody avoided having to step up with 'Nozzer' as undoubtedly it would lead to delays if not arguments between him and the instructor. For some reason or other 'Nozzer' was reluctant to get his long blond curly locks wet, resulting in him and whoever was on the side at the time having to repeat the manoeuvre. Some days were colder than others and on at least three or four different occasions the instructor and whoever was first in the queue had to break the ice at one end of the pool so as to allow for a suitable and safe area for the 'bounders' to jump into.

Harry's mindset was to get in and out as quickly as possible with two critical considerations. One was to avoid 'Nozzer' like the plague even though he was in the same barracks. Not even the most battle-hardened warriors would have chosen to jump in a second time as this really was brass monkey weather. The second consideration was to ensure that he didn't jump too far forward and get stuck under the ice. This was unlikely although, in Harry's mind, being entombed in a swimming pool-sized ice block was not how he saw his life ending, so he was careful to stay as close as possible to the edge. Harry couldn't work out if the impact of the freezing cold water taking your breath away was worse than actually getting out. Some bright spark suggested running back to the barracks, but the combination of the dropping body temperature against the raw wind coming off the Irish Sea meant even more freezing conditions and Harry found that, as an alternative, an energetic walk back to the hut was just as invigorating.

On reaching the barracks it was off with the wet trunks and getting the body dried and warmed up as quickly as possible. By now the heating in the hut had kicked in but the temperature was still around freezing. *This will make a man out of you,* thought Harry as he pulled on his second pair of socks. The trick was to try and find a warm place in the small building next to the pool which essentially was a drying room. Unfortunately, with the sheer number of trunks and towels, unless you were lucky to find the right spot, invariably when you collected the items at the end of the day they were still considerably damp. Also, some jokers thought it funny to hide the trunks altogether to cause a little consternation amongst the group. Harry soon realised that the trick was to arrive a little later at the drying room so he could move items that had already been placed on the warm pipes to one side. The downside to this was if the timing went awry, it resulted in arriving at the back of a long queue for breakfast.

It was instilled in the 'bounders' that breakfast was the most important meal of the day, so Harry made sure that he had as much as possible to get him through until the following morning. Whilst the itinerary for the month was more or less mapped out this could change from day to day and was dependant on the prevailing weather conditions. Breakfast time at the centre was very busy as well as noisy, particularly if 'Nozzer' was at the same table. Most of the talk surrounded the early morning 'dip' and who had made a fool of themselves by refusing to jump, or what was on the agenda for the remainder of the day.

The routines and exercises on a day-to-day basis varied greatly but, as the centre bordered an estuary, a significant amount of time was dedicated to outdoor water pursuits. This included sailing small two-man dinghies, one- and two-man kayaks and a larger, older sailing boat manned by a crew of a dozen. For health and safety reasons, before anyone was let loose on the river everyone from each group had to perform some basic manoeuvres in the swimming pool. One of the simplest tasks included staying afloat for two minutes with and without a buoyancy aid. Bearing in mind the time of year, the water was pretty cold but everyone seemed to sail through this part. Colin, a member of Shackleton group, was not a keen water enthusiast and disliked all water activities greatly. Harry could see that he lacked confidence when in and around the pool but thought he was an okay guy as he tried his best and did not whinge and whine like 'Nozzer'. Once everyone had mastered the two-minute staying afloat trial, the instructor moved onto something a little more technical and hazardous, bringing into the pool a short snub-nosed kayak. This was an introduction to the 'Eskimo roll', which Harry had never heard of before and which everyone had to complete before they were allowed out onto the open river. This was done with the individual wearing a buoyancy aid as they would when out on open water.

Andy, the instructor, demonstrated how it should be done. To him, it was as easy as tying a shoelace as he had done it a thousand times before. He got into the small kayak and positioned it in the centre of the pool. Holding onto the sides, he flipped himself sideways so he and the kayak were upside down in the pool. He waited a couple of seconds before tapping his hands three times onto the bottom edge of the canoe. This was an indication that he was okay and about to release himself. Part of the kit involved the 'spray-deck' which had two parts to it; one that fitted around the canoeist's waist and a further part which fitted around the cockpit rim. This piece of equipment was designed to prevent water from splashing into the canoe but, when performing an 'Eskimo roll', the rim part had to be released to allow free exit from the kayak. Occasionally, this meant being upside down longer than anticipated as the spray-deck could become snagged. Harry learnt that as soon as the kayak capsized the occupant needed to bend the body forward as far as possible to release the spray-deck from around the cockpit rim. It was also a good idea to partially release the rim before tapping the bottom of the canoe, thus allowing the occupant a little more time. Tapping the underneath three times showed control over the event but, in the main, it was to exit as quickly as possible before the lungs collapsed. Most of Shackleton group mastered this exercise but Colin was experiencing what would be referred today as, a 'panic attack'.

Several times Colin sat in the kayak in the middle of the pool with everyone urging him on. 'Nozzer' just sat cross-legged on the edge of the pool looking totally bored with the whole proceedings. Twice, Colin bottled out and paddled to the side to be reassured by Andy that this was mind over matter and he was convinced that Colin could do it. Finally, the young bank worker manoeuvred the kayak gently to the middle of the pool for a third time. The rest of the group gave vocal encouragement and started a count down from ten. By the time they reached the number three Colin's hands were visibly trembling from the sheer amount of strength he was exerting to hold the sides of the kayak. The group screamed "GO!" at which point Colin tipped the canoe to his left leaving him upside down in the water. Harry and the rest waited for the hand-tapping motion but it never came. They waited and waited... but still nothing happened.

The silence was deafening before Andy screamed, "Get him out!" at which point Harry and two others dived and jumped into the pool. Colin was still hanging upside down from the canoe being held in by the spray-deck which was still in place. Colin seemed rigid so Harry and the others released the spray-deck, simultaneously pulling Colin out in a downwards motion before bringing him up for air. With the help of the others who were at the poolside, Colin was dragged out and laid in the recovery position. He seemed ashen faced and was shaking but at least he was breathing as he immediately started gasping for air. After a short visit to the on-site medical room where he was checked out, Colin was given the all clear to continue but, to Harry's knowledge, Colin never got into another kayak alone during the remainder of the course although he did accompany Andy in a two-man canoe when the rest of the group were deemed proficient enough to paddle the single kayaks on the river.

One of the most exhilarating events of the month's course for Harry was the combined rock climbing and abseiling. Led by experienced instructors, the group did this as a whole on at least three different occasions. The basic principles were first shown to the 'bounders' within the school where there was a specially built wooden tower. Shackleton group spent many hours on this structure in the first few days, learning about the different ropes and the importance of fixing a karabiner. Standing thirty to forty feet up with only two ropes for security took some while to adjust, but the tower had been specifically built with that in mind. After a few practice sessions everyone including 'Nozzer' seemed to have mastered the basics even though he couldn't complete the session without moaning.

Once Andy was happy with the whole group's degree of capability it was time to put this into a realistic setting, so Shackleton group set off for the coast. When they arrived, the tide was out and the mission was to get everyone down from the cliff top onto the sand and back up again by climbing the rock face via an alternative set route. This was clearly a spot used regularly by the school as most of the securing posts for the abseiling were already in place. The twelve-man team were split into two groups; fortunately Harry managed to avoid 'Nozzer' who was in the other group of six. They each abseiled over the cliff edge which started at a gentle angle but became more acute as the descent progressed. This was relatively fine until the last thirty-five or so feet as it became evident that the sea had eroded into the cliffs leaving a cave-type entrance. This meant that on reaching the lip of the cave the 'bounder' had to push off with both legs simultaneously releasing the 'holding' rope and, if things went according to plan, they would land safely on the sand below.

Needless to say, 'Nozzer' was one of those who couldn't master the technique which incorporated strength, co-ordination and a little courage as, if it was executed wrongly, it left the student either smashing themselves back against the cliff face or being left dangling in mid-air. The latter was probably the safest but took longer then to descend to the ground and it attracted a fair bit of ridicule from the rest of the group. Each 'bounder' took their turn whilst those who had already completed it waited at the foot of the cliff before an ascent could start in earnest.

Harry soon realised that this must be one of those tests set by the instructors as he noticed, along with a couple of others, that the tide was turning and the sea was beginning to come in. They still had two from each group to make the descent before they could start thinking of climbing back up, so time was of the essence and the pressure began to mount. Colin was one of those still waiting to abseil down, Harry hoped for everyone's sake that Colin would be okay and not panic at the sight of the incoming sea. Once the last person was down, the instructors abseiled down in less than thirty seconds. The whole group had to then negotiate their way around a slight promontory before reaching the point where they each took turns to climb up the cliff.

For safety reasons only two members of each team were allowed on the cliff face at any one time; this meant that when the first ascending team member reached halfway the second could start and so on. They drew lots to see what order they would take. Harry was more than content when he drew second place and knew he would not still be standing on the beach when the tide came in. Both groups set off and Harry watched intently as a lad called Mick, who also happened to be a banker, started slowly but surely. After about ten minutes, Mick had reached halfway, so Harry set off knowing that he had to get up as quickly as possible to allow the others following to start their ascent. The rocks were very slippery and freezing cold, making the fingers sting each time they were caught on a sharp bit of rock. Although each 'bounder' was attached to a rope which was secured from the top by an instructor, there still was a sense of danger as by the time Harry reached halfway it seemed a long way down.

As Harry reached the halfway point, he was aware of some shouting from below as well as from above. He looked up, only to see Mick a few yards in front and holding onto a rock for dear life. He could not work out why Mick was stuck at this point and this meant that as two from the same group were still on the cliff the next team member couldn't start their climb. Harry reached Mick in another few moments and rested on a ledge just below him. "I can't move," said Mick, still gripping the side of the rock for all his worth. Harry was perplexed and quietly talked to him thinking it might help but Mick had, in effect, got stage fright and was fixed rigid to the cliff face. Harry could hear those below shouting, and who could blame them as the sea was coming in. Out of nowhere Andy appeared like a present day 'Superman' having abseiled down from the top to Mick's ledge. Andy stayed with Mick and beckoned Harry to continue his climb. The remaining members took their turn in climbing; passing Mick and Andy en route to the top and all along Andy was giving Mick support and encouragement. Finally, with help from another instructor, Andy managed to get Mick to the top where he was given a medical check before returning to the Outward Bound School.

Harry got to abseil once more during the month which involved a disused mine shaft and a 120-foot drop into a dark abyss. Naturally, there was some whining from 'Nozzer' who thought it affront to have to be dropped from such a great height into a darkened quarry. Each 'bounder' was given a miner's hat which had a small lamp on the front that was powered by two small batteries from a power pack. The hats happened to be very temperamental and worked off and on at will. Again, there was a general feeling of excitement, yet a sense of the unknown; this was an opportunity, explained Andy, to get a flavour of conditions that some miners had to endure in their daily routine. As Harry set off he wondered what it would have been like working in the coal mines years and years before. After literally a few feet he discovered complete blackness, so much so that Harry could not see in front of his eyes. He could now turn his lamp on by means of a small switch attached to the battery pack. *Not a lot of difference,* thought Harry, but the further down he went the darker, colder and quieter it became. He looked around but all there was to see was black walls of coal. After what seemed like an age, Harry reached the foot of the mineshaft and his lamp immediately picked out an animal which seemed like a large ferret. It turned out to be a polecat which apparently lived in the dark and dingy conditions. The journey back to the surface was considerably more comfortable as the group used the existing lift, even though 'Nozzer' still moaned about it.

Towards the end of the course, once Shackleton group had sufficiently bonded, they embarked on a three-day trek across mountainous terrain minus their instructor. They had to take adequate provisions for at least two nights away from the school with at least one of those nights being spent near to Llyn Cau, reputedly a bottomless lake at the foot of Cader Idris. Harry questioned whether it would be possible to put up with 'Nozzer' for three whole days and two nights; at least he didn't have to share a tent with him. The team set off mid-morning and would camp out that night at a pre-determined location before making their way up Cader Idris the next day.

The first day passed without incident and the group pitched the six tents that evening in a valley beside a small stream before having a hearty meal of dried food and fruit. The following morning, at around seven, any of the group that were still asleep were awoken abruptly by the sound of two huge fighter jets flying at very low altitude through the valley. The roar of the engines was deafening and the breaking of the sound barrier was enough to wake the dead. With some of the 'bounders' already out their tents there was an unexpected return a few minutes later as the two jets roared past for a second time, making even more noise. It was as if they were giving the group an early morning alarm call. Harry was completely mesmerised by the sound, but even more startled at the height they were flying and the distance between them.

After breakfast, the group mapped out the best route to the lake but this caused a clear division in the ranks. One half felt that the more direct route upwards was the quickest which would afford more time to set up camp at the other end. The other half felt that a slightly longer but easier trail up was the best option as it would be less physically demanding and they would still have time to set camp up before night fell. Taff, who was in charge of the team, agreed that Shackleton group could split into two teams of six. He accepted that this probably went against protocol and safety rules but he saw no particular issue as they would all hopefully end up in the same place. Taff took his group of six including Harry the longer but less physical route, and 'Nozzer' and five others went the most direct route. As with all other similar stories about tortoises and hares, needless to say that Taff's group reached the rendezvous point at the edge of Llyn Cau quite a while before the other team; this was predominantly due to the fact that their intrepid map reader 'Nozzer' had taken them the wrong way and they lost time having to double back. Camp was set, a fire was started and a feast of dried food and fruit was had that evening before they all settled down for the night.

There is a tale amongst locals that Cader Idris is haunted and anyone who spends the night on or around the top of the mountain will wake up either a madman or a poet. It was mooted by one or two of the group that a ghost existed in these parts, but no one was able to relay the full story so it was disregarded out of hand. However, at around two a.m. Harry was aware of something or someone tugging on the guy-ropes of his tent; sensing this was one of the others playing the fool he chose to ignore it. It then happened again and again. He signalled to his tent mate who was by now awake, but neither spoke a word. As quietly as they could both 'bounders' slipped out of their sleeping bags. They positioned themselves by the end of the tent where it was zipped up the middle. When the next bout of guy-rope tugging commenced, the zip was undone in an instant and both Harry and his tent mate leaped out like leopards, switching their torches on as they did so. Had the culprits been anyone from an adjoining tent they would have been caught hook, line and sinker in the torchlight – but there was absolutely nothing. They considered the possibility of it being an animal of some sort but again, as they exited the tent, surely they would have seen it? There was not even any wind so that theory was discounted as well. The two had a quick look round the campsite and were conscious of not waking any of the others. The only odd thing of note was a giant-sized swirl of mist hanging down off the side of Cader Idris which appeared not to move. It looked out of context with the rest of the mountain and there was a mystical presence about it. There was little they could do but to return to bed; fortunately there were no reoccurrences that night but it was always a mystery as to who or what was responsible for their guy-rope incident.

The following morning, after breakfast, the group packed up and headed back to the Outward Bound School. The one good thing about this three-day trip was that they all missed the early morning dip in the iced pool. Out of all the attachments which Harry completed as a senior it was the Outward Bound one which taught him the most; it was mainly in relation to mind over matter and giving things a try for the first time. It was all about working as a team and achieving the goals that had been set, but dealing with adversity and challenges along the way. During those times, when he found it difficult, Harry would always mutter those words of encouragement to himself, "Harder yet!"

Chapter Twenty-Two

The Cheshire Home

The Leonard Cheshire Homes for the disabled started in 1948 with the former war hero volunteering to take in someone with a disability into his own home and care for them. This developed into a national charity and at one point there were no fewer than 100 Cheshire Homes across the country providing expertise, nursing and medical assistance for people with physical and sensory impairments, people with learning disabilities, children, older people and people with an acquired brain injury.

Harry spent two weeks together with Butch at the local Cheshire Home in the north of the county. This was a residential home where the majority of guests suffered from multiple sclerosis or muscular dystrophy. Some visited on an ad hoc basis once or twice weekly and received the same level of care and overall range of services and assistance. The consequence for Harry and Butch was that they instantly became volunteers nominated by the constabulary whether they liked it or not. Both were given bedrooms which, in Harry's case, negated any form of travelling to and from Fordham on a daily basis and secondly the food at the home could be no worse than was presented by Beryl Blackett. He seemed quite content until he realised that he could be called upon in the middle of the night to assist if the need arose.

This was a different kettle of fish to the hospital attachment where it was anticipated and likely that patients admitted were treated, were likely to recover and then leave. Unfortunately, for a lot of the residents at the Cheshire Home, this was likely to be their last staging post in life as sadly there was no cure for those diagnosed with either multiple sclerosis or muscular dystrophy. "There can't be many more things worse than being confined to a wheelchair for most of the day," thought Harry and he would not wish it on his worst enemy. Harry thought no less of Butch despite them having fought in one of the previous boxing matches and for the two weeks they got on really well, although they were on different shifts so only saw each other for short periods each day.

Some of the nursing staff lived in and others who lived locally worked shifts on a daily basis. The cadet shifts comprised of seven thirty a.m. to three thirty p.m. or one p.m. to nine p.m., meaning that when Harry worked one, Butch was on the other and they alternated for the second week. This meant that at the busiest time of the day both cadets were available at one p.m. when lunch was served for everyone irrespective as to whether the residents lived in or whether they were visiting for the day. The whole fortnight was a real eye-opener and Harry was fascinated to try and understand the different specialist skills utilised for patients with varying degrees of progressive neurological conditions and acquired brain injury, although in fairness he had absolutely zip idea of which doctor specialised in what. Harry was really impressed by all the full-time staff and recognised what a difficult task they had.

Harry learnt that multiple sclerosis occurs when the immune system attacks the nerve cells in the brain and the spinal cord. The resulting damage from this autoimmune activity can lead to problems with vision, bowel and bladder control, sensation and muscle function. It is not clear what causes the initial attack of the nerve cells but the bad news for sufferers is that there is no cure. According to the Multiple Sclerosis Foundation, it is not a fatal disease and MS patients can have the same life expectancy as the general population.

There are more than thirty different kinds of muscular dystrophies varying in symptoms and severity. Some are inherited disorders that lead to abnormalities of specific proteins within the muscle cells and over time these defective proteins cause loss of muscle function. Sufferers often have hormonal and metabolic abnormalities, such as low testosterone levels and insulin resistance. Unlike multiple sclerosis, muscular dystrophy doesn't damage nerves in the central nervous system.

Generally, for the first couple of days until Butch and Harry became acquainted with all the different residents and staff within the home, they were asked to assist at mealtimes to feed those who required help. This involved spoon feeding a plate full of mushy solids to the patient, who occasionally got very frustrated at the speed at which Harry, in particular, was trying to force them to eat. In Harry's defence, he had no experience of people suffering from either condition, and it took some time for him to realise that they had entirely different eating habits than he did and the sooner he understood that, he would be able to empathise more with them. Sometimes the residents were too ill to eat in the dining room, so had to be fed in their rooms

Harry was introduced for the first time to the wonderful but dubious music of Frank Zappa, an American jazz singer/songwriter. Harry was more of a Diana Ross follower and had never heard of the artist but tried to show an interest for Phil's sake, who was one of the younger residents who suffered from muscular dystrophy. Phil had been diagnosed only for a couple of years and the disease had steadily worsened but for all the adversity in his life he had a very positive outlook and a wicked sense of humour. Phil, who was sadly confined to a wheelchair but had a limited range of use of his upper body, was an avid Zappa fan. Phil's girlfriend who he was due to marry just before he was struck down with the disease visited him every day at the home, which Harry thought was highly commendable given his dire situation. He was sure that many a woman would have given up on someone in his predicament. Phil was one of the brighter and inspiring residents that impressed during Harry's fortnight.

Another one of the older characters was Brian who had been at the home for a year or so and who Harry thought was really grumpy and pernickety. It seemed that most of Harry's shifts saw him spending more and more time attending to Brian's needs and Harry suspected that it was a plot of some sort by the regular staff to 'dump' Brian on Harry's plate so as to speak. Brian, like Phil, had limited use of his arms and was confined to a wheelchair for most of the day. As time went on, Harry would help to get Brian out of bed in the mornings, he would assist him to get dressed, take him to the toilet, and clean his wheelchair when it was not in use. He would also give him advice on what clothes to wear but, given Harry's taste in fashion, this was contentious and Brian would often end up wearing psychedelic shirts which made him even grumpier.

After the embarrassment of Anna at Fordham Hospital Harry made the conscious decision not to try and woo any of the staff at the Cheshire Home although there was one particular nurse who caught his eye. He tried to flirt with her early on but she was having none of it and for the remainder of the fortnight he treated her with the utmost respect and dignity even though, on the odd occasion, he caught her sneaking a peek at him with a glint in her eye. Perhaps it was tears of joy that he would be leaving very soon. All the other nurses were extremely professional in their roles. They never moaned or groaned except occasionally when Brian became demanding, which seemed to be every day in one way or another.

Towards the end of the fortnight Harry became a little blasé about the whole attachment. It wasn't necessarily due to his lack of enthusiasm; it was more to do with the fact that most of the residents would not be walking again, which was something that Harry found difficult to accept and it started to prey on his mind. For an eighteen-year-old to see such pain, anguish and suffering at first hand but not be able to fix the problem was something he was finding hard to come to terms with, particularly as he had forged new friendships with people such as Phil and to a lesser extent Brian. Harry was a fit, healthy young man who was always on the go, and dealing with those with disabilities on a day-to-day basis was beginning to make him a little tetchy.

One of Harry's last shifts was working one till nine p.m. and it had been particularly busy. At around eight thirty p.m. Brian called Harry from his bedroom as the youngster walked past his room along the corridor. Brian was preparing himself for bed but at the last minute decided he needed to use the loo for a number two, which left Harry with little option but to help as all the other nurses were busy. Harry had mastered this art, which necessitated navigating the bulky wheelchair into a position alongside the toilet before placing Brian into a hoist. Remembering to unzip Brian's trousers and pull them down with his underpants, Harry ensured that the strapping was in place before hoisting Brian up, out of his wheelchair and swinging the hoist across in line with the toilet. He then released the hoist slowly, enabling Brian to sit snugly to do what he had to. The hoist could be quite temperamental and the control required a delicate touch; any heavy handedness could result in the hoist jolting downwards causing a moan and groan from the occupant. Having completed this several times before on his own, Harry was quite accomplished with the process. The wheelchair was moved to one side to afford more room and Brian was duly left to get on with his ablutions. Harry passed him the cord which Brian knew to pull once he had finished; this would show a red light outside the door and make a little buzzer noise to indicate to staff that he was ready to be helped out. Harry wished him well and left Brian to it, closing the toilet door behind him as he left.

For some inexplicable reason, Harry forgot all about Brian. It may have had something to do with a game of football being shown on the television, which Butch, who was off duty, was already watching in their room. It may have also been due to the fact that another resident required some assistance with getting ready for bed, but Harry genuinely believed that when Brian was ready he would pull the cord to indicate this fact. At nine p.m. the night shift came on duty and Harry made his way up to the room he shared with Butch to have a cold Skol beer and watch what was left of the football match. After about forty minutes, Butch came into the room telling Harry that he was wanted downstairs by the nightshift nurse in charge but didn't say why. Reluctantly, Harry pulled himself away from the football but could not understand why she wanted to see him. He was met at the bottom of the stairs by the night nurse who had a face like thunder and appeared very annoyed. "Have you forgotten anything?" she said inquisitively.

Harry thought for a second or two before saying, "I don't think so."

She then said, "Come with me," turned and walked towards the corridor that led to the residents' rooms. Harry followed, wondering what on earth could be up. As she got level with the toilets she stopped abruptly almost causing Harry to walk into the back of her; she turned to the cadet and flicked her eyes to one side indicating the toilet door. It still hadn't dawned on him what the problem was so she grabbed the door handle, almost wrenching it off its hinges to reveal Brian still sitting on the loo. *Oh my God,* thought Harry. Brian was less than impressed with having been left for well in excess of an hour without a cord to pull. The nurse, angered by this clear breach of neglect, was almost seething and muttered to Harry, "You deal with it!" before turning her back on him and walking away.

Harry could not apologise enough to Brian, who was still fuming and believed this was a deliberate act by Harry to punish him for his belligerent attitude during Harry's attachment. This could not have been further from the truth. Yes, Harry had become slightly intolerant of Brian because of all the attention he craved, but the youngster would never have done anything like that to get back at him. It then dawned on Harry that Brian had not pulled the cord to indicate he had finished and mentioned this to him as he was cleaning him up. Angrily, Brian retorted, "That's because you didn't give me it." Harry felt hurt as he knew full well that before leaving him he wound the cord once around his hand to ensure it did not escape his clutches. Brian had apparently drawn the attention of the night nurse by calling out continuously and it was pure luck that she heard him. After returning Brian to his room and putting him to bed, Harry went in search of the nurse who informed him this was a serious matter as Brian was making an official complaint about his behaviour. Harry mentioned the cord to her; she explained that when she went into the toilet the cord was hanging in the corner in its normal place out of his reach with Brian complaining he was not given it in the first place. Harry tried to explain but, as she had clearly made up her mind, there seemed little point in annoying her even further. She suggested Harry went to bed and the matter would be dealt with the following morning. Harry, feeling quite disconsolate, returned to his room, told Butch the story and had another Skol before retiring to bed.

Harry did not sleep well that night as he mulled over the incident in his mind. This was Brian's word against his. Who would they believe? The following morning, Harry reported at the usual time and at nine a.m. was invited to the matron's office who asked him for an account which he gave. He maintained he had handed the cord to Brian in order that he could alert staff as to when he had finished. This was something that had been drummed into Harry on commencement of the attachment but also before that, during his time at Fordham Hospital. The matron listened intently. She informed Harry that this was a very serious matter but she had spoken to Brian who no longer wished to make any complaint and it would not be taken any further. Harry could not work it out; if Brian had deliberately let the cord go in order to make a malicious and unfounded complaint against him, then Harry believed he really was a vindictive individual. Alternatively, if Brian had accidentally let the cord go, why did he not just mention that to the nurse at the time instead of trying to blame Harry? Perhaps Brian just wanted to put the young upstart in his place and show him who was boss. For the remaining couple of days things were a little frosty between them and it came as a relief when Harry completed his time at the Cheshire Home and returned to work at Fordham. It certainly was an eye-opener and made him feel extremely grateful for his own health.

Chapter Twenty-Three
The Shaftesbury Society Home

The last attachment in the diary for Harry was two weeks at the Shaftesbury Society Home in Dovercourt. Here he joined forces with Kimbo who he shared a room with, similar to the Cheshire Home set-up. For the duration of the fortnight Kimbo and Harry ate all meals on site with the visitors. Although they were not allocated specific shift patterns it was generally expected that the two cadets would muck in with routines from breakfast time through till evening.

The Shaftesbury Society differed from the Cheshire Home as all the visitors had most of their faculties and could walk unaided or with the assistance of a walking stick or crutches. No one suffered from any debilitating disease but most of the visitors were elderly and either lived alone or in sheltered accommodation in a cross section of London boroughs. Harry was not entirely sure how this group had been chosen for this fortnight, but he knew it was an ongoing arrangement throughout the summer period and was aimed at those less well off, or in aid of a little 'pick me up'. Fred Cotton was the man in overall charge and, whilst there were Shaftesbury helpers who accompanied the holidaymakers to the Essex coast, Kimbo and Harry were expected to fully take part in all activities and assist wherever they could. Fred had worked for the Shaftesbury Society for a number of years; he was a born leader and a very caring man. He went about his business in a calm manner; he wanted all and sundry to enjoy the moment and would do everything within his power to try and please everyone and inspired the helpers to achieve the same level of service. There were one or two notable incidents during this holiday period involving the two seniors.

The first involved Harry on the second day when a group of less-abled visitors were escorted down to the seafront in the minibus which belonged to the home. It was a beaten-up old Bedford CA van which had seen better days but was the only realistic mode of transport for the holidaymakers. The five or six wheelchair-users were taken off the carrier and wheelchairs were assembled for them. The group then headed off towards the promenade. Harry had the pleasure of pushing a large-built elderly lady who probably could have benefited from a crash course at Weight-watchers. The path down was a little steep and the tarmac in places was patchy with one or two potholes along the way. As they came to a low kerb, Harry was pushing with all his might to maintain a suitable momentum, which would allow him off one kerb and then up another in one continuous motion without having to stop. He completely misjudged the angle of the kerb so, as the wheelchair went down, it toppled to its right. Given the weight of the woman combined with the wheelchair speed and the angle at which it left the kerb, there was only one possible outcome. How Harry was able to prevent the wheelchair from fully toppling over is bewildering to this day, but stop it he did. The picture, had it been today would have got thousands, if not millions of views on YouTube. It was a precarious predicament at the time but generated a good old laugh when everyone got back into the safety of the minibus for the return journey back to the home. It certainly was a talking point that evening when everyone congregated at mealtime. If there is one thing that pensioners are always good at it is mickey taking, which they did in abundance over Harry's lack of driving skills with a wheelchair. He viewed it slightly differently; had it not been for his adeptness and strength the expression 'beached whale' could have taken on a whole new meaning.

One of the funniest and most interesting characters that Harry met during the two weeks was a frail but very stoical little lady from Pinner named Alice who was in her late seventies. She always seemed to be behind Harry when he was helping another visitor and when he wasn't fully occupied she was bending his ear about something or another. For some, unbeknown reason she felt safe in Harry's company and confided in him, telling him some very personal and tragic stories relating to the War and about her husband who sadly had passed over. Alice had a story for almost every eventuality and was such a happy soul, encouraging others at every opportunity to join in. Mealtimes were such a hoot if you happened to sit on the same table as Alice, which Harry seemed to do more and more as the days went past.

On the first weekend, Alice was visited by her daughter and her very attractive granddaughter who was a few years older than Harry. The two struck up a friendship. Kate was amazed at how Harry had made such an impression on her grandmother, something which apparently not many had achieved since her late husband. It came as a bit of a shock when Kate asked if she could write to Harry from time to time if only to keep him updated on how Alice was doing. Who was he to refuse such a polite and pretty young lady? Besides, the letters from Lena had by this time started to dry up. And so it came about that Harry became pen pals with Kate who regularly sent him letters after the fortnight's holiday updating him as to her grandmother's antics. It was a very sad day when, about three years later Harry received a letter from Kate informing him of Alice's death. He attended the funeral before going back to Kate's house for some hilariously funny stories about Alice's life. Kate's mother thanked Harry for giving up his time and attending the funeral and also told him that Alice had sung his praises ever since their first meeting at Dovercourt. One of Alice's secret wishes before her death was that Harry and Kate could have taken their pen-pal friendship to the next level. She saw Harry as a perfect match for her granddaughter but it was never destined to be, although, if they had, the story of how they met could have been the makings of a romantic novel.

Bill was an ex-serviceman who liked to keep himself to himself; it was identified quite soon after his arrival that Bill was very much a loner and reluctant to accept help in any way, shape or form. It was clear that Bill was not the most hygienic of people and washed when he felt the need, which noticeably was not every day. Harry was detailed by Fred Cotton along with one of the senior Shaftesbury helpers to give Bill a bath, which was going to be a monumental accomplishment if they could get him anywhere near the bathroom. After lunch one day,

Harry and the helper approached Bill who usually sat on his own because of his dire body odour. They broached the subject of when he last had a bath. "About four months ago," he said quite pleased with himself.

"When did you last have new clothes?" asked Harry. Bill pondered before explaining that the clothes he was wearing were about three years old, including his underwear, and these were the only ones he possessed. The helper raised her eyebrows worriedly; it was evident, she thought, this was a task too far but she was equally determined as Harry to try and get Bill into a bath if only to supply him with some clean underwear. He told them in no uncertain terms that he did not wish to bath and there was nothing they could do to make him.

For the next day and a half, Harry and the helper persisted in trying to persuade this doddery old-timer to take a bath and they tried all sorts of tactics in their efforts. Bill finally succumbed to all the pestering from the helper and the cadet and agreed to take a bath the next morning at eleven a.m. on one condition. They both almost simultaneously said, "Name it," thinking there could be absolutely nothing that would prevent them from going ahead with a bath for Bill.

"You can't cut my toenails," said Bill. "If you agree, I will have a bath," he said.

Harry looked at the helper who quizzically asked, "What is wrong with your toenails?" Bill explained that since the War he hated having his toenails cut as it gave him bad memories and as a consequence he did not like to cut them. Harry and the helper were in a slight quandary; they desperately wanted to give Bill a bath but didn't want to do so under a false pretence where he thought they might have duped him. They reluctantly agreed not to touch his toenails.

The following morning everything was made ready for Bill's rare excursion to the bathroom. Some second-hand clothes were arranged for him from a local charity shop, but he was insistent on retaining his old boots. A hot bath with some nice-smelling crystals was prepared and Bill entered the bathroom with a little trepidation. He was unaware how Harry and the helper were going to view him as he undressed. Bill removed his shirt and trousers. The smell seemed to fill the room instantly. Harry thought Bill's underpants were a light yellow colour when in fact they used to be white, but the repetitive staining over the years had made their mark and probably now were irremovable. *What a life,* thought Harry, comforted by the fact that he had showered that morning and was wearing a brand new pair of boxer shorts, but this was not about him, everything was centred on Bill. Last to be removed were Bill's heavy woollen socks. Again, the smell was unbearable but what greeted Harry and the helper was something out of this world. Bill's toenails, as he had intimated, were not cut regularly, in fact they were all so long that they intertwined other toes on the same foot. The nail on the big toe of one foot was so long it had grown around his little toe on the same foot and it must have been between nine and twelve inches long. Harry looked on in awe, wondering if this was some kind or record, but at the same time thinking this must be a health issue. Bill quite happily jumped into the bath, at which point the helper scooped up his clothes and removed them from the bathroom. "Where has she taken my clothes?" asked Bill angrily.

Harry explained that some second-hand ones had been obtained which were much cleaner and would feel fresher on his cleansed skin. Harry was still thinking about the extraordinary toe when the helper returned with Fred. A discussion ensued with Bill in the bath about the length of his toenails. Finally, after about forty minutes and with the water cooling rapidly, Bill agreed to have his nails clipped the next day. He seemed to have accepted his fate and was duly provided with nice clean attire but kept his old army boots. The following day he had a foot bath before having his toenails clipped, which wasn't a straightforward task as normal 'pinkie' scissors were just not strong enough. He retained his old clothes, which were washed thoroughly with the exception of his disgusting underwear, which was disposed of. Bill became a relatively new man again; suddenly other holidaymakers started talking to him and even sat with him at the same table at mealtimes.

After a hard day's toil, Harry and Kimbo were pleased to see their beds. Generally speaking, all the visitors had retired to bed by ten p.m. and there was serenity within the whole building. Male holidaymakers were placed into a dormitory-type room containing four beds on one side of the building, whilst the females shared a four-bed room on the other side. Single rooms were available but only in exceptional circumstances, although Fred Cotton had one to himself. The only lights on at night were the small corridor nightlights; when dimmed, these lights just about gave sufficient brightness for the light to be seen underneath the bedroom doors. At around two fifteen one morning Harry woke from his sleep. He had no idea what had caused him to wake, but lay with his eyes wide open and his ears straining in an effort to try and hear what had woken him. You could hear a pin drop, and all that he seemed to achieve was an increase in his heart rate. After about five minutes of intent listening Harry quietly called Kimbo's name, the reply came, "What"' Harry stupidly asked if he was awake. There then followed a frivolous conversation whispered between them as to what had caused them to wake and whether the other could hear anything outside. After another few minutes of debating they both agreed that it was probably best to go and investigate. There was an air of trepidation as they both had a sixth sense that something was not quite right. The dimmed night-lights suggested that no one was up but the two cadets needed to be sure. They walked slowly along the corridor deciding whether to turn on the main lights or leave them in state of twilight. They opted for the latter but, as they approached a point where two corridors met, they noticed something on the floor which they soon identified as blood. The trail came from one of the bedrooms where the door was ajar so, instinctively, they followed it into the room. The nearest three beds were all occupied but curiously the occupants were all fast asleep. Harry and Kimbo, still following the blood trail wandered slowly across the room to the bed in the corner where the occupant was missing. The bed linen was all folded back and there was a pool of thickly congealed blood on the bed sheet. Without wanting to wake the others in the room the two turned around, following the trail back to where they had first noticed it, before following it along the corridor which led towards the dining room and lounge. It seemed as if Harry had been holding his breath forever, his heart was still pounding; he tried to remain calm but the incident they were experiencing had all sorts of thoughts spinning in his head.

They reached halfway along the corridor when the blood trail came to a halt outside a toilet door. For some reason Harry knocked on the door but this was no time for being reserved. There was a muffled reply from within so the two cadets entered to find Bert, an elderly man, sitting on the loo clearly in discomfort. "Can you help please, I think my piles have burst," he asked. He looked very pale and it was evident that he was in need of urgent medical attention. Unfortunately, neither Kimbo's nor Harry's first aid training extended to treating something of this nature; if he was suffering from hypothermia or needed an arm placing in a sling, then they probably could have helped. This was a case for super Fred, who was duly woken and summonsed to the toilet. He was curious to know why both cadets were up at that time of the morning, which they found difficult to explain. An ambulance was called and rushed poor Bert to the local hospital where he underwent emergency surgery. Harry had never seen so much blood in one place before and wondered how Bert was still alive. He and Kimbo cleared the blood up before removing the stained linen from the bedroom whilst the three other occupants slept like babies, totally unaware of what had taken place. The two cadets went back to bed feeling as if they had been through a bad dream. Neither could fathom out why they had woken up when they did but it was just as well they did as the outcome could have been so very different. The following afternoon Harry and Kimbo accompanied Fred to visit Bert in hospital. He was pleased to see them all, particularly the seniors who he congratulated for helping him in his hour of need. They were just grateful that things had turned out well for him and that he was on the road to recovery.

Fred Cotton had a heart of gold and partly due to their assistance in helping Bert he showed his gratitude to Harry and Kimbo by giving them a day off. If that was not sufficient he also allowed Kimbo to take the beaten-up old Bedford CA van out for the day as long as they brought it back in one piece. Kimbo had not long passed his driving test but was quite experienced, given all the times he had ridden his motorbike illegally. Harry suggested they might like to go up the coast to his parents, which was a one and a half hour drive away and he knew the route well, as it was one he had taken many times before when catching the ferry from Harwich to Holland for past holidays.

The sun was out so Harry was confident of having a nice day; they set off after breakfast with Kimbo at the wheel. The peculiar thing about this vehicle was the gearbox, as every time Kimbo changed gear he had to deploy the double d-clutch method when going up as well as down the gears. Although Kimbo had passed his test, it was evident from the moment they set off that this relatively short trip was going to be a challenge; from the outset the sliding front doors wouldn't stay closed, allowing the wind to whistle into the vehicle with impunity. Harry had not been in many vehicles like this before and, although he did not know much about shock absorbers, he had a general idea that each bump they encountered should not have left his spine tingling from top to bottom. Even after an hour of driving, Kimbo was beginning to feel a tingling sensation in his hands and arms from the vehicle's dubious suspension system. The two intrepid travellers managed to make the thirty-five miles up the coast where they spent the rest of the day at the beach, visiting the hotel where Harry's father worked or at Harry's house with his mother, who made them a wonderful cake to accompany a plate full of sandwiches and numerous cups of tea.

The time came for them to leave. It was still light and assessing their options and, providing there was not too much traffic, they thought they could be back by around six p.m. The initial part was fine but as they neared Ipswich the light began to fade so, as any newly qualified driver would do, Kimbo turned on the lights. He turned the switch several times but nothing appeared on the dashboard to indicate the lights were on. He decided to pull into a lay-by to check them out, only to find they were not working and some of the fuses were missing, but Kimbo was not qualified enough to know which ones were which. "Oh my God," was the feeling from them both as their hearts sank; they believed they were doomed until Kimbo, who was fiddling with every wire he could find, managed to get the sidelights to flicker on… but there was no sign of the headlights playing ball. It was a moment of madness but Kimbo decided to continue as they had little option. Fearless to the end and maybe stupidly, and with the light fading, he drove the beaten-up old banger of a Bedford van slowly back to Dovercourt on nothing but sidelights along unlit roads. Harry felt completely helpless and, fearing there may be an accident, could do little but to hang on and try and keep the cold wind out. After several hours of negotiating double bends and country lanes they limped into the car park of the Shaftesbury home quiet, downbeat and cold. Harry was greatly impressed with Kimbo's ability that day and Fred Cotton was extremely pleased to see them back in one piece before telling them that there was a problem with the lights, hence them never taking the old banger out after dark. *Typical,* thought Harry. *What a way to end a wonderful day.* Harry reflected on the fortnight's experience: he had met some real characters, no more so than Alice who shared some precious memories with him. Reality soon kicked in and it was back to Fordham to Betty Blacketts home cooking and to continue as he had started for the next couple of months.

Chapter Twenty-Four

Boys into Men

On completion of his final year as a senior at Fordham, Harry took another well-earned summer break returning to his east coast home. Again, this gave him plenty of time to reflect as he caught up with Ernie. Unfortunately there was no visit from the wonder of Warwick and their relationship slowly diminished as time progressed.

There were plenty of other things to keep Harry and Ernie occupied such as their nineteenth birthdays which they celebrated together. Harry had also become acquainted with a receptionist called 'Cat' working at the same hotel as his father. She was very lovely and forthright and totally different to Lena with short, dark curly hair. The good thing from Harry's perspective was that she could drive and had her own car; a white Hillman Imp which was her pride and joy. Now, Harry could not at this point of his life consider himself as an expert driver; the only time he had done so involved his mum's Mini when she asked him to put her car in the garage, but things didn't go according to plan. Cat's driving was, however, haphazard and dangerous in his opinion. She drove with one hand most of the time, she constantly smoked and midway between the hotel and his house she would invariably change her shoes whilst at the wheel. Buses and cars that had right of way would hoot and flash their lights before Cat took immediate evasive action. How she actually managed to avoid all those vehicles – and in some cases pedestrians – was a complete mystery.

Harry and Ernie returned to their respective forces at the beginning of September 1974 when they were sworn in as constables during a week's induction course. Harry could not quite believe that two years had flown by since he first started out as a cadet and now he was being offered a full-time role as a police officer. It was at headquarters that Harry renewed acquaintances with Ed who had taken the advice given following his untimely departure earlier that year when he was given an ultimatum over resignation. Coincidentally, Harry and Ed from Tinkers Hill and Ernie from Kanga Force then embarked on the same intensive ten-week training programme at an Oxfordshire law college where they further discovered the world of policing, learning all the necessary laws, rules and regulations that they needed to know about in order to become real-life police officers. It was also here that Ed showed what an exceptional runner he was by winning the course cross-country race.

From the time they started their last year at school to this point, three whole years had elapsed which in comparison to a whole lifetime seemed like a drop in the ocean. Yet these three exciting, tough and eye-opening years taught both Harry and Ed and many others like them, thoroughly invaluable and priceless lessons that would remain with them for the rest of their lives. Although their DNA was already written from birth, their upbringing, schooling and their formative teenage years had a great bearing on how they would turn out. Many would say the cadet corps gave them a substantial grounding which they took forward into later life; at the time it was probably viewed by the police hierarchy as a good method of recruiting. Others simply referred to cadets as robotic and not having the necessary life experience to make good police officers, as was suggested to Harry at his very first interview. Not everyone survived the ordeal, not everyone achieved their ultimate goals, and not everyone went on to have long and successful careers in the police. However, Harry and Ed were eternally grateful for the opportunity and would always remember the journey they took with others – but most of all they will never forget the short, irritatingly funny man with the hardened look and always remember his notable and prodigious catchphrase: "Harder yet!"